What Others Are Saying About Vickie McDonough and *Whispers on the Prairie*...

Vickie McDonough has another winner! Her knowledge of the Old West and the people who settled it shines in *Whispers on the Prairie*. With its well-drawn setting and cast of endearing characters, this delightful story will play tug-of-war with your emotions right up to the very last page.

—*Carol Cox*
Author, *Love in Disguise* and *Trouble in Store*

Whispers on the Prairie is a heartwarming historical romance with a great cast of realistic characters who will capture your heart from the first page. Charming, inspiring, and delightful—prairie romance at its best!

—*Carrie Turansky*
Award-winning author, *The Governess of Highland Hall*

Against a backdrop of the growing pains of the post-Civil War United States, Vickie McDonough weaves a tapestry of words depicting life on the plains and the changes that were quickly becoming the norm. Her characters leapt to life in my mind and my heart, and they stayed with me long after I finished reading this wonderful tale. Just the kind of book I will keep on my bookshelf.

—*Lena Nelson Dooley*
Award-winning author, *Maggie's Journey*, *Mary's Blessing*, *Catherine's Pursuit*, and *Love Finds You in Golden, New Mexico*

The story of Sarah Marshall and Ethan Harper tugged at my heartstrings, and it will echo in the heart of any reader who has ever yearned to belong and be wanted. *Whispers on the Prairie* is a title to cherish, and I eagerly await the next book in the Pioneer Promises series.

—Laurie Kingery
Author, *Hill Country Cattlemen*

When you avoid loving the one God desires for you, watch out—just ask Sarah Marshall and Ethan Harper. This story of two people determined to go their own way had this reader engaged faster than jelly slides on peanut butter. With *Whispers on the Prairie*, McDonough begins this new series on such a strong base that I was left wanting the next book right away.

—Diana Lesire Brandmeyer
Author, *Mind of Her Own*, *A Bride's Dilemma in Friendship, Tennessee*, *Hearts on the Road*, and *We're Not Blended, We're Pureed: A Survivor's Guide to Blended Families*

Vickie McDonough has created a wealth of intriguing characters in this heartwarming tale of brotherly conflict and family loyalties set on the Kansas plains. Combining just the right amount of romance, faith, and honest emotions, Ms. McDonough has penned another winner that you won't want to put down.

—Margaret Brownley
Best-selling author, *Dawn Comes Early*, *Waiting for Morning*, and *Gunpowder Tea*

Gifted author Vickie McDonough blends authentic details of stagecoach stops, the hardships of the Santa Fe Trail, and the beauty of the prairie to give readers a heartwarming story of family, friendship, and true love.

—Amanda Cabot
Author, *Waiting for Spring*

A good plot, good writing, and characters so real, it seems as if you know them—Vickie McDonough delivers all of that and more in *Whispers on the Prairie*. I especially enjoyed the way she handled the relationship between the three Harper brothers. I'm looking forward to future books in her Pioneer Promises series.

—*Dorothy Clark*
Award-winning author, the Pinewood Weddings series

Vickie McDonough paints a vivid picture of Kansas, 1870s style. Here is a wonderful story rich with emotional tension, lively characterization, exciting plot twists, and the perfect dose of spiritual teachings. Well worth every page-turning minute!

—*Sharlene MacLaren*
Best-selling author of three series: Little Hickman Creek, The Daughters of Jacob Kane, and River of Hope

From a setting that comes alive to characters who could have walked off the page, *Whispers on the Prairie* is an incredible story. It made me smile, laugh, and even tear up at times.

—*Nancy J. Farrier*
Author, *Painted Desert*, and coauthor, *The Immigrant Brides*

Author Vickie McDonough delivers a delightful tale in *Whispers on the Prairie*. Filled with high drama that tests the characters' faith, as well as their mettle, the story transports you back in time, right onto the Santa Fe Trail. Get those chores out of the way, set the DVR to record all your favorite shows, and don't start reading too close to bedtime, because you won't be able to put this page-turner down!

—*Loree Lough*
Award-winning author of more than 100 books

VICKIE McDONOUGH

WHITAKER
HOUSE

WHISPERS ON THE PRAIRIE
Pioneer Promises ~ Book One

Vickie McDonough
vickie@vickiemcdonough.com
www.vickiemcdonough.com

ISBN: 978-1-60374-841-4
eBook ISBN: 978-1-60374-842-1
Printed in the United States of America
© 2013 by Vickie McDonough

Whitaker House
1030 Hunt Valley Circle
New Kensington, PA 15068
www.whitakerhouse.com

Library of Congress Cataloging-in-Publication Data

McDonough, Vickie.
  Whispers on the prairie / By Vickie McDonough.
    p. cm. — (Pioneer promises ; bk. 1)
  ISBN 978-1-60374-841-4 (alk. paper)
  I. Title.
  PS3613.C3896W45 2013
  813'.6—dc23
                    2013011103

No part of this book may be reproduced or transmitted in any form or by any means, electronic or mechanical—including photocopying, recording, or by any information storage and retrieval system—without permission in writing from the publisher. Please direct your inquiries to permissionseditor@whitakerhouse.com.

1 2 3 4 5 6 7 8 9 10   ⊔⊔   19 18 17 16 15 14 13

Dedication

A very special thanks goes to Tim Talbott,
director of the Mahaffie Stagecoach Stop & Farm
Historic Site in Olathe, Kansas. Mr. Talbott took a good
hour and a half to give my husband and me a private tour
of his wonderful facility. I loved the Mahaffie Stagecoach
Stop and its wealth of history, which sparked many ideas
for this book. Thanks, Mr. Talbott, for your gracious
hosting and for answering my many questions.

Prologue

1868 · Kansas

Don't you love springtime?" Della asked as her horse approached a shallow brook. Rather than ride through it, she tapped her mare with her quirt and leaned forward. "C'mon, Jezebel. Let's go."

Ethan Harper clenched his jaw as the black mare deftly jumped the creek, and in spite of using that crazy-looking sidesaddle, Della sat the jump as well as any man riding astride. With her safely across, he relaxed, then reined in his buckskin to walk the gelding across the stream. Della knew no fear—and that made her far too reckless.

He surveyed the gently rolling hills covered in lush, ankle-high grass, still littered with patches of white from last week's snowfall. "Yep, spring is nice. Sure will be glad to not have to fork hay to the livestock anymore, at least not till next winter."

Della turned and rode back toward him. "I was talking about all the pretty wildflowers. Just look at them! Violet, yellow, snow-white, crimson, lavender...."

"Aren't violet and lavender the same thing?"

She giggled. "Of course not, you silly goose."

He didn't particularly care for his sister-in-law's name-calling, but he let it slide, like rain off oilcloth. Della could be childish at times, but his family tried to overlook that. "No one is perfect," his ma was fond of saying.

He decided to change the subject. "All that hard work sure built some muscles." He grinned and flexed his arm. "They're almost as big as Aaron's now, don't you think?"

She drew closer, reaching out to squeeze his upper arm. "Why, Ethan Harper! You'll be the belle of the ball."

He snorted a laugh and then shook his head. "I certainly hope not."

Grinning so wide that her dimples flashed, Della shrugged. "You know what I mean. Surely, you've noticed all the marriageable young ladies batting their eyes at you whenever you go to town." She cocked her head, her blue eyes glinting, and flapped her lashes like she'd been in a dust storm. "Why, Sally Ann, don't you just adore that Ethan Harper?" she gushed with a flippant flick of her wrist. "Isn't he the handsomest man in the whole county?"

He looked away, his ears warming, but Della reined her horse around to his other side.

"Why, yes I do, Minnie Sue! I've set my cap for him, so you best go find some other man to flirt with."

Ethan chuckled. "Your husband might take issue with that."

Della pursed her lips. "My husband? Whatever do you mean? My name is Sally Ann, and I've got my sights set on you."

Nudging his horse forward, he blew out a breath, tired of her pretending. Time was wasting. "I have chores waiting, and you have two children who are probably missing their ma right about now."

"Oh, pooh." Della tucked in her chin and pushed out her lower lip. "You and your two brothers sure can be spoilsports at times. Men down South enjoy a game of theatrics now and then."

"Well, this is Kansas, and men here don't have time for such foolish pastimes. We have work to do."

"Hmpf. I'm going to tell Aaron you were cranky today."

"Go ahead. He's your husband. He should be the one escorting you." Ethan generally enjoyed Della's vivid imagination and her vitality for life. Unfortunately, that same vitality often kept her from her mothering duties and, more often, her responsibilities at the stage stop. Every chance she got, she visited neighbors or spent her time on some "important" cause in Windmill—any excuse to get her away from the stage stop. As the youngest Harper son, Ethan usually drew the short straw and was designated as her chaperone. During the winter, he got a reprieve since she hated the cold, but, come March or April, Della always had spring fever and had to get out. She was fun; he just wished she'd take more interest in her two young'uns and help his ma with the cooking and cleaning.

"Let's race home, Ethan." She reined her mare around and hunkered down, grinning wickedly.

"Huh-uh. I'm responsible for your safety. Aaron would have me tarred and feathered if anything happened." He shook his head. "Plus, racing is too dangerous for the horses. The ground is still too soft."

"You can be such a stick-in-the-mud at times. The ground is fine." She swatted her mare with her quirt. "C'mon, girl!"

"Della, no!"

She flashed him a grin over her shoulder. "Last one home has to wash the supper dishes."

Ethan's gut clenched as painfully as if Aaron's fist were squeezing it. He kicked his horse with his heels. "C'mon, boy." Wrestling with what to do, he urged Alamo into a trot. His pa had drilled into him the importance of not taking any chances with the horses. They were valuable, and it was a man's duty to care for his mount. But he'd also been charged with watching over Della, and people were more important than animals. Hunkering down over Alamo's neck, he kicked him into a gallop. "Heyah!"

Della rode over the nearest hill and disappeared down the other side. Ethan kept to the road, hoping that the packed dirt would be solid enough, in spite of the recent snow. He crested the hill, and Alamo, a faster horse by far, quickly closed the gap.

Della's jubilant laughter taunted him. "You won't catch me that easily. I know a shortcut." She reined the mare away from the road and across the open prairie.

"Della!" Foolish woman. Aaron never should have fallen for a city girl.

Ethan didn't know whether to follow her across the damp fields or stick to the road. Obey his pa or keep his word to his brother.

A sudden screech jerked his gaze back to Della, and his heart leapt to his throat. The mare had stumbled and fallen to her knees. Della flew over the horse's head and rolled several times across the new grass.

"No, no, no!" Ethan jumped off of Alamo and ran. He sped past the squealing, thrashing mare and stopped over Della's still body, lying facedown in the wet grass. He dropped to the ground at her side, the dampness seeping into his pants. With a trembling hand, he brushed her hair away from her cheek. Should he move her? Leave her be?

He had to do something, or she wouldn't be able to breathe. "Oh God, please…." *Please let her be all right.*

As carefully as he'd once held his brother's newborn son, he gently rolled her over. Her head lobbed to one side, and she didn't open her eyes. He yanked out his handkerchief and dabbed at the blood on her forehead. "C'mon, Della. Wake up." He wiped the mud from her cheek, but she didn't react at all. She'd be so upset when she awakened and discovered how dirty she was.

He shook her shoulders, tears welling in his eyes. "Della, wake up."

She was so still. He squeezed his eyes shut. "God, please don't take her. Aaron will never forgive me."

With tears running down his cheeks, he gathered her in his arms and gave her another gentle shake. Her head hung back over his arm in an unnatural manner. No amount of prayers or wishing could bring her back. She was dead.

A deep, searing pain burned within his chest. He'd failed everyone—his brother, his father, his young niece and nephew. Della.

An agonizing squeal rent the quiet afternoon. Jezebel writhed in pain where she had fallen. Ethan gently set Della's body down among the wildflowers she had loved, and then he stood, feeling as if his own life was seeping away like the last of the snow in the warmth of the spring sun.

Things would never be the same.

He and his brothers had always been close, but never again. Aaron would hate him. Della may not have been the perfect wife, but Aaron had loved her from the first day he'd seen her.

Ethan marched toward the mare, angered at her for stumbling, even as he pitied her pain. He ran his hand down her swelling fetlock. Broken. Pulling out his gun, he aimed it at the mare, hands shaking.

If only someone could put him out of his misery.

Chapter One

March 1870 · Chicago

The toddler's whimpers rose to an ear-splitting scream as the little girl pushed against the chest of the woman holding her captive.

"Here, let me have her, Abigail." Sarah Marshall reached for Mary, and her friend handed over the fussy child. The girl persisted in her cries, so Sarah crooned to her, swaying in time to a waltz playing in her mind as she rubbed circles on the toddler's back.

"I don't see how you can have such patience with her. That obstinate child cries more than all the others in this orphanage combined." Abigail bent down and reached for a handsome three-year-old boy, who came rushing toward her with a big smile that showed his dimples. "Personally," Abigail raised her voice over Mary's ruckus, "I prefer the quiet ones."

Sarah smiled. "I prefer the needy ones." She leaned her cheek against Mary's head. "All is well, little one. All is well."

After a few more minutes, the wails finally subsided, and the girl began to relax. She sniffled, her whole body shaking as she finally fell into an exhausted sleep.

"Poor little one." Sarah's heart nearly broke for the child, recently orphaned by the death of her mother. At least, at such a young age, she stood a chance to adapt more easily than Sarah had when her parents died. Though the accident that claimed their lives had happened over a decade ago, she still missed her father's big smile and her mother's comforting arms.

"You'll make a good mother one day." Mrs. Rayburn leaned against the door frame, looking tired. "Are you sure you don't want to move in here?"

Sarah smiled. "If my aunt was in better health, you know I would take you up on your offer. And I do hope to be a mother someday. If I'm good, as you say, it will be only because I learned from the best."

Mrs. Rayburn swiped her hand in the air, but Sarah could tell the comment pleased her. If not for the generous care of the well-to-do widow, the six orphaned children who resided under her roof would most likely still be out on the cold Chicago streets, begging for scraps to eat, working for some cruel taskmaster—or worse.

Abigail glided to the center of the bedroom that had been converted into a nursery, holding Tommy on her hip, and pretended to dance with him. "Sarah may take a giant step in the direction of motherhood this very night."

"Abigail!" Heat marched across Sarah's cheeks as she thought of Walt and how he'd hinted at proposing—again—at her birthday dinner tonight. "I don't want that news getting out."

"Why not?" Abigail spun the boy in a circle, eliciting a giggle. "You aren't going to turn the poor fellow down again, are you?"

Sarah glared at her best friend, wishing she would learn when to hush. She hoisted Mary higher on her chest and carried her to the adjoining bedroom. Stopping beside Mary's bed, she rocked the girl from side to side to make sure she was asleep. Though she would never admit it to Abigail, the toddler's wails did grate on her nerves from time to time, especially when she hadn't slept well the night before. Holding her breath, she lowered Mary into her bed and then pulled the small quilt over her.

Sarah kept her hand ready to pat Mary's back, should she stir. Thankfully, she didn't. Straightening, Sarah checked on the two napping babies. She then tiptoed across the big room to adjust the blanket covering Ian, the six-month-old whose father had deposited him on Mrs. Rayburn's doorstep last fall. The poor man had lost his wife and couldn't care for an infant. Sarah's heart ached for each one of the youngsters. She knew how hard life could be without parents. Still, she counted herself among the lucky ones—she'd been taken in by family, though she hadn't lived in a house as fine as Mrs. Rayburn's mansion.

Bending, Sarah filled her apron skirt with rag dolls, balls, and other toys, then deposited them in the toy basket as the mantel clock in the parlor chimed two o'clock. She tiptoed out of the nursery and back into the playroom.

"Time for you girls to head home." Mrs. Rayburn crossed the room and clapped her hands. "Tommy, would you like to hear a story?"

The three-year-old lunged into the older woman's arms. She hugged him and then set him down. "My, but you're getting heavy."

"Too much porridge, I imagine." Grinning, Sarah turned to Abigail. "Are you leaving now, too?"

"Yes, Papa is sending his driver for me. See you tomorrow, Mrs. Rayburn." Abigail waved good-bye as she walked from the room. She stopped in the doorway and faced Sarah. "Do you want a ride to your uncle's shop?"

"Thank you, but I'll walk."

Tommy ran out of the nursery, lifted his little hand, and waved. Mrs. Rayburn followed him into the upstairs parlor and took hold of his hand. "I don't know how I'd manage without you girls and your friends who volunteer in the evenings. I fear I'm getting too old to manage so many young children."

Mrs. Rayburn had said the same thing for the past two years, and yet she hadn't turned Mary away when a neighbor had brought her last week. Still, Sarah couldn't help wondering if the day would come when the kind woman would feel it necessary to close her door to the orphans. What would happen to them then?

She and Abigail donned their cloaks and left the warmth of the cozy home behind as they stepped out into the blustery chill of March. The gusty wind off Lake Michigan whipped at Sarah's skirts, and the gloomy sky released a light drizzle. Abigail's driver stepped out from under the shelter of a nearby tree and opened the door of her carriage.

"Are you sure you won't let us give you a ride? It's a miserable day to be out."

"Thank you, but I'll be fine. I'm headed home, anyway, and that's the opposite direction for you."

"So, you're not clerking for your uncle this afternoon?" Abigail accepted her driver's hand and climbed into the buggy. "How did you get out of doing that?" She sat, leaning toward Sarah, her eyebrows lifted.

"I'm going home to help Aunt Emma get things ready for my birthday dinner." Sarah turned so the wind was at her back and wrapped her fist around the edges of her cloak to hold it closed. "You're still coming tonight?"

Abigail nodded, grinning. "I wouldn't miss seeing Walt propose again. I don't know why you don't just accept. Your uncle will probably throw you out one of these days, and then where will you be?" She motioned to her driver, who closed the door and scurried up to his seat.

Sarah walked quickly toward State Street. She hadn't missed how Abigail had poked her with her barbed comment about her uncle casting her out. That very possibility had been in the back of her mind. Uncle Harvey had barely tolerated her presence all these years. He'd never wanted children and wasn't happy when his wife's only sister died, leaving behind a daughter. It was a miracle the stingy man had agreed to let her live with them in the first place.

She blew out a sigh of relief at the sight of the horse-drawn trolley, just a block away. Hurrying to the middle of the street, she waited until it drew near, then grabbed the rail and stepped aboard. The sides of the carriage blocked the wind, to a degree, but the chilly air still seeped inside, bringing with it the aromas of baking bread and roasting meat.

The rain picked up, and she was glad she'd decided not to walk home. She stared out the window at the Chicago city streets, teeming with horses and buggies, fancy carriages, freight wagons, and even a man pulling a handcart. Busy people bustled up and down the boardwalks. She loved this town and hoped never to have to leave it.

If she married Walt, most likely she wouldn't. Yet she struggled with the notion of being his wife. He was a good friend, yes, and she'd hate to disappoint him. Still, shouldn't a woman have stronger feelings than friendship for the man she married?

Her uncle would be beside himself if she turned Walt down again. Maybe she should just say yes this time. At least then she'd be assured of having a home of her own—and of freeing herself from the heavy sense of owing her uncle. One would think the hours she'd spent doing chores in his home and clerking at his watch repair shop would be sufficient to cover any debt she owed, but she could never do enough to please Uncle Harvey. Still, she was grateful to have lived in his home these last twelve years. She should be satisfied and not wish for more.

And yet she did. She longed to marry a man who made her laugh like her papa had, one whose broad shoulders were strong enough to protect her. But she hadn't yet met that man. Maybe she never would. Maybe she needed to give up on wishing and just be satisfied with Walt.

⌒

Sarah sat back and rested her hands in her lap, smiling in satisfaction with the meal. She stole a glance at the sideboard loaded with food she'd helped her aunt and the cook prepare—roast leg of mutton and currant jelly, mashed potatoes, creamed spinach, fried parsnips, and glazed carrots. Just the thought of it all made her stomach ache, and they had not even served dessert yet.

Walt wagged a finger at the servant standing at attention.

The servant hurried to the table from his post in the corner of the room. "Sir?"

"Bring me some more of those parsnips."

Sarah winced at his commanding tone, then looked to the head of the table. Uncle Harvey was seated next to a stranger—Mr. Gibbons—who'd appeared at the door just before they'd sat down to dinner. The two were having a private discussion, but Sarah had overheard enough to know it was about the benefits of living on the western frontier. She couldn't imagine what anyone found interesting about the untamed prairie, with its wild Indians and abundance of dust.

At the other end of the table, Lizzie Monahan and Betty Phillips engaged her aunt in a lively chat about the latest styles in fashion, while Abigail sat infatuated with Howard Shibley, Walt's best friend, who babbled on about a recent report that the population of Chicago had reached 300,000. Sarah nearly rolled her eyes.

"What was that look for?" Walt dabbed his lips with his napkin.

Sarah leaned closer to him, so not to be heard. "If Howard has any hope of winning Abigail's heart, he should find a more interesting topic of conversation."

"I doubt romance has even entered his mind."

"Obviously." Sarah shook her head.

Walt rested his chin in his palm and caught her gaze, his hazel eyes gleaming. His ash-blond hair had been slicked down and combed back from his forehead. "Speaking of romance, are you ever going to agree to marry me?"

She sucked in a sharp breath and glanced around the table once more. Nobody cast an odd look her way, so she assumed that no one had overheard the oh-so-unromantic proposal. She had pretty much made up her mind to say yes, but his casual manner of asking made her want to shake her head. Schooling her features and straightening her posture, she replied. "I don't know."

Walt blinked, obviously taken aback. Seconds later, he scowled, then glanced across the room and motioned to the servant again. The man rushed to his side. "I seem to be out of parsnips again."

Why couldn't Walt have just kept quiet? She liked him well enough, but his frequent proposals were producing the opposite of their intended effect; they made her more inclined to avoid him than marry him. She snuck a glance at Abigail, still trying so hard to get Howard to notice her, while the man, clearly oblivious, just kept spouting his knowledge.

Sarah peeked at Walt again. He wasn't particularly handsome, but he wasn't ugly, either. He would be a good provider, being the sole heir to his father's shoe factory, but she had a feeling that life with him would be just as boring as their evenings together. She wanted to marry—to finally be free from her uncle's overpowering presence and stern glare—but she wanted a man who thought she was the only woman in the world for him. Yes, Walt seemed to feel that way, but something held her back. Was there something wrong with her?

An hour later, she stood at the door to see Walt on his way. Everyone else had already gone.

Walt hung his head and twisted his hat in his hands. "I…uh, won't ask you again." He lifted his gaze to hers, pain evident in his eyes.

She'd hurt him, and that was the last thing she'd wanted to do.

"I'm twenty-nine, Sarah. I'm ready to marry and start a family. I need to know if there's any hope that you'll say yes one day."

"And I just turned nineteen—today."

He closed his eyes and exhaled a heavy sigh. "All right. I'll give you a few more months to make up your mind."

Sarah bristled. What if she still didn't have an answer? "And then?"

He stared at her with a serious, no-nonsense expression she'd never seen before. "And then I'll be forced to look elsewhere. I mean to be married before I turn thirty." He slapped his hat on his head and stepped out into the blustery evening wind.

She watched him jog down the steps with more purpose than usual. He wanted to get away from her, and that was just fine, as far as she was concerned. She shut the door. Some birthday party that had been.

The sound of raised voices drew her to the parlor. Her aunt and uncle rarely argued, mainly because Aunt Emma's chronic illness made her too weary to fuss over trifles.

"Harvey, please. You can't be serious about this."

Sarah held her breath, all manner of ideas racing through her mind.

"You might as well come in here, Sarah. I know you're out there."

She jumped at her uncle's stern command and was tempted to slither away, but her curiosity forced her to do as bidden. "I was just saying good night to Walt," she explained as she entered the room.

"Sit down. I have something to tell you."

Aunt Emma didn't look up from the sofa but anxiously wrung her hands.

Sarah sat next to her and laid a steadying hand over her aunt's.

Her uncle paced in front of the fireplace, where a cozy blaze heated the front half of the room. Still, a shiver clawed its way down Sarah's spine. Whatever news she was about to hear, it wouldn't be good, from the looks of it.

Uncle Harvey stopped in front of the hearth, rested one hand atop the mantel, and stared into the flames. "You met Gibbons tonight." He straightened and stared at her, an unreadable expression in his brown eyes. "He's a wagon master. Been lead-ing wagon trains down the Santa Fe Trail for the past twenty years."

Sarah's thoughts whirled. Again she wondered about her uncle's interest in such a rugged man as Mr. Gibbons. He hadn't even worn proper attire for a dinner party.

"Oh, dear. Oh, dear." Aunt Emma fanned her face. "I fear I'm not feeling well."

Sarah's uncle narrowed his gaze at his wife. "You may be dis-missed as soon as I'm done."

Aunt Emma gave him a meek nod, keeping her head down.

Uncle Harvey cleared his throat, drawing Sarah's gaze again. "The truth of the matter is that my brother has written me from Kansas City to inform me that he's moving his family to the New Mexico Territory, by way of the Santa Fe Trail."

"New Mexico?" Sarah pressed her lips closed, knowing her uncle wouldn't appreciate her outburst. She sidled a glance at her aunt. Why was she so distraught? Turning her attention back to her uncle, she voiced the question that wouldn't go away. "Why would your brother want to move to such an uncivilized place?"

Uncle Harvey's nostrils flared, and Aunt Emma uttered a piti-ful moan.

"Because there is great opportunity there," her uncle insisted. "Bob says that one day, the New Mexico Territory will become a state. He has been to Santa Fe and plans to return to open a mer-cantile there."

Sarah blinked as she absorbed the information. The truth finally dawned, and she gasped, staring wide-eyed at her uncle. "Surely, you don't mean to go there, too."

He lifted his chin, revealing his wrinkled, white neck from its hiding place beneath his beard. "I most certainly do. Chicago has dozens of watchmakers. According to Bob, Santa Fe doesn't have a single one. I plan to set up shop next to his store. We'll build a door between the two, so that we can assist each other when things get busy."

Sarah could see her well-ordered life spiraling out of control. She'd already lost her parents. How could she stand to lose Aunt Emma, too? Sarah stood and started pacing the room. "You already have as much business as you can handle. And how could you expect Aunt Emma to endure such a difficult trip?"

"I've talked to the doctor, and he says the warmer climate will be much better for her. Lydia will be there to take care of her if she falls ill."

Falls ill? Didn't he realize his wife was nearly always unwell? She'd been sickly ever since she'd survived a bout of scarlet fever a year before Sarah had come to live with them. The sickness had left her frail and had robbed her of her hearing in her right ear.

Sarah doubted Aunt Emma could survive such a rugged journey. "Won't you reconsider, Uncle?"

He shook his head. "My mind is made up."

"And what about me?" Could she stay in this big house alone? He'd always expected her to pay her own way, and she could hardly afford a place as nice as this two-story brownstone.

He shrugged. "I expect you to marry Walt, and then you'll be his responsibility. I've already sold the house, so you can't stay here."

Her aunt gasped and stood. "How could you do such a thing without consulting me?"

Sarah's heart ached for her aunt. How could Uncle Harvey be so insensitive?

"Now, Emma. It's my place to make such decisions. You'll see once we arrive in Santa Fe that this move was for the best."

Emma screeched a heart-wrenching sob and ran from the room, her dark green silk dress swishing loudly.

Sarah had never once stood up to her intimidating uncle before. This time, concern for her aunt stiffened her spine, and she turned on him. "How could you be so selfish? Such a trip will probably kill Aunt Emma! Is that what you want?"

His nostrils flared. "She is no concern of yours." He walked to the dark window and stared out through the panes. "I never wanted you to come here, you know. I never wanted children. They're nothing but a nuisance. I will concede that you've been good for Emma, but she needs to learn to get along without you." He turned back to her, his eyes narrowed. "Marry Walt. He's a decent fellow."

She'd always known her uncle hadn't wanted her, but hearing the words spoken out loud pained her as badly as if she'd been stabbed in the heart. Out of respect for her aunt, she didn't lash out at him as she wanted to. "I'm not ready to marry yet." Uncle Harvey may have housed her all these years, but that didn't give him the right to force her to wed a man she didn't love. "I...I can find a boardinghouse to stay in."

He smirked. "And how do you intend to pay for it?"

A wave of panic washed over her. She had a few coins her aunt had given her—nowhere near enough to live on, even for a short time. "I'll find another job. Since I've worked for you for so long, I've honed my office skills and have plenty of experience."

"Hmpf. What employer would hire a female clerk when he can so easily find a man to do the task?"

Sarah dropped back onto the sofa, realizing the truth of his statement. What would she do? Where would she live? How could she manage without her aunt's loving guidance? The last time she'd felt as empty and confused as she did now was when she'd learned that her parents had died.

Quick footsteps sounded outside the room, and Sarah and her uncle both looked to the door. Her aunt had returned, her eyes damp, her face red and splotchy. With a trembling hand, she held a handkerchief below her nose. Sarah longed to embrace her aunt, but she would wait until her uncle left them alone.

"I see it's too late to change your mind," she said, her voice quavering. "You've wounded me deeply, Harvey. I hope you know that."

He started toward her, his expression softening, and took her hands. "Haven't I always taken care of you, darling? Have you ever lacked for anything?"

Her aunt didn't respond, but Sarah could tell by her expression that she didn't share her husband's perspective. Steeling her gaze, Emma stared up at him with rare determination in her eyes. "I won't go without Sarah."

"What?" Sarah and her uncle exclaimed at once.

"I won't go unless she goes, too." Emma hiked her chin.

Sarah didn't know what to say. This was the first time she had seen Aunt Emma stand up to her husband, and she couldn't bear to tell her that her efforts were wasted. But the last thing Sarah cared to do was leave Chicago and travel on a wagon train to Santa Fe.

Even marriage to Walt would be preferable to that.

Chapter Two

Sarah stood with Aunt Emma in the shadow of the train depot in Kansas City, Missouri, while Uncle Harvey supervised the unloading of their belongings. At his brother's request, he'd purchased numerous crates of goods for the Santa Fe mercantile. He'd also brought all of the personal items they would need, as well as several pieces of furniture her aunt couldn't bear to part with. How would they manage to convey half a boxcar of items all the way down the Santa Fe Trail? Too bad there wasn't a train that ran that far.

Aunt Emma fanned herself with her hand. "Mercy, but it's hot here."

Sarah wiped the perspiration from her forehead. "Yes, it is. The moisture in the air is so thick, you almost need a machete to walk through it."

In spite of her discomfort, Emma tittered. "You will never know how much I appreciate your coming this far, Sarah. Are you sure you won't continue on with us? I don't know how I'll bear going on and leaving you all alone."

She smiled. "Chicago is my home. I have no desire to live anywhere else. But I do hate to be parted from you. I appreciate all that you've done for me, more than words can say, Aunt Emma."

"I would never leave you if I had a choice." Tears glistened in her aunt's eyes. "I hope you know that."

Sarah patted her hand. "Of course I do. This journey wasn't your idea." She scowled at her uncle. How could he be so selfish?

Anyone could see that the train ride had brought Aunt Emma to the point of exhaustion. How did he expect her to endure the remaining miles traveling by wagon, a far harsher mode of transport?

Was she being selfish to refuse to go with her aunt? She'd already done far more than she'd originally intended by traveling this far, but she'd wanted to care for Aunt Emma until Lydia was able to assume that responsibility.

Her uncle sure didn't dote on her. In fact, there was a niggling concern in Sarah's mind that maybe he'd planned this trip just so he could be rid of his ailing wife and a niece he'd never wanted.

Dodging puddles left and right from a recent rain, she walked to the edge of the platform and scanned the people making their way through the mud toward the depot. Bob Stone, her uncle's brother, was supposed to come for them with a wagon. She had seen him only once before, when he had been passing through town and had stayed overnight with them. He bore a striking resemblance to her uncle, with the same brown hair and bushy eyebrows, although by now her uncle's was mostly gray.

Kansas City was far bigger and more civilized than she'd expected, but it was no Chicago. The depot looked brand-new and still smelled of fresh wood. A wide street spread out before her, lined on both sides by buildings of brick and wood, most of the structures several stories tall. She had expected something far more rugged.

Sarah cupped a hand over her mouth to hide a yawn. The long train ride had worn her out, as well. Still, she wanted to take the next train back to Chicago, so she stepped into line at the ticket counter. She was anxious to get back home and see how the orphans were doing. Did little Mary miss her? Had Abigail continued helping Mrs. Rayburn, even though Sarah wasn't there?

Blowing out a breath, she searched the crowd for her uncle. She spotted him at the far end of the dock beside a massive pile of boxes and pieces of furniture, waving a finger at one of the men unloading their belongings. Sarah's attention drifted past him, to a man leading a sleek black horse out of the next freight car and down a ramp. Just beyond the end of the train was a corral filled with cattle, probably waiting to be loaded.

"Can I help you, miss?"

Sarah turned back to the depot clerk and purchased her ticket home. Minutes later, she wandered away from his window, her attention drawn to an announcement board where papers flapped in the light breeze. She trapped a yellow page with her hand and read:

> *Owing to the rainstorm last night, the concert announced by the Beethoven Club at Turner's Hall was not given. It has been postponed to Monday evening next. Tickets sold for last night's concert will be good for Monday evening.*

"Hmm, imagine that. A Beethoven club."

She studied another page, her curiosity piqued.

> *A great treat for the lovers of Shakespearian drama will be the presentation this evening of the celebrated tragedy of Othello by the extraordinary Company of Artists now playing at Frank's Hall. Mr. M. S. Bingham will play Othello; Mr. James Dyer, Iago; C. H. Davenport (Dolly Davenport), Cassio; Mrs. Augusta L. Paragon, Desdemona; and Mrs. Larren in her great character of Emilia. Let those who wish to see this great play go tonight. It is the only opportunity they will have, as this Company closes here this week and will not repeat the program.*

Shakespeare and Beethoven. She was duly impressed. What didn't impress her were the puddles of water covering the depot deck, the mud being tracked up the steps, and the foul odor blowing in her direction from the cattle pens. Holding her hand over her nose, she walked to the edge of the platform again and gazed out upon the bog of murky water that pooled along the front of the depot. Down the road, a trio of men pushed against the back of a wagon with its rear wheels halfway sunk, trying to shoulder it free. She could hear their yells and grunts from a hundred feet away. How would she and her aunt ever manage those muddy streets in their long skirts?

"Sarah!"

She spun around at her uncle's call. He strode toward her, that ever-present scowl wrinkling his brow.

"This unloading is taking far longer than I expected." He yanked out his handkerchief and swiped his forehead as he surveyed the depot. "Bob must not have received my telegram, or he'd be here already. We need to get Emma out of this heat." He pulled a piece of paper from his pocket and studied it for a moment, then held it out to her. "I want you to go to Bob's house. Let him know we've arrived and tell him I said to come and bring the biggest wagon he has. Two, if possible."

"You want me to go without an escort? In a strange town?" Sarah glanced down at the slimy street.

"You'll be fine. Men in towns like this one watch out for women."

Watch out? Just what did he mean by that?

"How will I find the place?" Sarah studied the vague directions, then looked up and compared them to what she could see of the town. She still wasn't convinced she could find Uncle Bob's house. "I don't know my way around."

"There's a map on that paper. Turn it over."

She did as told. Sure enough, there was a map. The depot was clearly laid out, and it looked as if she had only a few blocks to walk. But was it truly safe for a woman to venture out alone in these parts?

"Go on, girl. Do you want your aunt to faint from the heat?" He took her by the shoulders, spun her around, and gave her a shove.

She stumbled forward, then glanced around to see if anyone had noticed.

"Be quick about it. I don't want any vandals absconding with our valuable effects."

Sarah worked hard to maintain a neutral expression, so as not to reveal how much this errand irked her. If she were his daughter, would he send her off, unescorted, in an unfamiliar town? She sincerely doubted it.

She picked her way down the steps, holding her skirts in one hand and the railing with the other, trying to avoid the worst of the slop. All too soon, she reached the street. No matter which way she went, she'd be ankle-deep in the nasty stuff.

A tall, thin man who'd just helped an older woman from a buggy strode toward her on a sidewalk she hadn't notice from the platform above. "Here, miss, let me carry you across the road so you won't sully your dress. Unless, of course, you are waiting on someone."

Sarah shrank back at the thought of a stranger carrying her anywhere. "Thank you for your offer, but no."

He scowled but didn't look offended. "Are you sure? You'll have a difficult time managing the muck with all those petticoats."

Cheeks flaming at his mention of her undergarments, she ducked her head. "I'll be fine, thank you."

He nodded, lips pressed tight, then jogged up the stairs.

She exhaled a sigh, glad to have him gone. Then, steeling herself for the inevitable, she stepped into the street. Her foot sunk, but not as deep as she'd expected. With skirts held high, she lifted her foot from the goo and carefully took another step. On a positive note, the nasty mess cooled her feet; yet she feared her shoes would be ruined. She glanced to the left to make sure no one was coming, then made her way to the middle of the road, where she paused to catch her breath. If she could just make it to the boardwalk....

"Hey, look out!"

Sarah whipped her head toward the warning, and her heart leapt up to her throat at the sight of a runaway horse charging toward her. She jumped back as it ran straight at her and flew past so close she could feel the heat of the creature's body. Arms flailing, she fell backwards, landing in the muck with a *splat*.

"Ah!" Her dress! She lifted her hands, now caked with mud and who knew what else. Behind her, laughter echoed across the depot's platform. Never had she been so humiliated.

A man on horseback rode toward her at a fast trot. This time, she wouldn't refuse assistance. He slowed the horse and gazed down, his brown eyes showing an odd mix of concern and amusement. Was he laughing at her, too?

"You all right, lady?"

She closed her eyes. "Do I look all right?"

"You're not hurt, ma'am?"

"Only so far as the pain of humiliation."

"Good." He nudged his horse in the side. "Then I'll go catch my stallion. He's real valuable."

"Catch your stallion? Of all the...." Sarah stared at the man, her mouth wide open. A fly buzzed dangerously close, so she snapped her lips together, then watched the man chase after his precious horse. She flung the mud from her hands. Never had she encountered a more insensitive brute.

⌣

"Are you feeling better now that you've bathed and dressed in clean clothing?" Lydia Stone stared at her with concerned gray eyes.

"Yes, much better. Thank you." Sarah smiled. "And I'm terribly sorry for the muddy mess I made in your washroom."

She swatted a hand in the air. "Trust me, it isn't the first time. We haven't had rain for so long that everyone has been praying for it, and then we get three months' worth in one hour this morning."

She shook her head. "Too bad you couldn't have arrived yesterday. The streets were dry as hardtack."

Sarah finally took time to study the parlor. Furniture almost as nice as her aunt and uncle's filled the room. She blinked as a sudden thought wormed its way across her mind. Why wasn't the furniture packed?

Turning back to Lydia, she asked, "Has Aunt Emma arrived?"

Lydia nodded. "She's in bed, resting. She sure looked all tuckered out."

The front door handle jiggled, and her uncle and his brother stomped in, mud flying. Lydia gasped and hurried toward them. "Bob, why didn't you enter through the back and leave your filthy boots on the porch?"

Her husband looked down, then back up at her, regret in his eyes. "Sorry, Sugar. We were talking, and I just didn't think about it."

Lydia heaved a sigh. "Well, don't move another foot. You'll ruin my carpets if you get that muck on them. Go ahead and take off your boots."

Uncle Harvey frowned with obvious irritation, but Bob bent to do as bidden, nudging her uncle in the thigh with his elbow. "You best get those off, Harv, or Lydia may not let us have any of her mincemeat pie, and you sure don't want to miss that."

Sarah's uncle removed his shoes, but she could tell he didn't like it. In stockinged feet, he followed Bob into the parlor and both men sat.

Bob shook his head. "I feel real bad about all this. I don't understand why you never got my telegrams. I sent a second one, just to be sure. Think I'll go back to that telegraph station and demand a refund."

Sarah wondered what he was talking about, but good manners kept her from inquiring. "Did you get everything moved?"

Bob shook his head again. "No. It's impossible with all that mud. We rented a storage room at the depot and hired several men to transfer the crates and furniture to it. Should be safe there. They have a guard that watches the depot at night."

She hoped he was right. What would her aunt and uncle do if they lost everything?

Bob rested his elbows on his knees and hung his head. He seemed as relaxed and friendly as her uncle was stuffy and surly.

Lydia returned to the room with a colored servant carrying a tray with a teapot. She motioned for him to set it down on the drum table. "Thank you, Simeon. I'll serve the tea. Please have Eliza come clean that mess at the door."

"Yes'm, Miz Stone." He turned and left, Uncle Harvey's eyes watching his every step.

Something had definitely upset her uncle. He looked as if he would lash out at the first person to say the wrong thing.

No one spoke until the tea had been served. Bob took a sip, then set his cup and saucer on the table beside his chair. "I feel real bad about this, Harv, especially after the way I needled you to come with us."

"I do, too." Lydia lifted a couch pillow into her lap and rubbed the fringe with her fingertips. "But we couldn't have anticipated the Martinson and Cooper children coming down with whooping cough." She shrugged. "There's nothing to be done. Months could pass before everyone is well again. We'll just have to postpone our trip."

Sucking in a sharp gasp, Sarah glanced at her uncle. *Postpone their trip?* No wonder he was upset. He wasn't the kind of man to change course midstream.

She looked out the parlor door to the entryway, and the stairs leading to the second floor, where Aunt Emma rested. Who would take care of her, if not Lydia? Would Uncle Harvey delay their journey until his brother and sister-in-law were ready to travel, or would he forge ahead to Santa Fe? A rampant rush of questions ran through Sarah's mind. If only Uncle Harvey hadn't sold the house, he might have been inclined to forget his crazy plan. But it was too late now.

"So, what will you do?" Bob asked.

Leaving his tea untouched, Harvey stood and paced the room. He assumed the familiar pose of standing by the hearth, one hand rested on the mantel, and staring out the window. "We'll continue on. There's really no alternative. We can't go back to Chicago."

"Why don't you wait and go with us? Of course, you're welcome to stay here until that time. Since our Alice is married now, we have her old room available for guests." Lydia glanced at Sarah.

"Oh, don't be concerned about me." Sarah straightened and scooted to the edge of her seat. "I'll be heading back to Chicago two days from now."

"You mean, you're not going to Santa Fe?" Lydia looked aghast. "Where will you live? How will you support yourself?"

"She has a fiancé," her uncle offered before she could respond. "But Sarah will have to travel with us now. Emma will need her assistance."

Sarah shot up from her chair. "I can't! Mrs. Rayburn and the children at the orphanage need me. I promised I'd return by next week." The fact that she was not officially engaged to Walt didn't seem a matter worth arguing about at the moment. "I can't go, Uncle. Surely, you understand."

He caught her gaze. "That Mrs. Rayburn has sponged off of your free services for far too long."

"Now, Harv, hang on." Bob rested his chin in his palm and tapped his cheek with his index finger. "I have an idea."

Uncle Harvey glared at his brother but kept quiet.

"There's a widow woman in Windmill, across the Missouri River in Kansas. She's a friend of Lydia's."

His wife clapped her hands. "Of course! That's the perfect solution. Susannah Baker would be happy to travel with you and look after Emma."

Bob nodded. "Her son and his wife are down in Santa Fe, about to have their first child. Susannah wasn't happy about the delay."

Sarah's uncle rubbed a finger across his mustache. "And you vouch for this woman? She'll tend to Emma, if need be, and won't be a bother to us otherwise?"

"I'm sure of it," Bob said. "Susannah has her own wagon and driver. She'd be good company for Emma, and that way Sarah wouldn't have to change her plans."

Sarah blew out a relieved breath. Two more days, and she'd be back in Chicago. Back to the children.

"All right. If you're positive." Uncle Harvey stared at Sarah for a long moment. "You can return to Chicago—but only after you accompany us to Windmill."

Sarah's whole body stiffened. "No! I can't. I told you, I have commitments back in Chicago." She turned to Bob. "How far is this Windmill town?"

"Not more than a week's travel."

She sat back, stunned. A week there and a week back—and how would she make the return journey? And then she'd have to wait for another train. It would be nearly a month before she was in Chicago again. Tears stung her eyes, but she wouldn't cry—not in front of her uncle.

"You'll travel with us to that town, and if that woman agrees to go with us, you can return to Chicago."

She knew it would do no good to argue. Uncle Harvey never changed his mind, especially when doing so would convenience her. "Please excuse me." Sarah stood and exited the room, wanting desperately to run from her uncle's sight. She stepped out onto the back porch and gazed up at the brilliant blue sky. Prayer wasn't something she'd done much, not since her parents had died. And yet she had nowhere else to turn. "God, could You send someone else to help my aunt? Chicago is the only place I've ever called home—the only constant in my life. Please, I need to return home."

Chapter Three

Sarah followed her uncle and Bob down the boardwalk. Though the sun shone bright today, a North wind had blown in overnight, leaving a bite in the air. Yesterday's sun had dried out most of the mud, and one of Lydia's servants had been able to rescue Sarah's muck-encased boots. Thank goodness she'd been wearing a dark blue dress, or it would have been ruined. Other than her dignity being bruised, she'd fared rather well after her tumble in the street.

She yawned. Sleep had been elusive the night before, as she'd lain on a cot in an upstairs storage closet, wrestling with her fate—and her guilt. She should be glad to spend another week with her aunt, but she could hardly wait to be free from her uncle's dominating ways.

She'd be with the women now, if Lydia hadn't suggested she go along with the men this morning to help purchase supplies and buy some clothing and other things she would need for the extended trip. The kind woman had slipped her some coins but had still ordered Uncle Harvey to see to it that Sarah had whatever she needed, since he was the one who'd insisted she travel with them further. Missouri, Kansas...Abigail would never believe it when she told her she'd traveled so far from Chicago.

They stopped outside of a large mercantile, and Bob pulled his pocket watch from his vest and looked at it. "Ethan Harper is supposed to meet us here at ten. He'll help get you outfitted. His family runs one of the last stage stops along the Santa Fe Trail before you head out onto the prairie, and many a wagon train's stopped at his place to overnight."

"Good." Her uncle nodded. "When do you think we'll know about joining up with another wagon train?"

"Not sure." Bob shrugged. "Ethan might know of one you can join."

Sarah watched a trio of women about her age stroll the boardwalk on the far side of the street. They were dressed in hoopskirts and hats. She'd stopped wearing those years ago. A tall, broad-shouldered man stepped out the door of a hotel and nearly ran into the three women. He stopped short and lifted his wide-brimmed hat. Sarah couldn't hear what was said, but it was obvious the trio was enamored of him. They watched as he took his leave and crossed the street, coming her way. One of the women snapped open a fan and waved it in front of her face, then leaned toward one of the other women, as if to whisper something.

Returning her gaze to the long-legged man, Sarah had to admit there was a rugged appeal to him. Of course, he wasn't neat and polished, like the Chicago men she knew, but his skin had a sun-kissed tone, and his chin was covered with just enough dark whiskers that she found him oddly alluring. If ever she'd had an image of a cowboy in her mind, this man fit the bill. Wearing dark pants, boots, a loose-fitting linen shirt, and a lazy grin, he made her mouth go dry. All she could see of his face was that smile, because his hat blocked her view of his nose and eyes. She forced her gaze away, lest he caught her staring.

She glanced at Bob and saw him smiling—right at the man. So, this must be whom they were waiting for. If the men in charge of the wagon train looked like him, then perhaps they would all fare better than she'd expected.

"Morning, Ethan."

"Bob."

Her uncle's brother turned to her and Harvey. "This is the man I told you about—Ethan Harper. He can help get you outfitted." Bob waved a hand at Uncle Harvey. "This is my older brother, Harvey Stone, and his niece, Sarah Marshall."

Her uncle held out his hand, and the man shook it, but his head swiveled toward her. Sarah's heart beat faster. The man lifted his hat. "My pleasure."

Sarah tilted her head back to look him in the eye. Suddenly she felt as if a horse had sat on her chest. "Not you!"

Confusion dimmed the gleam in his eyes, but then they sparked again. "Ah, the mud maiden. I see you fared well. No lasting damage."

"No thanks to you."

He set his hat back on his head, but, this time, she could see his face fully—and a handsome face it was. "I apologize for not stopping to help you, but you seemed fine, except for having some ruffled feathers, and I needed to catch that stallion before he got away."

Surely, the man had not just compared her to a chicken! She supposed she shouldn't be surprised, considering his rudeness yesterday. Still, she felt a measure of disappointment to discover that he was like her uncle, favoring money over manners.

"How is it you two know each other?" Bob asked.

Mr. Harper had the gall to grin. "She had a run-in with one of my horses yesterday."

"Ah." Bob smiled. "Not the reason for all that mud in my house?"

"Yes, it is." Sarah glared at the uncouth man and lifted her chin. "He chose to chase his horse rather than help me."

Bob brushed his hand over his mouth to hide a smile. "Well, horses are worth a pretty penny. We've had a shortage ever since the war."

"I see." Sarah turned away, sensing she would not win this battle. She couldn't pinpoint just why she was disappointed, but she was. Had she hoped Bob would stand up for her? No one ever had, not since her father's death; she wasn't sure why she expected it now.

"Let's get down to business. What do we need to purchase?" Uncle Harvey asked.

Mr. Harper pulled a piece of paper from his pants' pocket and unfolded it. "First off, you'll need a sturdy wagon and a healthy team. You don't want to pinch on money where they're concerned. And there's a list of food supplies, but don't overbuy, because you need to keep the load as light as possible."

"They'll need two wagons, since we've bought supplies for a store we plan to set up down there," Bob said.

"Hmm." Mr. Harper looked at Sarah, and she tried not to squirm. "Have you ever driven a wagon?"

She pursed her lips and lifted her nose. "Of course not. We've always had a driver."

He had the nerve to roll his eyes. "Of course you did."

Sarah was certain that, if they'd been alone, she would have smacked the lout.

"You'll need to hire a driver or two. If there's a family on the train with some older boys, that should work."

Uncle Harvey scowled, and Sarah could see him adding up the dollars in his head.

They followed Mr. Harper several blocks to a livery. Out back, the owner had two corrals, one with a dozen or so horses and mules, the other with huge cows.

"I recommend oxen first, then mules. Oxen are a bit slower, but they're more dependable, less likely to be stolen by Indians, and more likely to survive on the available vegetation. If you use horses, then you'll have to buy grain, and that costs more money and takes up space in the wagons. Oxen are the least expensive and the best deal overall."

A tall, thin man with a long black beard walked out of the livery and approached them. He waved at Mr. Harper. "Mornin', Ethan."

"Marcus." Mr. Harper nudged his chin in Sarah's direction. "Brought you some customers, if the price is right."

The man smiled, his brown eyes twinkling. "It always is, isn't it?"

Mr. Harper grinned and slapped the man on the shoulder. "I've got some folks here that are looking for a couple of wagons and teams of oxen."

Sarah eyed the huge creatures with sharp horns and shivered. She had no desire to get friendly with one of those. "Um…Uncle Harvey, excuse me, but you're familiar with horses and know how to handle them. Wouldn't they do better for us?"

Her uncle frowned at her, then glanced from the horses to the oxen and back. "As much as I hate to admit it, she does have a point."

Sarah's heart skipped at his unexpected assent. She hadn't purposely plotted to undermine Mr. Harper, but it did make her feel good to think her uncle might side with her for once. Besides, if the horses weren't strong enough to pull the wagon, then maybe her uncle would forget this whole mess and return to Chicago.

"I am familiar with horses," he said. "I know nothing about oxen."

"Most city folk don't, but herding oxen is easy enough to learn." Mr. Harper's eyebrows dipped. "It's your choice, but with all the equipment you have to haul, you'll need two wagons, and I highly recommend the oxen to pull them. They hold up better in times when grass and water are scarce, and there'll be plenty of places like that along the Santa Fe Trail."

Her uncle walked over to the oxen corral and studied the ugly animals for a long moment. Then, he returned to the horse pen and hung his arms over the railing. "What are you planning to use, Bob?"

"I bought mules, but Mr. Harper, here, knows what he's talking about. I might reconsider, especially since Lydia wants to take the cupboard and desk her grandfather built."

Mr. Harper stood back, not forcing his opinion, and for that, Sarah gave him credit. But why should he? It wasn't his money that was being spent, or his family who was traveling. Shouldn't they be able to buy what worked best for them? She walked up to the railing, careful to avoid the muddy depressions in the ground. Her gaze landed on a pretty, silver-colored horse. "What about that one?"

Footsteps sounded behind her, then Mr. Harper and the livery man joined her.

"If you're pointin' at that gray, she's a ridin' mare. Too small to pull a wagon." Marcus nodded his head backward. "You need stock horses, like those big ones in back."

"And if you're planning to buy a freight wagon," Mr. Harper added, "you should at least get mules for that."

Marcus nodded. "That's right."

"All right, then. Set me up with half a dozen mules and your best stock horses." Uncle Harvey turned to Mr. Harper. "Where are the wagons?"

"Just down the street. You might want to consider getting another pair of mules for your freight wagon."

Her uncle pressed his lips together and shook his head. "Six will be enough."

Sarah nodded at their guide, feeling a bit smug that her uncle had listened to her and chosen horses instead of oxen. She shouldn't feel that way, she knew, but after what happened yesterday, it felt good to gain the upper hand.

The group set out for the wagon shop. Peeking out of the corner of her eye, Sarah noticed that her uncle's lips were still pursed. Was he upset about their decision?

Blowing out a sigh, she increased her pace to keep up with Mr. Harper's brisk steps. A true gentleman would slow his to match the lady's, but it was obvious this cowboy or frontiersman—whatever he was—had not been raised with proper manners. Otherwise, he never would have left her wallowing in the mud yesterday.

She peered sideways at him. He had a nice profile: straight nose, solid jaw line, and nice lips. He turned his head and caught her staring, but instead of the cocky grin he'd given her earlier, he seemed to have retreated behind a wall of disdain. Maybe he was like her uncle even more, in that he didn't like to lose.

Ah, well. What did it matter, anyway? After today, she'd never see him again.

⌒

Ethan shook his head as he plowed forward. Why did city folks such as these seek him out and ask his advice if they weren't going to take it? He'd seen others like the man and his niece, who thought they knew everything. Della had been like that, and look where it had gotten her. He hated to think of the pretty woman whose eyes had flashed fire at him yesterday as she sat in the mud meeting the same fate as Della. Women like those two were better off in the safety of a city, where they didn't have worry about encountering Indians, rattlesnakes, or prairie dog holes that could break a horse's leg. Why would she even want to leave the security of the city for someplace as rugged as Santa Fe?

He'd never understand. All he could do was try to talk them into buying the safest, sturdiest equipment and adequate supplies. If they didn't want to listen, it was no hair off his scalp.

Miss Marshall's silk dress swished beside him as she hurried to keep up. He really ought to slow down, but he wasn't exactly in the mood to be accommodating. Still, memories of his mother scolding him for not being a gentleman made him slow his pace. He hoped the snippet of a woman had packed some more serviceable dresses, because that one would be snagged to pieces after a week of walking across the prairie.

He turned the corner and stopped at Williams' Wagon Shop. He doubted they'd had time to build a new wagon since his last trip to town, but maybe they'd have some decent used ones on hand from city folk who left them after wising up and heading back East. How long before these two greenhorns did the same?

Ethan greeted Frank Williams and his two sons, then introduced them to Harvey Stone and his niece, and they followed Frank out behind his shop. "I've only got four vehicles, and one of those I wouldn't sell to my worst enemy. Cracked axle." He waved his hand across the near-empty yard. "That one over there."

Ethan strode over to the freight wagon and examined it. "This would do nicely for your second wagon," he said to Mr. Stone, "providing Frank can raise the walls. As it is, it won't hold enough to bother taking it out on the trail."

Frank rubbed his chin and nodded. "We could do that. Might take a few days. Gotta finish the wheels for that wagon in the shop first."

Mr. Stone nodded. "How much do you want for it?"

Frank quoted a fair price, and Mr. Stone grimaced, but then he nodded again. The man sure didn't like to part with his money.

Ethan walked past the Conestoga wagon that had once been red but now resembled the color of one of his niece's pink dresses. Behind it was a farm wagon that looked to be in decent condition. He checked the wheels and peeked underneath at the floor and axle. "This one looks solid."

Both of the Stone men walked toward him, but the woman split off, walking around the pink wagon. She stood on her tiptoes and peered inside the ramshackle Conestoga.

Ethan resisted rolling his eyes and focused on the men. "What do you think? Other than needing a new canvas on top, I think this farm wagon would suit you well."

Both men circled the wagon, meeting up with Miss Marshall on the far side. "This one is larger, Uncle Harvey." She nodded at the pink monstrosity. "Wouldn't it make sense to get the bigger one, since you have so much to haul?"

He swiveled his head back and forth between the two wagons. "It does look a good fifteen to eighteen inches wider."

Bob Stone nodded. "There might even be enough room that the women could sleep inside it, and Emma could lie down during the day if she felt faint."

They approached the pink wagon and peered inside.

Ethan looked at Frank, who shrugged. "It's an all right wagon, I reckon. The other one is better, but that painted one should hold up fine."

"*Should*" was the word that concerned Ethan. What if it didn't? Little Miss Priss would be stranded on the open prairie, and that thought bothered him—a lot.

"Besides, just think how much easier it will be to find ours among all those wagons that look exactly the same."

Miss Marshall may be creative in her persuasive techniques, but color was a foolish reason for choosing a wagon. Ethan strode toward the men, hoping to sway them before they had their minds made up. "That other wagon is a better one. More solid. And, with as far as you have to go, you want better."

Mr. Stone once again looked back and forth from one wagon to the other. "We need the bigger wagon. It won't pay me to leave behind half of the supplies I've already bought." He looked at Frank. "We'll take the freight wagon and this one, provided you can have them ready in two days."

Frank sidled a glance at Ethan and then nodded. "As long as you're certain. Once you drive them off my property, they belong to you."

Mr. Stone gave a swift nod, pulled out a double eagle gold coin, and handed it to Frank. "There's my down payment."

Frank pocketed the coin, then held out his hand, and the two men shook on the deal. Ethan watched Miss Marshall trace her fingertips over the side of the pink wagon, as if she'd found a special treasure. The naive woman had no idea of the hardship she would soon face. She caught his gaze and lifted her chin, a tiny smirk pulling at her lips.

He forced his feet into motion, and her gaze grew wary at his approach. "Your uncle has the list of supplies. You seem plenty efficient at purchasing things, so I'll bid you good day."

Ethan said his good-byes to the men and strode off, glad to get away from the know-it-all greenhorns. He was ready to get back to his family and home and be done with people like the Stone men and Miss Marshall. The problem was, they'd probably overnight at his family's stage stop on their way down the trail. Well, if so, he'd just have to make himself scarce.

⟋

Sarah watched the long-legged man stride away. She'd been thrilled that her uncle had actually listened to her reasoning, for once; but Mr. Harper had spoiled her victory. The friendly man they'd first met had hardened when they'd declined his advice. She looked at the smaller wagon and shook her head. What if she'd made a mistake?

Chapter Four

Aunt Emma's rattling cough echoed out the back of the wagon. Sarah wished she could do more to help her— make her more comfortable, take her cough and aches away. Erase the pain of her husband selling her home. *Something.* Surely, Uncle Harvey had noticed that all the dust and debris stirred up by the animals' hooves and wagon wheels were making her condition worse. Sarah had tried closing the flaps, but the heat inside the wagon had become unbearable.

She swiped at a trickle of sweat and glanced at the brown smudge on the back of her hand. The mess reminded her of a mud facial mask, a popular treatment for wealthy Chicago women willing to pay a small fortune to enhance the beauty of their skin. Sarah doubted the dirt clinging to her face would make it look any better, so she pulled a dingy handkerchief from her sleeve and wiped her forehead and cheeks.

The sight of the dirty cloth made her wince. After a week on the trail, she could only imagine how much dirt had accumulated in her hair. No doubt it looked more brown now than blonde. They were scheduled to arrive in Windmill today, and she was prepared to part with a few of her coins in exchange for a nice, warm bath, wherever one could be found—even if she had to go knocking on residents' doors.

Yawning, she eyed the tailgate of the wagon. She would have ridden inside with her aunt, in spite of the dreadful heat, but the shaking and jarring had nearly loosened every tooth in her mouth, and so she walked. Too bad they couldn't have bought that pretty gray mare back in Kansas City for her to ride.

A shout rang out. The news trickled down the line to the last dozen wagons like water bubbling its way along a creek bed. They'd reached Windmill.

Ten minutes later, Sarah followed the wagon train into the small town. Sure enough, right in the middle of the town square was a windmill that looked just like one a Dutchman might have built in Holland. Windmill was exactly what she'd expected Kansas City to be like prior to traveling there, with only three streets of one- and two-story buildings made of wood or stone. She passed two saloons, a doctor's office, one of the smallest banks she'd ever seen, a boardinghouse, a mercantile, a church, and a handful of other establishments. A smattering of houses spread out beyond the businesses. If she had to guess, no more than two hundred people lived here.

Business owners strolled out of their shops, some watching, others waving. She wondered if they were especially friendly or just hoping for customers. Her heart dropped a few inches when she realized she hadn't seen a bathhouse.

The man leading the wagon train, Mr. Wayne, trotted past on his horse and waved to her uncle, who was driving their Conestoga. "Continue on out of town, then circle the wagons," he shouted. "We'll camp there for the night."

Sarah cast a wistful glance at the boardinghouse. She'd hoped they might be able to stay there tonight. To bathe in a tub of warm water. To sleep on a real bed. To eat food without crunching dirt between her teeth.

In another day or two, the wagon train would move on toward Santa Fe, and she'd at least be able to stay at the boardinghouse until she could catch the stagecoach back to Kansas City. Bob and Lydia had graciously invited her to stay with them until the next train heading east.

At the thought of the wagon train's departure, something pinched her heart. She dreaded saying good-bye to Aunt Emma. She had an ominous inkling that she would never see her aunt again. Though her uncle had treated her with indifference, her aunt had always been loving and comforting. It would almost be like losing her mother again. Her throat tightened.

The wagons circled, and Sarah hurried to check on her aunt. She peered over the tailgate. Emma lay on a thin mattress that rested atop tightly packed crates of dishes, blankets, food items, and personal belongings. The cabinet Emma's father had built rose up on one side, the carved bed frame on the other. Wouldn't Mr. Harper have a fit of apoplexy if he saw those heavy items? The thought brought a smile to her face. "How are you faring, Auntie?"

"Like every bone in my body has been rearranged. I'm afraid to sit up, for fear I'll flop around like a rag doll—" She broke into a hacking cough that brought tears running down her cheeks.

"Let me get you some water." Sarah rushed around to the side of the wagon, wrestled the lid off of the water barrel, and dipped in the ladle. Carefully, she carried it back to her aunt, who sipped until it was gone.

"Thank you, dear." Her aunt handed the ladle back and studied her.

A lump formed in Sarah's throat.

"You've grown into such a lovely young lady, Sarah. I want you to know I'm proud of you." Her gaze filled with emotion. "I don't know how I'll manage without you, but I want you to know that isn't why I'll miss you. I love you, dear, and I haven't told you nearly enough."

Sarah glanced down, batting her lashes to keep from crying. "I love you, too, Auntie. I wish Uncle Harvey would forget this foolhardy scheme and return home."

Her aunt smiled serenely. "Men need their dreams, dear, and we women must allow them, and follow wherever they go. I'm just surprised Harvey hasn't wanted to do something like this before now."

Sarah lowered the tailgate. "But how will you bear it?"

Emma sat up, wobbling a little, then crawled to the back of the wagon and took Sarah's hand. "I know you think Harvey is a mean ol' curmudgeon, but I love him. He wasn't always like that."

"It's my fault, isn't it?" Nibbling her lower lip, Sarah looked away, watching the other travelers unhitching their teams and setting up camp. She needed to get busy before her uncle snapped at her. At least this would be the last time she had to mess with the smelly animals.

"No, dear. It has nothing to do with you, but I am sorry for how grumpy he's been toward you. He's set in his ways." She covered a cough. "He wanted a son, you know. And when our little Harvey Junior died, shortly after his birth, it broke Harvey's heart. I never could carry another baby to full term, and, somewhere along the way, my husband decided he didn't want children."

Sarah stared at her. All those years she'd lived with her aunt and uncle, and yet she never knew they'd had a son—and lost him—much less several babies. "I'm sorry, Aunt Emma. I can't imagine how painful that must have been for you both. And then, you got stuck with me."

"You're a blessing, not a burden." Her aunt cupped her cheek with her hand, her eyes caressing her face. "I haven't said anything to you about Walt, but I feel I need to."

Sarah stiffened. She didn't need another person pushing her toward him.

Her aunt fiddled with the cuff of her sleeve for a moment. "Sarah, don't marry Walt if you're not certain he's the man God has chosen for you. Don't get me wrong—he's a nice man; but I don't see stars in your eyes when he comes around. You don't rush to the mirror and pinch your cheeks or fix your hair when he arrives. You don't act like a woman in love."

Sarah's mouth gaped open, but she quickly closed it. "Forgive me for saying so, but you don't either, Auntie."

Emma gave her a wan smile. "The excitement of marriage tempers with time, but a young woman in love should be beaming with it."

Sarah considered that for a moment. "Do you think it's better to wait for the possibility of love when you have a perfectly good man who wants to marry you?" A movement caught her eye, and she turned to watch two young boys chase after a runaway goat. They zigzagged one way and then the other, barely missing a woman bent over a campfire. She jumped out of the way, waving a wooden spoon at them. They laughed as they dodged around her. How would it feel to be young and carefree like those boys?

"Sarah, I'm not too good at speaking what's on my mind. I don't want you to make a mistake and marry Walt just because he's the only man showing interest. If he doesn't stir your heart, then wait for the man who does."

Ethan Harper barged into her thoughts—tall, loose-legged, handsome. She shook her head, thinking she must be losing her mind. A man like him wouldn't give a citified woman like her a second glance.

⟶

Ethan skidded to a stop and did a double take, his heart jumping clear up into his throat. He would recognize that pink covered wagon—and the lovely woman standing behind it—anywhere. He had to give her credit for making it this far, because he'd had serious doubts.

Miss Marshall assisted a woman out of the back of the wagon, then dragged a crate to the edge of the tailgate, lifted it out, and set it on the ground. With Miss Marshall's help, the older woman dropped onto the wooden box, looking wrung out from the effort. No one had said anything to Ethan about traveling with an ailing woman, as he assumed her to be; she was too young to be moving so slowly otherwise. Just another factor working against these city folks.

Miss Marshall's uncle and a younger man had almost finished unhitching the mules from the Conestoga, but no one had started on the team pulling the pink monstrosity. Ethan stepped forward without a second thought and walked toward it. As he drew nearer, and Miss Marshall caught sight of him, her eyes widened. With one hand, she hastily tucked some wayward strands of hair behind her ear.

A fist tightened in his gut. The dainty woman who'd been spotless in her silk dress a few days ago now stood before him once more, looking as if she'd fallen into yet another a mud puddle. Her cheeks were smudged with dirt, and her cotton dress, which he suspected she'd bought new in Kansas City, was filthy. She resembled a street urchin he once saw in an alley. He didn't want to feel sorry for her, but he did. He'd never understand why someone so refined would leave her comfortable home to endure the rigors of the Santa Fe Trail.

"Evening, Miss Marshall." He tipped his hat to her, then glanced at the other woman. He guessed she was in her mid- to late forties, but she was even thinner than Miss Marshall.

"Mr. Harper." She nodded. "This is my aunt, Emma Stone." She turned to face the woman. "He's the man who helped us buy our wagons and stock."

He nearly snorted a laugh but held himself in check. He'd *tried* to help them. "Would you mind if I unhitched your horses for you?"

Miss Marshall jutted out that pert little chin of hers as if it were a weapon. "Why would you do that?"

"Because I often help people that need it."

"Oh." The poor woman looked exhausted. "Thank you, but my uncle would probably be upset if I didn't do it."

Ethan strode forward. "If he gets upset, he can come see me, and I'll set him straight. In the West, men help women, not the other way around." He paused, glancing at Mrs. Stone. "I apologize, ma'am. I shouldn't have said that about your husband." At least, not in front of her.

"No offense taken, Mr. Harper." Though she smiled, it did nothing to hide her exhaustion. "I'd be most grateful if you'd help Sarah. She tries to take on too much at times."

"You do realize I'm standing right here, Auntie."

Mrs. Stone's soft gaze turned serious. "Let the kind man help, Sarah."

"Fine." She rolled her eyes, and one corner of her mouth turned up. "You may unhitch the horses."

Ethan grinned at her less-than-enthusiastic acquiescence.

"And invite the nice man to dine with us, Sarah."

Miss Marshall's lovely blue eyes went as round as saucers. "But all we have to eat are beans and some leftover biscuits." She visibly shuddered.

"That sounds just fine, ma'am."

She narrowed her eyes, and he grinned again. Why did he enjoy goading her so much?

"Weren't you going to tend our horses?"

He tugged his hat down. "Yes, ma'am. I was just fixin' to do that." He walked toward her, holding her gaze, then shook his head and chuckled. *Sarah.* He liked her name.

"'Fixin'—just what kind of word is that?" she mumbled, just loud enough for him to hear.

He didn't think she expected a response, but she watched him for a moment before busying herself with meal preparations.

He unhitched the lead horse and led it to the far side of the wagon. Not since Della had he met a woman with so much spirit. Aaron would like the feisty city gal. Ever since Della had died, Ethan had been determined to find a new wife for his oldest brother. Maybe when the wagon train stopped at his family's stage stop, Ethan could introduce them. But then, what would be the point? Miss Marshall wouldn't be staying for more than one night.

⁓

As Sarah dished up the beans leftover from lunch, Uncle Harvey marched into camp wearing five layers of dust and a scowl. After he'd finished unhitching the mules, he'd headed off toward town without so much as a wave. What could have happened to upset him so?

Sarah handed her aunt a plate, then searched for Mr. Harper. He was just leading the sixth horse around to the far side of the wagon, so she handed his plate to her uncle. He glowered at her, and her nerves danced as if they were on fire. What was wrong? Had one of the mules gone lame?

"I went into town and tracked down that Susannah Baker. Turns out that she joined up with the last wagon train that left town."

"What?" Sarah froze, the food no longer tempting her stomach. "Isn't there someone else in town who can go with you?"

He shook his head and shoved a spoonful of beans into his mouth. "I asked around."

No. No. No.

"You'll just have to go. There's no other alternative."

She backed up. "But I can't. I have obligations to fulfill back in Chicago."

He dropped the plate onto the tailgate and started toward her. "Your obligation is to us."

"I promised Mrs. Rayburn I'd return. I simply can't go with you any farther." Tears ran down Sarah's cheeks as she saw the life she loved blowing away like Kansas dust.

"You *will* go. You owe us that much for all we've done for you."

She opened her mouth, but nothing came out. Would she never be done owing him? "I—I don't even have any clothes, other than the few things I brought for the trip. All my possessions are at Abigail's."

"Now, Harvey, don't force her to go. Her friends are all back in Chicago." Emma gave Sarah a sympathetic look, which only made her feel guilty. "I'm sure there will be people on the wagon train you can pay to help me."

Harvey lifted his chin. "Why should I have to pay anyone when I have family who can do the same job for free?"

With her uncle, everything always came down to money, and he referred to her as family only when it benefitted him to do so. He never gave a thought to what she might want, and so he didn't care one speck that she had no desire to go to Santa Fe. Had she no say in the matter?

"Sarah shouldn't have to move all the way to New Mexico if she doesn't want to." Emma shoved the corner of her biscuit into her mouth, as if she realized she'd said too much and was afraid to say more.

Sarah offered her a weak smile. While she appreciated Emma's coming to her defense, she knew her aunt's efforts were in vain. Whether she wanted to or not, she'd be going to Santa Fe—if she didn't get scalped or blown to kingdom come by the perpetual wind first.

"She will do as I say," her uncle insisted. "I've fed and housed her all these years. It's the least she can do to show her appreciation."

It's the least she can do. How many times had she heard those words?

What would it take for her debt to be fully paid?

Chapter Five

Sarah raced past her aunt and uncle, past the wagon. She hurried around the horses, which had been tied to a line running from the wagon to a nearby tree, as her eyes blurred with tears. Her life was over. She'd failed Mrs. Rayburn, and now her aunt thought she didn't want to care for her. She would be stuck in a tiny, backwoods town with no friends and no means of escape. How could things have gone so terribly wrong?

She glanced over her shoulder to make sure her uncle hadn't followed, and ran smack into a solid wall of man. His arms lifted to steady her, and she glanced up into Ethan Harper's concerned brown eyes.

"What's wrong?"

She pressed her lips together and shook her head. He released her but then took her arm, leading her away from the wagons and people, out onto the prairie. The tall grass tugged at her skirts like the hands of the children at the orphanage, vying for her attention. She sucked in a sob. She'd probably never see those children again. Stopping, she buried her face in her hands. She wished Mr. Harper would leave, and yet she felt oddly comforted by his presence. He must think her such a ninny.

After she'd cried away the immediate pain of her situation, she wiped her eyes and dared to look up at him. He stood with his hands resting lightly on his hips, his face pointed toward the sky. "What are you doing?" she asked.

He looked down at her, his gaze filled with compassion. "Praying for you."

Sarah stared at him, surprise overcoming her misery. "Praying? For me? But you don't even know what's wrong…or did you happen to hear what my uncle said?"

He surveyed the rolling hills surrounding the valley they'd camped in. The sun cast bright shafts of light into the sparse clouds as it came close to ducking down behind the horizon. "I heard some of it, but not because I was trying to. I'd just unhitched the last horse and was brushing him down." He shrugged. "Sorry. I didn't mean to eavesdrop."

"It doesn't matter, anyway."

"So, you never planned to go to Santa Fe?"

Her chin quivered, and she shook her head. "No. I never wanted to leave Chicago in the first place. But my aunt hasn't been well, and she needed my assistance, so I was supposed to come as far as Kansas City, then return home." She sniffed as tears filled her eyes again. She had no control of her own life. "Things keep changing."

"You can't always control circumstances. You have to learn to not fight the wind. God often uses unexpected situations to do a good work in us."

He sounded as if he spoke from experience. Had he faced an impossibly difficult task, like she did?

"Have you ever been to Santa Fe?" she asked.

He drew his mouth into a tight line.

Her heart lurched. The town must be dreadful.

"Twice. I needed to get away from home for a time, so I tagged along with a friend of my father's and did some scouting for a couple of wagon trains he led. It's an old town with a strong Mexican influence, but things are changing down there." He smiled. "A few years ago, a man started a music group called La Banda de Santa Fe. They're pretty good."

Sarah sighed. One band did not an orchestra make, but at least it was something.

"It's not Chicago, I'm sure, but it's a nicer town, and bigger, than many down that way."

"Thank you for trying to ease my worries, Mr. Harper. I suppose I must accept the fact that I won't see home for a very long while." She started to walk back to camp but then stopped and turned. "Did I understand you correctly? You've traveled the Santa Fe Trail twice—and returned? So, it would be possible for me to come back after seeing my aunt safely there?"

"I reckon, but you wouldn't want to travel like we did. We rode fast, with long hours of travel; slept after sunset and rose before dawn. That's too rough for a woman. You couldn't make such a journey, anyway, unless you knew your escorts were men of character who would insure your safety." He pierced her with a stern stare.

She cocked her head and smiled. "You seem a nice enough man. Could I ride back with you?"

He stiffened, and a muscle in his jaw tightened, as if the thought repulsed him. "No. I'm afraid that's not possible."

She cocked her head. "And just why not? Don't you think I could keep up with you?"

Shaking his head, he backed up. "No, I don't, but that's not the reason. I won't be held responsible for another woman. And, besides, I'm only traveling as far as Harpers' Stage Stop, where my family lives."

He turned his back on her, and she thought he'd leave, but he didn't. What did he mean when he said he wouldn't be responsible for "another" woman? Disappointment washed over her to learn he wouldn't be traveling with them. She didn't know why, but that news bothered her.

Sarah pushed her feet forward. She didn't need him.

She didn't need anyone.

⌇

The wagon train rested a day so that the travelers could do some final shopping in Windmill. Early the next morning, before the sun had peeked its face over the eastern horizon, the wagons set off down the Santa Fe Trail, creaking and groaning as if they knew what they would face and didn't like it one bit. Sarah's feet, which had just begun to stop hurting, ached again. If only there were a cool stream to soak them in. Blisters had formed on blisters. The sturdy shoes she'd purchased in Kansas City were only making things worse.

Late in the afternoon, the wagons ambled past a big two-story house, white with green trim. A score of rocking chairs sat on the wide front porch, moving eerily forward and back in the brisk breeze. She couldn't help wondering if they were occupied by the ghosts of people who'd passed through here and perished on the trail. A black-and-white dog lay at one end of the porch but never uttered a bark. A young girl and an even smaller boy sat on the front steps, waving at the wagons. This must be Harpers' Stage Stop, and Mr. Harper must be related to those children somehow. He didn't seem old enough to be the girl's father. But hadn't he mentioned having a brother?

The wagons circled in a level area west of the big barn. A man rode his horse down the line, shouting for the drivers to turn their critters loose in the field. He waved to his right. "If you'd care for a home-cooked meal, Mrs. Harper's fine food will have your tummy kissing your feet just for making the walk up to the house." Chuckling, he rode on.

Uncle Harvey strode toward Sarah. "Get those horses unhitched. How's Emma?"

"Doing well."

"Good. Tell her we're eating at that house tonight." He spun around and hustled back to the freight wagon.

If she hadn't been so tired, Sarah might have laughed. Thoughts of a home-cooked meal had him moving faster than she'd seen him go in two weeks. But she understood. This dinner was the first thing to excite her all week. No burnt cornbread and, hopefully, no beans tonight.

An hour later, after the animals had been cared for, and Sarah and her aunt and uncle had cleaned up, they waited with the group of twenty or so who were going to the Harpers' house to eat. A man strode toward them, and her heartbeat increased, until she realized he wasn't Ethan Harper. He walked up to the wagon master, shook his hand, and said something. Then, he turned toward the group.

When he took off his hat, Sarah could see that he did bear a resemblance to Ethan Harper, though his eyes were blue instead of brown. "Welcome to Harpers' Stage Stop. I'm Joshua Harper. We're glad to have you folks pass through, and, believe me, you're in for a treat. My ma is the best cook in the county."

He seemed a friendly sort, unlike his brother. They followed him toward the big house, but instead of escorting them inside or to tables set up under the big pecan trees, he guided them around the side to some steps leading down into the basement. Sarah glanced at her uncle and found the scowl she'd expected. Her own second thoughts were chased away by the stomach-tingling aromas wafting up from the stone-walled space.

Her uncle balked at the door, but Sarah pushed past him and helped her aunt down the stairs. The basement was a large, surprisingly pleasant room, not the dingy hole she'd expected. She took a seat next to her aunt, her mouth watering at the sight of baskets of sliced bread, and bowls of peaches and pickled beets. She sipped cool water from the glass she'd found next to her plate and studied the room. The walls were made of flat limestone rocks in various shades of gray and brown. Long, narrow windows near the ceiling lined one wall, allowing light in, and lanterns overhead illuminated the four tables, which were lined up end to end.

A woman came down the narrow staircase on the far side of the room, followed by the little girl Sarah had seen earlier on the porch. Ethan Harper, wearing a gold calico apron that surely belonged to his mother, followed them, carrying a large bowl. Sarah bit back a grin. Her uncle took a seat and slid the nearest bowl of peaches closer to him. He wouldn't be caught dead in such feminine accoutrement.

The woman gazed out at the group with a wide smile and friendly brown eyes. "Welcome, everyone! I'm Karen Harper, and this is my youngest son, Ethan. I do believe most of you have already met him." She glanced at him with a proud gleam in her eye, and then she looked down and patted the girl on the head. "And this is my granddaughter, Cora."

"Corrie, Grandma." The girl flung one of her two dark braids over her shoulder as soft chuckles echoed around the room.

"Yes, we do call her Corrie." Mrs. Harper offered the child a tender smile, then focused on the group again. "Before you leave, I'm sure you'll meet my husband, Nick, and my other two sons, Aaron and Josh. I hope y'all are hungry."

Corrie tugged on her grandma's skirt. "Don't forget Toby."

"Oh, heavens! No, we certainly can't forget dear little Toby. He's my young grandson and Corrie's brother."

Ethan set the bowl filled with steaming potatoes on the table, then walked over and opened a small door of what looked like an inset cupboard of some kind. He tugged on a rope, and Sarah watched, intrigued, as a small cabinet lowered. A dumbwaiter—how interesting. She never would have expected to find such a device in a place this remote.

The aroma of roast beef hit her nose just before Ethan Harper set a platter of sliced meat right in front of her. Corrie went from person to person, handing out warm biscuits, while Mrs. Harper refilled empty water glasses. Ethan rolled the dumbwaiter back up, then took the steps two at a time. What a sight the muscled man made in his linen shirt, black pants, boots, and apron. He must be very confident of his manhood to don such a getup.

He returned after a moment and emptied the dumbwaiter of several bowls, then squeezed in between Sarah and Aunt Emma and set down a bowl of buttered carrots and another of peas so green they made her mouth water. Sarah glanced up at him, and he had the gall to wink at her.

"You look lovely in gold." The words slipped out before she could stop them.

"Thank you." Grinning, he leaned closer. "Ma says it goes good with my eyes."

Sarah dipped her head, her shoulders bouncing as she worked to contain a chuckle. The man was a jester. He carried several bowls to the other tables, then resumed his spot next to his mother and niece.

Mrs. Harper held out her hands. "I hope y'all are pleased with the meal. If you need anything at all, just ask one of us. Ethan will lead us in a prayer of thanksgiving, and then please enjoy."

All of the diners, with the exception of Uncle Harvey and one other man, bowed their heads.

"Dear heavenly Father, thank You for bringing these folks to our home. I pray that You will bless them on their journey, that You will watch over them and let them arrive safely in Santa Fe. I ask Your blessing on this meal. In Jesus' name, amen."

"Amen!" yelled one of the Mason boys at the far end of the table.

Her uncle reached for the peaches, taking more than a fair amount before passing them to her aunt. Sarah let the man on the far side of the table start the carrots while she waited for the peaches. She tore off a hunk of biscuit and ate it. Why couldn't she get hers to turn out this light and flaky?

Far too soon, all the bowls were emptied. Ethan's brother, who'd joined them halfway through the meal, helped remove them. Ethan reached for Sarah's plate, brushing her sleeve with his arm and causing her sated stomach to lurch. Before she could analyze why his accidental touch had affected her so, his brother placed a generous slice of custard pie in front of her. She wasn't sure she could find room for it, but she was certainly going to try. It was a good thing they'd have to walk back to the wagons before bedtime.

After the meal, Sarah and Emma thanked their hosts, and her uncle paid the more than fair fee for the supper. As they filed outside into the warm evening air, Sarah realized just how comfortable that basement had been. Had they all been stuffed into a dining room in the house, they probably would have been hot and not nearly as comfortable. Whoever had thought up the basement café had a brilliant idea.

Corrie was sitting in the grass next to the house, playing with a tabby kitten.

"Oh, how sweet." Sarah stopped beside her. She loved small animals, but her uncle had never permitted her to keep one. "May I pet it?"

Corrie glanced up with eyes as dark as her uncle's. "Sure. You can hold him, if you want."

"I'd love to." She scooped up the tiny cat and held it in the crook of one arm, watching her aunt and uncle follow the people returning to the wagons. Either they hadn't noticed she had stopped or they'd decided not to wait. That was fine with her. The wagons were within sight, so she would be all right walking back alone. She scratched the kitten under his chin, and his eyes closed. "You're a sweet little thing, aren't you?"

"That's what the ladies keep telling me."

Sarah whirled around. Ethan Harper stood there, wearing the same cocky grin he'd worn back in Kansas City.

"I wasn't talking to you."

"Ah, that's a pity." He slumped his shoulders and stuck out his lower lip, as his niece might have done when pouting.

She had a hard time not smiling.

"There's four more in the barn. Would you like to see them?"

Sarah handed the kitten back to Corrie, then glanced toward the wagons. "I probably should get back."

"I saw your aunt with your uncle. It might do him good to tend her awhile."

She wanted to scold him for being so forward, but, in truth, she felt the same way. She loved her aunt and didn't mind caring for her, but Aunt Emma needed her husband's attention at times. Feeling emboldened, Sarah nodded. "All right. But I need to get back before dark."

She walked beside him, noticing that he'd slowed his pace this time. "You have a lovely home here. Whose idea was it to host travelers in the basement?"

"That was actually my pa's. Ma wasn't too thrilled with the notion of having strangers traipse through her house all the time, so we thought up another way."

"Well, it works out well. It's so cool and comfortable down there."

He nodded. "Yeah, and in the winter, the fireplace keeps it nice and warm, though we don't get nearly as many travelers then. Too much cold and snow."

"Do you get a lot of snow here?"

Ethan shrugged. "Generally one to two feet each winter."

"That doesn't sound like all that much."

"I don't guess it is for Chicago, but we're further south."

Sarah gazed at the field across from the barn, where a large herd of cattle grazed. "I don't suppose we'll get *any* snow in Santa Fe."

"Don't be so sure. Did you know it's up in the mountains? I've never seen snow when I've been there, but it does get chilly at night."

Sarah shook her head. "I guess I thought it was in the desert."

"Maybe you'll find that you like it more than you expect to."

She sincerely doubted that would happen, but the fact that Santa Fe was in the mountains intrigued her, at least. She followed Ethan into the big barn. The west-facing door was open wide, letting in the final rays of the setting sun, which illuminated a parade of dust motes. A golden horse nickered to them, and Ethan walked toward it.

"Hey, boy. Are you ready for some dinner?"

"He's pretty. What kind of horse is he?"

"A buckskin."

"His golden color makes a beautiful contrast with his black mane and tail."

Ethan covered the horse's ears. "Stop using words like 'pretty' and 'beautiful.' You want to turn him into a sissy?"

She bristled for a second before she realized he was joking. A giggle bubbled up from deep within. "You're goofy, you know?"

He grinned. "It comes from being the youngest and having to clown around to get any attention. At least, that's what Ma says. Do you have brothers or sisters?"

"No. I mean, I did, but they both died when they were babies."

"Sorry to hear that. We'd better visit the kittens before we lose all the light." He gave the horse a final pat, then strode across the barn to another stall. Inside lay a tabby cat with a quartet of kittens, their fur ranging from solid black to yellow calico.

Sarah crouched down. "Oh, they're so darling." She picked up the black and cradled it in her arms. It looked up at her with watery eyes. "Aren't you just a sweet little thing!"

"I thought we had that discussion already."

Sarah shook her head, ignoring Ethan's comment. She didn't quite know how to take his joking. Walt was always so serious and businesslike; he never teased.

"I'd offer you a kitten, if you weren't traveling so far. A pet would just make things more difficult for you."

She set the kitten down and stood. There was no sense in getting attached, even though, if given her choice, she'd pick the little black one. Maybe one day, when she had a home of her own, she could get a pet. "I'd better be getting back. Aunt Emma will be tired from the walk up here and back and will want to get ready for bed."

He gently grasped her elbow and guided her out of the barn. "It's kind of you to take such good care of her."

Sarah shrugged, uncomfortable with his compliment. "She took me in when my parents died. It's the least I can do."

"And yet you don't feel the same way toward your uncle."

Pausing, she gazed up at his handsome face. The last rays of sun reflected off of his bronzed cheek. "My uncle can be very selfish, even cruel at times."

His jaw tightened. "He hasn't hurt you, has he?"

"Not physically. The wounds he inflicts are more internal. Emotional pain."

"I've known other men like him. They take pleasure in putting others down—bullying anyone smaller or less well off. If he ever does hurt you physically, let me know."

She studied him for a long moment. Why did he care what her uncle did to her? "That might be hard to do, with you here and me in Santa Fe."

"Well, no matter where you are, God is always with you. Remember that. Call on Him when you have problems." He glanced toward the sunset, which had turned the underbellies of the clouds a bright pink hue. He shook his head and chuckled. "Those clouds remind me of your wagon."

"It's not *that* pink." She smiled back at him, then sobered. This was probably the last time she'd ever see this man, and yet saying good-bye to him seemed harder than saying farewell to Walt. "I should go."

He drew in a deep breath, exhaled, and trapped her gaze, his now serious. "Take care, Sarah Marshall. Stay close to the wagons.

Hitch the horses like I showed you, and be sure to give them some grain every night."

Sarah bit her lip, afraid to tell him that her uncle had refused to buy grain. He'd said the prairies were covered in grasslands, so there was no need.

"Don't wander away from the wagons for any reason." He placed his hands on her shoulders, as if she meant something to him. "You'll be passing through Indian lands, but, chances are, they won't bother you. Just don't let them catch you alone. You hear me?"

"Yes, I hear you." What would happen to her if she were caught by Indians? The thought sent a shudder down her spine.

He walked her to the edge of camp, but he seemed in no hurry to leave.

"Thank you for all your help, Mr. Harper. I don't know how we would have managed without it."

"You're very welcome. It gives me pleasure to teach people and to know they'll be safer because of what they've learned."

She like that about him—that protecting people was so important. She hadn't truly felt protected since her father's death.

"Sarah? Is that you?" her uncle's deep voice called as they drew near.

"Yes, Uncle. I'm coming." She turned back to Ethan. "I must go. Thank you for showing me the kittens."

"My pleasure, ma'am." He touched the brim of his hat, far more a gentleman than she'd first given him credit for being. "God go with you."

Abruptly, he spun around, as if saying good-bye to her was just as hard for him. She watched him until he blended with the shadows and disappeared. She'd known him only a few weeks, and yet she wished more than anything that he was traveling with them to Santa Fe.

Chapter Six

By the light of the campfire, Sarah penned a letter to Abigail. She'd already written a short missive to Walt, explaining why she wouldn't be back and urging him to find another woman to marry. In one way, it hurt to tell him, but in another way, it brought freedom. Her brief attraction to Ethan Harper proved that she had no business marrying Walt. He was a good man, but not the man for her. Maybe that man lived in Santa Fe, or maybe he was on this very wagon train. She'd overheard Ethan telling someone that this was an average-sized train, with seventy-three wagons in all. There were bound to be some men her age—not that she was particularly interested in marrying.

Dear Abigail,

You won't believe how much my life has changed since I last wrote you. The woman who was supposed to care for Aunt Emma had already gone West with another wagon train before we arrived in Windmill. Thus, Uncle Harvey ordered me to continue on with them. My life is over. You wouldn't believe how dreadful I look dressed in thin, dirty calico and clumpy shoes. What will I ever find to do way down in Santa Fe?

Mr. Wayne, who led our small train from Kansas City to Harpers' Stage Stop, came by after supper tonight to introduce Mr. Winfield, who will lead the wagon train to Santa Fe. He also said he'd be by in the morning to collect any mail we might have and give it to the Harpers, who would see that it was sent to the post office, so I'm staying up late to write all my friends.

How are the children? I miss them terribly. I think of Mary, in particular. Has her perpetual crying decreased at all? I plan to write to Mrs. Rayburn, too, if I can stay awake long enough. I feel awful for promising her I'd return, only to be incapable of keeping that promise.

Instead of rocking children to sleep or clerking at my uncle's shop, I now spend my days hitching horses—yes, I truly do—walking endless miles, preparing meals over a campfire, and then falling asleep, exhausted, on the ground beneath the wagon. Can you imagine that—me, sleeping on the ground?

I awoke one morning, and a giant walking stick—I mean three inches long—was on my pillow, right in front of my face. I screamed so loud that I woke up the whole camp. Men came rushing barefoot out of their wagons, pulling up their suspenders with one hand and holding a rifle in the other. I was mortified, but it gave me a good chuckle later.

Life here is so different. I've resigned myself to going along, since I really have no choice. The only consolation is that I won't be separated from Aunt Emma. I felt guilty for not wanting to go with her, and then I found out she didn't want to go any more than I did. At least I can do my best to keep her comfortable and see that she eats. I haven't mentioned this to anyone, but I have a nagging fear that she won't survive the trip. I don't know what I shall do without her.

Mr. Harper, that man I wrote you about—the one who left me sitting in the mud—ended up being a rather nice fellow. He taught me how to harness the horses. I feel bad for having urged my uncle to go against his counsel. It was rather childish of me.

I'd better end this letter, so I can write to Lizzie Monahan and Betty Phillips. I hope it isn't a bother for you to hang on to my trunk for a while. I'm hoping to return as soon as I get Auntie settled. If I can find a way back.

Sarah signed her letter and sealed it, then put it with the one she'd written to Walt. She yawned, hearing her bedroll beckon, in spite of her distaste for sleeping on the ground. She quickly penned a short note to her other close friends, explaining again why she wouldn't be back, then put away her writing desk and crawled under the wagon.

Before they'd set out, her uncle had made it clear that he would be sleeping with his wife, leaving Sarah the options of the freight wagon or the ground. After two uncomfortable nights trying to sleep on boxes of different heights in the sun-heated wagon, she decided on the ground, unless there was rain. She peered through the rungs of a wagon wheel and stared up at the dark sky. Thousands of stars flickered, reminding her of the lights of Chicago at night. She'd never known there were so many stars. Had she ever really looked at them?

A bump beneath her blankets pressed against her shoulder. She scooted over to a smoother spot on her pallet. Her bed was one thing she dearly missed, but it had been sold with the house. Who was sleeping on it now?

Sarah yawned again, but images of Ethan Harper tramped through her thoughts, driving sleep away. She wouldn't mind getting to know him better, but that wasn't to be. Tomorrow, and each day after, would put more and more miles between them.

"God go with you," he had told her. She glanced up at the sky again. "Will You, God? Go with us?"

Above her, the wagon creaked; either her aunt or uncle shifted on their cramped bed. At least it was cooler and less crowded outdoors. She turned onto her side and stared out at the black prairie, unable to quiet her curiosity. She'd attended church with her aunt every Sunday, but the messages were so confusing, and were preached with such vehemence, that she'd rarely understood them. Mr. Harper had prayed a simple prayer, as if he were merely talking to a friend. Was it actually possible to relate to God in such a casual way?

She turned on her side and closed her eyes. Tomorrow would be a long, troublesome day that would only take her farther away from all that she loved, with the exception of her aunt.

                                    ~

A rooster crowed. Sarah moaned and rubbed her eyes. She'd barely slept at all last night, between worrying about their travels and wondering where they'd live in Santa Fe, if they even made it that far. She had an uncanny sense they wouldn't. The wagon groaned again, and she rolled out from beneath it. She didn't want her uncle to awaken and find her lollygagging.

Her morning routine until a few weeks ago had been to labor through her toilette, taking time to fix her hair just right and trying on several day dresses until she found the one that suited her whim. Now, she threw a handful of water on her face and rinsed her mouth. No need to worry what to wear, since she'd slept in her dress. She donned her apron, tossed the few sticks she had picked up yesterday onto the embers of last night's fire, and then placed kindling around them, as Ethan had shown her. She stirred the ashes with a stick, blew on the red-hot coals, and poked the kindling against them. Soon, a fire had flamed to life. Pride welled up within her. Maybe she could learn to be a pioneer, after all— not that she cared to be. But she'd learned long ago to face things head-on and just get through them. Circumstances didn't change just because you wanted them to.

The coffee was warming by the time her uncle climbed out of the wagon. Sarah watched for her aunt, but she didn't follow. "Is Aunt Emma coming out for breakfast?"

He shook his head and continued buttoning his shirt. "She doesn't feel like eating. Still full from last night's meal, I suppose."

Sarah frowned and walked over to the tailgate. Her aunt was still in bed. How could she possibly be full from last night, when she had eaten so little? Sarah nibbled her lip as she dug out a bowl to make a quick batch of biscuits. She couldn't dawdle, because Mr. Winfield wanted an early start, and he'd threatened to leave behind those who weren't ready. With the bacon frying and the biscuits baking, she rolled up her pallet and gazed at the Harpers' home. She'd never thought she would envy someone who lived in the middle of nowhere, but she did. They had a large home, huge gardens, cattle and horses, and a big family to share it all with. She had none of those things. Shaking her head, she stuck the bedroll in the back of the wagon. There was no point wasting energy on covetousness.

An hour later, with breakfast over and the animals hitched, they started plodding down the trail. In spite of the dirt being hardened from all of their wagons and the ones that had preceded them, Sarah was coated in grime well before noon. Every time she licked her lips, her tongue was covered with grit. She'd given up trying to keep it off, because her efforts had proven futile. All she could think of was that four hours of walking were over and done with. Only about fourteen hundred more hours to go.

The monotony of walking all day and worrying about Walt's response to the letter she'd given Mr. Winfield to mail kept her mind occupied. Supper was a quick affair of cold leftovers from breakfast. Aunt Emma still wasn't feeling well enough to eat, although she did drink some tea. Her forehead felt hot, but how could Sarah tell if she were running a fever in this heat? And, if May was this warm already, how hot would it be by August? She'd never thought she'd miss the pestering winds that blew in off Lake Michigan, but she longed for a cooling breeze.

The sun touched the western horizon, and they made camp again. They hadn't passed a single house or farm all day. Sarah shuffled with several other tired women to a nearby creek and dipped her bucket in the water. If only she could soak her sore feet and wash the dirt off her face and from her hair. She would have to be satisfied with just cleaning her hands, which reeked from picking up buffalo chips all day—something she'd learned from Mrs. Scott, the lady in the wagon behind theirs. They needed the nasty buffalo flops for fuel, because there was little to no dried wood to be had. The few trees she'd spied in the boring flatlands cuddled the creeks and rivers, so their wood was green.

Once the buckets had been filled with water for cooking, the women plunged their hands into the warm creek. Sarah scooped a handful of sand from the bottom and scrubbed her palms so hard that they stung. She untied her apron and swished it back and forth in the water. Then, she stood, wrung out her apron, and grabbed her bucket. When she turned to go back to the wagons, she realized all the other women had already returned without her.

Her heart skipped a beat, and she quickened her steps, remembering Mr. Harper's warning. Tall sunflowers weaved back and forth in the light breeze, and a roadrunner darted across her path. She studied the brush around her, but it didn't look thick enough for an Indian to hide in. Still, being alone on the prairie gave her the creeps, after having grown up in a crowded city with tall buildings surrounding her, and people everywhere. She'd never felt alone in Chicago. But out here…. All but running, she hopped over the wagon tongue and entered the camp, blowing out a breath of relief. The last time she'd run anywhere had been to catch a good sale in downtown Chicago just before Christmas.

For supper, she boiled some potatoes, carrots, and bacon to make a stew. It tasted good with the corn bread she'd cooked in a pan over the fire. She managed to talk her aunt out of the wagon, but, after slurping a few spoonfuls of stew, Emma took to her bed again. She'd been sickly for a long while, but never like this. It was almost as if she'd lost heart.

After Emma had gone to bed, Sarah approached her uncle. "I think we should have the doctor come and check on Aunt Emma."

He shook his head and stalked toward her, sticking his face in hers. "You keep your voice down. If these people catch wind that Emma could be sick, they'll kick us off this train. She's just pouting, is all. She'll get over it."

Frowning, Sarah glanced at the Scotts' wagon, where Mrs. Scott stood, her back to her. She was half tempted to yell out that her aunt had smallpox, typhus, or some other contagious disease, so that they'd be forced from the train and have to return home. Instead, she set about cleaning up the supper dishes, then dug out her bedroll and spread it out. One whole day over and done with. Only another fifty-five or sixty more to go.

Sarah shivered at the expanse of green nothingness stretching out before them. Not a tree in sight. The warm wind howled like a grieving widow, but then later played the bully, tossing dirt into every meal she made. Why had her uncle insisted on making this horrible journey?

She licked a layer of dust off her lips and studied the dirt under her broken fingernails. It wasn't really dirt, but she could never admit to her socialite friends that she'd collected buffalo chips all day. She barely believed it herself.

Sweat trickled down her back and made an awkward trail down her bosom. Certainly not a place a lady scratched in public. She glanced sideways to her right, at the wagon just behind theirs, still driven by Mr. Scott. His wife had decided to take an afternoon respite, which sounded wonderful to Sarah, but her uncle forbade her to ride in the wagon because of the additional weight. She yawned, then nearly stumbled to her knees on a big rock in her path. The uphill climb, though not all that steep, made walking more difficult. With all this land and wide open spaces, why wasn't there a railroad?

Uncle Harvey drew out his whip and smacked it against the backs of the horses pulling the pink wagon. The animals hung their heads, snorting and blowing, and their muscles rippled in their effort to pull the heavily loaded wagon up the grade. The lead team of horses trudged their way toward the top, but Mr. Scott had stopped his wagon on level land to take a break. Sarah held her breath. If their horses were having this much trouble on such a small hill, how would they manage the bigger ones they were sure to encounter? And wouldn't they be traversing some mountains?

Sarah watched the horses continue their struggle. The front wheel dropped into a deep rut, and a sickening crack echoed across the prairie. The wagon listed to the left.

"Whoa! Hold on." Uncle Harvey hauled back on the reins, then grabbed the side of the wagon in his effort to stay on the bench.

The horses fought the reins, evidently not comfortable stopping on the slant of the hill. One of them pawed the ground, then jerked sideways, as if trying to escape the harness.

Sarah hurried toward the big black gelding, her hands held out. "Easy, Shadow. Whoa, there." She took hold of his noseband and cooed to him.

Her uncle set the brake, then climbed down and inspected the wheels. He muttered a loud curse. When the horses had calmed, she walked around to see the problem for herself. As far as she could tell, the wheel looked fine. And, if it wasn't, they had spares. Still, the delay would upset her uncle.

Mr. Scott struggled up the hill on foot. "How bad is it?"

Uncle Harvey scratched his beard. "I'm not sure. The wheel looks all right, but I heard a loud crack."

Mr. Scott got down on his hands and knees, careful to stay away from the line of the wheels, and looked under the wagon. When he glanced up again, his lips were pressed hard together. "Rotten luck."

"What is it?" Uncle Harvey asked, bending over halfway.

Standing, Mr. Scott wiped his hands on his pants and shook his head. "You've cracked your axle."

Her uncle yanked off his hat and threw it on the ground. Then he glared at Sarah. "This is your fault. I never should have let you talk me into buying this eyesore of a wagon."

Sarah backed away. Of course he would blame her. Shadow dug at the ground with his hooves again, and she hurried back to the horses, tears stinging her eyes. What would this mean for them?

"We need to unhitch your team," said Mr. Scott. "I've got a couple of blocks we can put behind the back wheels to hold the wagon until we can lower it to level ground." He turned and jogged back down the hill.

"Get those animals unfastened. I need to get Emma out of the wagon." Her uncle looked as if he wanted to say more, but he lumbered away.

Sarah let out a sigh and began unhitching Shadow. Could the axle be fixed? She didn't remember their buying an extra.

The sound of horses' hooves pounded over the hill, and Mr. Winfield rode toward them. "What's the holdup here?"

"Broken axle," her uncle grumbled.

A muscle flexed in Mr. Winfield's jaw. "Too bad, folks." He dismounted. "I won't mince words, Mr. Stone. You have two options, as I see it. Abandon this wagon, after salvaging what you need most from both wagons and consolidating it in your other one, or go back to the Harpers' and see if they have another wagon you can purchase, then wait for the next train to come through. It shouldn't be more than a few weeks."

"A few weeks!" Her uncle paced to the back of the wagon and peered inside, as if trying to determine what he could part with. "But that means we'll be traveling in the heat of summer."

The wagon master pursed his lips. "This is why I always recommend purchasing a solid wagon. Just be thankful you're not in Indian territory. At least you have options, like I said. You make up your mind and get those horses unhitched. I'll recruit some men to help lower the wagon and send your driver back with your other one." He waved at Mr. Scott. "This land's solid enough, Scott, that you can take your wagon up that side. Let's keep things rolling."

Sarah's heart lurched. They were leaving them behind? With the horses calm again, she hurried to her aunt's side. "Do you want to sit down?"

Emma shook her head. "I'm all right, for now. But, Harvey, what will we do?"

"I don't know." He muttered another curse, then stomped up the hill. "Sarah! Get up here and help me."

She looked at her aunt. "You're sure you're all right?"

Emma nodded. "It actually feels good to get out and stretch."

"You shouldn't stand so close to the wagon. The brake could give out on the hill, or we might have more trouble with one of the horses." She pointed to a shrub with deep green leaves covered in white flowers. "Let me help you over to that bush. It will give you some shade if you decide to sit."

"Oh, of course. Thank you, dear, for thinking of that. I believe I could use your assistance."

Sarah took her aunt's arm and helped her walk the short distance, then eased her to the ground. She hurried to unhitch Shadow, since her uncle had already released the other lead horse.

Mr. Scott's wagon climbed the rest of the hill without trouble. At the top, Mrs. Scott turned around and waved. "I'll keep you in my prayers! And I hope to see you in Santa Fe in a few months."

Sarah waved back, knowing her uncle wouldn't respond. "Thank you. Safe travels." She hated to see the kind woman leave. She didn't know how she would have managed without Mrs. Scott's guidance.

She all but ran down the hill to keep up with Shadow's long legs. At the bottom, she followed her uncle's example and led him to a grassy spot out of the way, rolling a heavy rock over his reins. She hoped he would be contented to graze until she could get him hobbled, because there was no tree in sight to tether him to.

As she made her way up the hill for another horse, several men came striding over the crest. The first to arrive began unhitching the wheelers, as Ethan Harper had referred to the pair closest to the wagon.

A short man she didn't recognize tipped his hat to her. "Sorry about your troubles, ma'am. Why don't you have a seat with that other lady and let us handle this?"

She glanced at her uncle, who was leading another horse down the hill, and nodded. He might object, but she was so tired that she was willing to let the men handle things. "Thank you."

Sarah sat down beside her aunt in the shade of the shrub. "What do you think Uncle Harvey will decide to do?"

Emma turned to her. She still looked tired, but there was a light in her eyes Sarah hadn't noticed for days. "He has spent too much money to just ride off and leave a whole wagon full of supplies on the trail. He'll want to go back to Windmill and buy that other wagon, if it's still there."

Sarah's stomach tightened. Returning to Windmill would mean going past the Harpers', and she was certain her uncle would want to stop there in hopes of getting another home-cooked meal. That would mean seeing Ethan Harper again, along with his knowing smirk when he learned the wagon she'd chosen had already broken down. She might admit to herself that the possibility of seeing him again lifted her spirits and that she should have heeded his advice about the wagon, but she sure wouldn't admit it to him.

Chapter Seven

S arah watched as ropes were attached to the front of their wagon, and then as more than a dozen brawny men grabbed hold of each rope. A boy of about thirteen released the brake, then jumped off the side and rolled down the hill. The men slowly let out the ropes, lowering the wagon down the hill. When it was finally on level ground, a shout rang out, and the men relaxed. Several stretched their backs, and others congratulated themselves. Uncle Harvey hadn't helped, except to stand partway down the hill and motion the men forward, as if they'd needed his guidance.

The men turned as one and clambered back up the hill. Only Mr. Winfield and Robby Blake, the young man her uncle had hired to drive the freight wagon, remained.

Sarah glanced sideways. Her aunt's eyelids were fluttering shut. "We should get you down the hill."

"What? Oh, yes. I don't suppose we can stay here any longer."

Sarah rose, then held out her hand and pulled her aunt up. They slowly made their way down to the wagon. Her uncle paced around it, as if willing the damage to repair itself. She helped Emma walk to the wagon so she could lean against the wheel.

Mr. Winfield wiped his brow. "I'm sorry to have to leave y'all behind, but you understood that could happen when you signed the contract."

"Isn't there anyone on the train who could repair this?" Uncle Harvey asked.

Mr. Winfield shook his head. "It would take too much time. You folks will be all right. It's just a day's ride by horse back to the Harpers', and the trail is clearly marked."

Her aunt could never ride a horse that far, if at all. Sarah wasn't even sure she could. But what other choice was there?

"You folks take care. Build up a good fire at night and keep your animals and rifles close. Like I said before, there's no Indians in these parts, but you best keep an eye out, just to be safe." He nodded, then mounted his horse and rode up the hill. Soon he crested the top, took a final look back, and then rode out of sight.

All was quiet, and they were alone. The only sounds Sarah heard were those of the grass swishing in the light breeze and her uncle's hard breaths. One of the horses bellowed a loud whinny, as if complaining about being left behind.

"What about me?" Robby kicked a pebble, sending it skittering along the ground. "I hired on to drive your wagon so's I could get to Santa Fe to join my brother." He lifted his hat and swiped his dirty hand through his oily blond hair.

Her uncle's eyebrows dipped, and he pushed out his lower lip. "You hired on to drive my wagon, and I paid you half of the wages up front. It doesn't matter where I want you to drive, you just drive. Do you understand?"

Robby scowled back at Harvey, but then he ducked his head and nodded.

"Good, then go unhitch those mules."

The boy turned and shuffled away, his shoulders hunched. Sarah had a hard time feeling sorry for him when she was so relieved that she'd gotten a reprieve. Was it possible that God had actually heard her prayer?

"So, Harvey…have you decided…what to do yet?" Emma pulled her handkerchief from her sleeve and dabbed it against her forehead, her chest still heaving from the exertion of walking down the hillside.

He smacked his fist against the canvas canopy. "I don't know. I guess either the boy or I will have to ride back to the Harpers' and get help."

Sarah gazed at the emptiness around them. Gently rolling hills covered in wildflowers spread out before her, but there was not a single house or person in sight. Just grassy wilderness. In spite of the warm temperature, she rubbed her upper arms. Who knew what lived out there? And though Mr. Winfield said there were no Indians, she had read about renegade bands who roamed the prairies and did unthinkable things to white people. She moved a step closer to her aunt.

Uncle Harvey turned and marched toward the freight wagon. "Boy! Where did we pack that saddle?"

Emma put an arm around Sarah's shoulders. "Now, don't you worry."

"Who says I'm worrying?"

Smiling, Emma lifted her index finger and touched the very top of Sarah's nose. "You get a tiny V right here when you're stewing on something. God will take care of us. I see this breakdown as an answer to my prayers."

Sarah's eyes widened. "You prayed the wagon would break?"

"No, dear. I prayed that if it wasn't God's will for us to go to Santa Fe, He'd intervene, and I believe He has."

"But if we don't go there, what will we do? There's no home to go back to."

Emma shrugged. "I don't know. You could still marry Walt, I suppose."

The image that entered her mind was that of a tall, tanned cowboy, not the smaller city man. She shook her head. "Not after the letter I sent him. I told him to find someone else."

"Good."

Sarah stared at her aunt, surprised to see her showing so much gumption. "Why is that good?"

"Because I never thought he was the right man for you. He's a nice man, but I believe God has someone better for you."

"I'm not sure that I even want to marry."

Emma cupped her cheek. "You will when you find the right man."

Again, Ethan Harper marched across her mind, with his cocky grin and blatant self-confidence. What was it about the man that made her unable to forget him? He did ride off, after all, leaving her sitting in a pile of mud and sewage.

Uncle Harvey returned, carrying his saddle. Wheezing, he set it on the ground and then glanced at the horses. "I sure hope one of them is broke to ride." He turned back, his gaze landing on Sarah. "Pack up enough food for several meals. And find a canteen and fill it to the top."

"What are you going to do?" Emma asked.

"I've talked things over with Robby. He'll stay to guard you and the wagons while I ride to the Harpers' and back."

Emma pushed away from the wagon and laid a hand on his arm. "How will you find your way? We must have traveled a dozen miles since then. What if…?"

He scowled and swatted his hand in the air. "Don't you see those deep ruts that previous wagons made? I'm quite capable of following the trail, Emma. It will lead me straight to the stage stop. It took a day-and-a-half to get this far by wagon, but on horseback, I should be able to get back there by nightfall."

"But that means we'll be here alone all night." Emma glanced around, wide-eyed, as if she'd just realized how desperate their situation was.

Harvey glared at Sarah. "Why are you still standing there?"

She spun around and climbed into the back of the wagon. He still blamed her. Life with him would only get worse. All she could do was hope that this setback would make him realize how unsuited they all were for enduring such a difficult trip. She located a dish towel and filled it with four biscuits leftover from breakfast, along with two apples and several slices of cheese. There was no meat to send. Uncle Harvey wouldn't be happy, but it would have to do. She didn't doubt that Mrs. Harper would gladly supply him with food once he arrived.

"I'm sorry for all this, Emma."

Sarah froze. In all the years she'd lived with the Stones, she'd never heard her uncle apologize.

"It's all right," her aunt said. "I know you were just trying to do what you thought was best. I love you, Harvey, and I'll be praying for you."

Sarah shuddered. How could her aunt still love that man after he'd been so mean? After he'd sold her home without consulting her, and forced her into taking this awful trip she hadn't wanted to take? He'd be lucky if Emma survived.

"Sarah! Get out here."

She wrapped a length of rope around the bundle, making a loop so that it would fit around the saddle horn, and then hurried out of the wagon. Robby was saddling Mable, the smallest of the stock horses. He glanced at her and winked. Sarah stiffened and turned toward her uncle, handing him the bundle.

"You take good care of Emma. You hear?"

Sarah nodded.

"Make sure she eats. And watch out for the horses and mules. If anything happens to them, we're sunk."

"Yes, sir."

"Robby, you keep watch over the women and the stock, too. I should be back tomorrow evening at the latest."

He started to walk away, then turned back and kissed Emma on the cheek. "You take it easy and get some rest."

They watched him mount the horse and strap the canteen and food bundle around the saddle horn. Mable pranced around in a circle, but she took a rider well. Uncle Harvey reined her around and kicked her sides. The horse lunged forward into a trot and then sped to a gallop, leaving behind a cloud of dust.

When the sound of hoofbeats faded, Robby spun around. "When's lunch?"

Sarah glanced up at the sky. "Not for another hour or two."

He shrugged and walked toward the freight wagon.

"Where are you going?"

"To check the stock and make sure the rifle is loaded," he called over his shoulder.

"Why?"

"In case there's trouble."

"What kind of trouble?"

Robby turned around but kept moving. "I don't know. Robbers, Indians, wolves…."

Sarah shuddered, then turned back to her aunt. "Maybe we should get you back inside the wagon."

Emma nodded. "There's a pistol in a crate just behind the wagon bench. It might be wise for you to keep it with you until Harvey returns."

Nodding, she helped her aunt climb back into the wagon and onto her pallet. Then, she found the gun and took a seat just inside the tailgate. She studied the weapon but had no idea how to use it. She could only pray she wouldn't need to.

⌒

Sarah sat in the back of the wagon, staring out at the darkness that had settled over them like a heavy blanket. So much blackness. Clouds had set up a barrier, blocking the shimmer of the stars and moon. Not a single lamp or a carriage lantern illuminated the inky gloom. The hum of insects marred the silence, and off in the distance a coyote or a wolf—or was it an Indian?—howled. She shivered, hugging the pistol to her chest.

Had her uncle made it to the Harpers'? Or had he stopped to sleep along the trail?

She hadn't even thought to send a blanket with him. Though they sweltered during the day, the nights were chilly. As she peered into the pitch dark, she saw shapes—figures. Her hands trembled. Was it a band of renegades come to take their scalps? She'd read that Indians were especially fond of blonde hair.

Footsteps crunched in the grass, silencing the nearby insects. Sarah froze, her breath ragged. She tightened her grip on the warm wooden handle of the revolver. Who could be out there? The sun had set hours ago.

"Sarah?" Robby's voice warbled through the quiet. "Miss Marshall."

"What do you want?"

"Just want someone to talk to. Lonesome, I reckon."

She squinted, barely able to make out his skinny shape. "It's the middle of the night."

"Nah. Ain't even midnight yet."

"That's right. Time to be sleeping."

"You ain't sleepin'."

As he slithered closer, she caught a whiff of stale body odor. She lifted her shawl to cover her nose. "Shh. You'll wake my aunt."

He chuckled. "I doubt that. Not if she can sleep all day in that wagon."

His presence was highly inappropriate, but hearing another human voice bolstered her courage. She wasn't as completely alone as she had thought. "Why do you want to go to Santa Fe, Robby?"

"My brother's there, and I figure it's as good a place as any to get a fresh start."

How odd for someone near her age to be talking about needing a fresh start. What had he done that he needed one? She stiffened. He had eagerly hired on when he'd heard her uncle needed a driver, even though others had turned him down due to the low pay offered. What if Robby was on the run from something?

And here she was, all alone with him, except for her aunt.

"Why don't you come out? We could have us some fun."

She sucked in a breath. "I think you should return to your... uh...wherever it is you're staying."

"Just come out for a little bit."

"I am sitting here holding a pistol, Mr. Blake. Don't make me use it."

He huffed out a laugh. "Who'd drive the freight wagon if you did?"

"I imagine Mr. Harper would, or one of his brothers. If need be, I'll drive it myself."

He hacked another laugh. "I'd like to see that. You probably couldn't even climb up to the seat in all those petticoats."

"Good night, Mr. Blake."

"You're as crotchety as your uncle. I never should have signed on with him."

When his footsteps grew quiet, Sarah blew out the breath she'd been holding. She'd never expected trouble from Robby. That just showed how naive she was. Proved she had no business traveling across the prairie in a wagon train. Give her a comfy carriage with a driver any day.

For the next hour or so, she listened hard for the sound of Robby's return, but he must have taken to his bed. Still, his unwanted invitation only heightened her discomfort. The insects had long ago resumed their song. She desperately needed to make a trip outside the wagon for comfort's sake, but she was afraid to move. What if Robby, or someone else—something else—sat out there, just waiting for her?

She hated this place. Hated the openness. Like a bird caged for years whose door had been flung open, she was afraid to fly.

She yawned, her whole body heavy with exhaustion from the day's exertion and events, but she doubted sleep would come anytime soon.

A flutter jolted Sarah. Her eyes shot open, and she stiffened. She'd slept?

Something to her left moved—a black blur—and she lifted the pistol. A crow perched on the closed tailgate, silhouetted against the bright morning sunlight.

She exhaled a nervous laugh. Just a bird, not some savage bent on taking her hair. She waved the pistol. "Shoo."

The creature took flight, and Sarah glanced at her aunt. Emma's chest rose and fell in a steady rhythm. Standing, Sarah stretched and peeked out the back of the wagon. It must be close to ten o'clock, judging by the height of the sun. She looked around but saw not a soul. From this angle, she couldn't see the freight wagon. She climbed down, tended to important business, and then walked to the other side of the wagon to check on the horses.

Her steps faltered, her mouth going dry. The five horses grazed peacefully on the hillside, but where were the mules? Where was the freight wagon with all of the merchandise?

Chapter Eight

The rhythmic *swish, swish* of the white liquid hitting the pail as Ethan milked lulled him into a relaxed state. He didn't even care whether he won the friendly competition he'd started with his brothers to see who could finish milking his dairy cow first. No, this morning, his mind was on a certain city gal. How was she faring on the trail? Was that winsome nose of hers, so often stuck up in the air, sunburned yet? And why did she enter his thoughts so often?

Maybe God kept bringing her to mind so he'd pray for her. *Keep Miss Priss and her family safe, Lord. Watch over them and let them arrive safely in Santa Fe.*

"Ha! I win." Josh stood and backed away from his cow, carrying his bucket. "I'll take this on in to Ma." He glanced at Ethan. "You'd better quit lollygaggin', little brother, or you're gonna be mucking stalls."

Ethan made a face at his brother, but when he glanced at his bucket, he realized he had been so lost in thought that his bucket was only half full. He leaned his head against the cow's warm side and put more effort into his work, watching frothy bubbles form atop the milk in his pail.

"Where's your mind this morning? You've been mighty quiet," Aaron said.

"I don't know. Just thinking about stuff, I guess."

"You still bothered by those greenhorns that didn't take your advice?"

Ethan shrugged. "I guess. It just doesn't make sense, folks seeking me out, only to ignore my suggestions."

Aaron chuckled. "Get used to it. One day you'll be a father."

"Just what does that mean?"

"Every day I tell Corrie and Toby to do things, but they don't listen. Even at six and four, they think they know more than I do."

A smile tugged at Ethan's lips. "Yeah, I know. They're smart young'uns."

"I suppose that's because they live with a houseful of adults." Aaron sprang up from his stool, grinning. "I'm done, and that makes you the mucker today."

For some reason, he didn't mind losing to both his brothers today. No matter who won their competitions, it made monotonous chores go by quicker. "If you want to leave your bucket, I'll take it in with mine."

Aaron nodded. "All right. I'll take these two cows out to pasture."

Ten more minutes passed before Ethan finished. Finally, he stood and stretched the kinks out of his back. Milking wasn't one of his favorite chores, but it had to be done. He lugged both buckets back into the kitchen, his stomach grumbling at the tantalizing aromas wafting from the warm room.

"Ah, so you're the loser this morning." His pa poured a cup of coffee, a teasing smirk twisting one corner of his mouth. He added a small amount of sorghum sugar and some cream, then held the cup out to Ethan.

He set the buckets on the worktable, took the cup, and sipped the hot brew. "Mmm, just how I like it. Thanks, Pa."

Ham slices hissed in the skillet, while chunks of potatoes and onions sizzled in another pan. His ma glanced over her shoulder. "Breakfast will be ready in fifteen minutes. Fill up Josh's bucket, then take the rest of the milk to the icehouse. With the days warming so quickly now, I don't want to take a chance on it going bad before Corrie and I make butter later on."

"Yes, ma'am." He downed the last of his coffee, then looked at his pa. "What's on the agenda for today?"

Pa rubbed the back of his neck and gazed out the window, coffee cup in hand. "We need to move the cattle to the south pasture, then work with those yearlings some, and the garden needs tending."

"The young'uns and I can work in the garden this morning." Ma forked the ham from the skillet onto a plate, then set it on the table. "I'm ready to scramble the eggs. Nick, you'd best go wake up Corrie and Toby."

With a nod, Pa set his cup by his spot at the table and did as bidden. Pa liked to think he was boss of the whole stage stop, but Ma ruled the roost, and everyone knew it but Pa. Grinning, Ethan turned to refill his coffee, then set it down at his place. "I'll just run the milk out and wash up. Be right back."

Ma nodded but didn't take her eyes off the twenty or so eggs she was scrambling. "Ring the bell on your way out so Aaron will start heading in."

"Yes, ma'am."

"And you can leave the door open. I could use a breeze right about now." She fanned her face with her spatula.

Ethan carried the milk to the icehouse, a small stone structure with thick walls that was set partially underground. He entered the cool building and put the pail on a shelf, then covered it with a board and placed a rock on top. After securing the door, he headed to the well to wash up. He rinsed his face and hands in the cool water, then dried them with the towel his ma set out each morning. There was no sign of Aaron, so he headed for the back of the house, picked up the metal clangor, and ran it around the black iron triangle hanging from a leather latigo.

That task complete, he reached for the door handle but hesitated when a movement caught his eye. A horse moseyed out from behind the wagon parked just outside the barn. What was a horse doing loose? As he drew nearer, he realized it wasn't one of their horses—and it was saddled. He picked up the reins dragging alongside the roan.

Aaron walked out of the barn. "Have we got company this early?"

Ethan shook his head. "Ma didn't say so when I took the milk in. I just found the animal roaming free." He stepped back and squatted down, surveying the newcomer. Something about the animal bothered him. "Look—imprint lines on her chest. This horse has recently worn a harness."

"So, why is she now wearing a saddle?"

Ethan ran his hand over the horse's crusty chest. "Look at all this lather. She's been ridden hard."

"I'll check inside and make sure no one's arrived," Aaron said, already heading toward the house. "You take the horse in the barn and unsaddle her."

Ethan led the animal into an empty stall and unsaddled her. He set out a bucket of feed, then grabbed a brush and began grooming the mare's brown hide. After a few minutes, he crossed behind the horse, keeping his hand on the horse's rear end to let her know he was there. He lifted the brush to groom the other side, and his hand froze. The horse had a white mark in the shape of a diamond on her shoulder—just like one of the horses the Stones had bought from Marcus. He stepped back and looked the horse over again. This *was* the same horse!

And that could mean only one thing. Problems.

Ethan clenched his jaw and exited the stall. He took Alamo from his stall, saddled him, and then led him up to the house at a jog. After tethering Alamo to a porch post, he plowed through the door, and everyone turned toward him.

"Where's the fire?" Pa asked, his eyes gleaming with humor.

"No fire, but other problems, I suspect." He looked at Aaron, who stood near the table, tickling Toby's tummy. "Any guests?"

Aaron shook his head. "I told them about the stray horse."

Ethan turned to his pa. "It belongs to the Stones—one of the families that just left for Santa Fe. Something must have happened. I'm heading down the trail to see what the problem is. Can a couple of you follow with a wagon?"

Pa nodded. Ma grabbed a special bag she'd made for carrying food when they rode.

Josh jumped up from the table. "I'll fix you a canteen."

"Thanks." Ethan hurried to the table, dished up some food, and wolfed it down.

"I sure hope those folks are all right." Ma set the food pack on the table. "Corrie, run to the parlor and fetch your uncle a bedroll from out of the wardrobe."

"Yes, Grandma." The girl slipped from her chair and ran out of the room. Aaron set Toby on the floor, and he followed his sister.

Ma caught Ethan's eye. "You bring them back here, if something's happened. We'll take care of them."

He nodded, his lips pressed tight. He had a feeling in his gut something bad had happened. And although he wasn't responsible for those folks—not like he'd been for Della—he still felt that he could have done more to ensure their safety. He'd failed Aaron and Della, but he wouldn't fail Miss Marshall. He hoped that the worst that might have happened was a broken wheel, yet apprehension swirled in his gut.

Corrie dashed back into the room, lugging a bedroll. Ethan took it and kissed her head. "Thanks, squirt."

"I'm not a squirt. Toby is." Her brown eyes flashed.

"Nuh-uh," Toby quickly responded. He stuck out his tongue.

"That's enough from both of you," Ma said. "Sit down so we can eat. The men need to hurry."

"I'm gone." Ethan waved. "Pray for us."

"God go with you, little brother." Aaron followed him outside, carrying a rifle, which he shoved into the scabbard on the other side of Ethan's horse.

"I'm sure He will." He tied the bedroll to the back of his saddle, secured the pack of food, and then mounted.

"Be careful." Aaron looked up at him with solemn brown eyes.

Ethan offered a tight smile and a nod. He reined Alamo around, then trotted out of the yard and down the road. Things had never been quite the same between him and Aaron since Della's death. Aaron had lashed out at him that day she'd died, but he'd never said another word about it. Ethan knew his brother still blamed him, but he hoped that he'd forgive him one day. If only he could forgive himself.

Fast hoofbeats approached from behind. Ethan slowed his horse and looked over his shoulder. Josh rode up beside him. "Couldn't let you go alone, not knowing what you might be facing."

"I'm obliged." He clicked out the side of his mouth, and Alamo broke into a gallop. Neither of his brothers was as talkative as he, but, at the moment, that was just fine. He couldn't shake the feeling that something bad had happened—and he was responsible.

They rode on for a good hour, alternating between galloping and walking to rest the horses, following the tracks made by the wagon train. A flock of prairie chickens darted out of the brush on Ethan's right and took flight. This far out on the prairie, there was nothing but grass, critters, and wildflowers—lots of the same ones Della had admired. Ethan blew out a sigh, thinking again about his failure. He'd asked for forgiveness from his family and from God for not taking better care of her, and they'd all forgiven him, even Aaron. Still, he couldn't let go of the thought that if he'd done things differently, Della would still be alive. Aaron would still have a wife, and his children, a mother.

They crested a hill, and Ethan spied something in the road. He glanced at Josh, who drew his rifle; they slowed their horses and proceeded. Many a man had been fooled by a fake body in the road, only to be attacked by a band of outlaws lying in wait. But, as they drew near, Ethan's heart sank. It wasn't a trap. It was Miss Marshall's uncle. And, if he wasn't mistaken, the man was dead.

⌒

"Staring at the road won't make them get here any sooner, you know." Emma ran a brush through her long hair.

Sarah turned away from the horizon to glance at her aunt. "I know, but don't you think someone should have been here by now?"

"That's a long ride for Harvey, and it was almost noon yesterday before he left. Even if he arrived at the Harpers' before dark, which I doubt he did, nobody would have left until this morning to come for us. I wouldn't expect anyone until this evening."

Sighing, Sarah resumed her vigil out the back of the wagon. She dreaded falling asleep again. Slumber had been long in coming last night. Yet, once she'd fallen asleep, she must have been out cold, for how else could she have missed hearing Robby hitching up the mule team or pulling out in that creaky wagon? More pressing, how could she face her uncle with the news that Robby had absconded with all of his possessions, except for those in the pink wagon? He would hate her even more than he already did.

She'd rolled up the sides of the canvas covering the Conestoga to let in more air, and it had helped a bit. She leaned down to peek out beneath the edge of the canvas. The horses seemed to be content grazing. She counted them for the tenth time. What if someone stole them tonight? But then, they hadn't seen a single person all day. What a hauntingly lonely place this Kansas was.

She picked up the fan she'd set down earlier and waved it back and forth in front of her face. If only there had been a tree to park under to give them some shade.

Sarah glanced at the trail again. Who would come for them? Ethan and his brothers? His pa?

Pursing her lips, she blew a breath out her nose. Not Ethan. He would probably refuse because he had another horse to chase after. She dreaded meeting him again, seeing the gloat in his eyes. If only she'd listened to him. But that would mean they'd still be traveling with the wagon train, heading to Santa Fe, and she was having a difficult time being sorry they weren't. She just didn't like being stuck in the middle of nowhere.

How did the pioneers endure the isolation? The danger? The almost constant wind? She gazed out across the prairie, trying to understand why some found it so compelling. With the lack of trees, a farmer might be drawn to fields that didn't need to be cleared. She watched the grasses dance like ballerinas on a stage, waving back and forth; but there was no music here, unless one counted the whine of the wind.

Tired of being alone with her thoughts, she turned to her aunt. Emma was sitting up, reading her Bible. "What's so interesting in there?"

A soft smile curved her aunt's lips. "Oh, lots of things."

"Like what?"

"I've been reading First Corinthians this afternoon. Let me read you a verse. '*But God hath chosen the foolish things of the world to confound the wise; and God hath chosen the weak things of the world to confound the things which are mighty.*'" Aunt Emma smiled at her. "Our God is a God of great resources. I believe He will take care of us and deliver us."

Sarah stared at her aunt. The small speech from the normally quiet woman surprised her. "But what does that mean?"

"Just that God gave a humble shepherd boy the strength and gumption to slay a giant. God took a man who stuttered, born a Hebrew but raised in the palaces of Pharaoh, and used him to free His people from captivity."

Sarah blinked, unsure what those stories had to do with their predicament.

"He can use a broken axle to keep two women from having to travel somewhere they don't want to go."

Her heart leapt at the thought. "But don't you think Uncle Harvey will just buy a new wagon and join another train?"

Emma shrugged. "I hope that he's learned his lesson. That he's figured out we aren't the kind of people who should be traveling West."

Sarah sighed. "I sure hope you're right. But, even if he decides to not continue on, what will we do? We have no home to go back to."

"Neither did the Hebrews who wandered in the wilderness after being set free from slavery in Egypt. It took decades for God to get them to the Promised Land, but they eventually arrived—in His timing. He has a special place for us, too."

Sarah fidgeted, suddenly uncomfortable. Her Promised Land was Chicago, but it was looking like she might never return there. "I'd better go check on the horses." She crawled to the back of the wagon and swung her legs around, ready to scoot off the tailgate.

"Sarah, I haven't spoken much about God at home because Harvey doesn't like to hear it, but I'm sorry now that I didn't do it more. I feel like I've failed you in your Christian education. God loves you deeply, dear. He longs for you to call on Him when you're afraid or worried, or even when you're happy." She swatted the air with her frail hand. "God has a plan, even in this."

Sarah scooted off the tailgate and dropped to the ground, then glanced back at her aunt. "I hope you're right. I'm scared half to death what Uncle Harvey will do when he finds out the freight wagon was stolen."

"At least we still have the horses and this wagon. Try not to worry, dear. I feel in my heart that all will turn out well."

Striding toward the horses, Sarah shook her head. This situation was impossible. How could everything turn out right?

She moved the horses one by one to a fresh patch of grass. Each time she moved them, it took them further from the wagon. Maybe this evening, she should bring them in closer. She was torn between staying there to guard them and hurrying back to the wagon to protect her aunt from possible intruders. The gun weighed heavy in her skirt, but it was there if needed. She checked Shadow's hobbles, then patted the big horse on the shoulder. For some reason, she liked the black horse the most. At least Robby had ridden off with the mules—she didn't care much at all for the stubborn creatures. Maybe they reminded her too much of Ethan Harper. An ornery smile tugged at her lips.

Hearing a horse's whicker, she spun around. Her heart leapt for a mere moment before plunging clear down to her stomach. Three dark-skinned men wearing wide-brimmed hats sat atop their horses, grinning—and gawking—at her.

One man said something to the others, and they all laughed. The closest one pushed his hat up off his forehead. "Where is your man, senora? Or is it senorita?"

Sarah's mind raced. She had no idea what they wanted, but she knew that she was in danger up to her knees. These men didn't look like the Indians she'd seen in pictures; their skin was dark brown, not red, as she'd imagined an Indian's would be. Swallowing back her fear, she forced her voice to not tremble. "What do you want?"

The man grinned, his white teeth bright in contrast with his swarthy skin. "Perhaps we are hungry. You have food, *sí?*"

One of the men, wearing a colorful cape of some strange design, backed up his horse and trotted toward the wagon.

Sarah had to think of something, and quick. "You'd better tell your man to stay away from that wagon."

The leader, wearing pants the color of Ethan's buckskin horse and a dirty, white shirt with loose-fitting sleeves, stroked his long mustache. Two bands holding bullets crisscrossed his chest, forming an X. He glanced at the other man beside him and rattled off a string of unfamiliar words. Then the leader dismounted.

Sarah backed up and slowly slid her hand into her apron pocket. When the man tossed his reins to the other stranger, she yanked out the pistol.

"¡Ai carumba! Ramon, la chica tiene una pistola."

Ramon's head jerked around, his black eyes gleaming. "You mean to shoot me, pretty lady?" He crossed his arms over his chest, not even trying to go for his weapon. But the man on his horse slowly edged a hand toward his.

Sarah lifted the gun and looked him square in the eye, halting his hand. He tipped his hat to her and smiled. The heavy gun wobbled, her arm muscles threatening to give out.

She hoped Ethan was right when he'd said God would watch over them. She could sure use His help right now.

The man nearest the wagon dismounted. Just as he reached for the tailgate, Aunt Emma erupted in a bout of coughing. The man's hand stilled, and he looked back at Sarah.

"Tell your man he'd better stop now if he knows what's good for him."

"And why is that, senorita?"

"B-because...my aunt has...smallpox." To add emphasis to the desperate lie that had rushed into her mind, she scratched her shoulder and then her neck. "Why else do you think the wagon train left us behind?"

Ramon's smile disappeared, and he backed toward his mount. He lithely hopped onto the black-and-white horse, then whipped his hand in a circle over his head. "Vamanos. We take the horses."

Chapter Nine

No! We need them." Sarah didn't know what to do. If she tried to shoot one of the men, there were still two more who'd come after her. And she had to stay alive, even if it meant losing the horses.

"I also have need of them, senorita. Be glad I do not take you, too. I cannot risk taking the smallpox back to my home, not even for a senorita as beautiful as you." Ramon tipped his hat, then pulled a coiled rope from his saddle horn and tapped his horse with his heels.

What would she do now? If no one came to rescue them, they would be stranded.

A blast of gunfire to her right jerked her around. A lone rider charged toward her—blessed be, it was Ethan!—on his buckskin. He glanced at her, then galloped toward the thieves. They'd freed only one horse so far, but the gunfire startled the animal, so that it shied away from the men trying to steal it. Ethan chased them up the hill, firing shot after shot. When the men had disappeared over the crest of the hill, he slowed his horse to a stop and stared after them.

She hadn't wanted to see him again, but right now, she was so happy that she could have hugged him.

⌒

When Ethan saw the riders traverse the third hill without slowing their pace, he finally turned back and loped his horse toward Miss Marshall. He'd been so relieved to see her standing there, but his heart had clenched at the sight of the men who were attempting to steal her horses. Banditos. Why hadn't they taken her, as well? It made no sense.

He dismounted and hurried to her, taking her by the shoulders. His gaze roamed her dirty face and dusty dress, his heart pounding. She wasn't crying, which astounded him. How many city women could face down a trio of banditos without fainting, or even weeping? Maybe she was stronger than he'd given her credit for.

"Are you all right? Did they hurt you?"

She smiled, setting his stomach in a tizzy. "I'm fine. And, no, they didn't hurt me. I'm sure glad to see you, though." She looked past him. "Did you come alone? Where's Uncle Harvey?"

He glanced at the horses, avoiding her question. "I rode out ahead of the others. They're bringing a wagon, since we didn't know the state of yours."

Sarah nodded. "I should check on Aunt Emma." She pulled away from him but quickly spun back around. "What do you mean, you didn't know the condition of our wagon? Didn't my uncle tell you?"

He frowned and stared past her, clenching his teeth. He wasn't sure how to break the news.

"How did you know to come searching for me if my uncle didn't tell you?" She reached out and touched his sleeve. "What is it?"

He hoped his gaze conveyed the depths of his sorrow. "I'm sorry, Miss Marshall, but your uncle is dead."

She gasped, covering her mouth with her fingertips. Her blue eyes filled with pain but not devastation. He knew her uncle hadn't treated her well, but what would they do now without a man to provide for them?

"What happened?"

Ethan pursed his lips and shook his head. "I'm not sure. My brother Josh and I found him on the road. Josh took his…uh…his body back to the ranch. If we hadn't found your uncle's horse outside the barn, we wouldn't have known a thing was wrong. Found the gelding early this morning, just after we did the milking. The good Lord must have guided him back. I'm sorry for your loss."

"Thank you." She stared out across the prairie. "I don't know how I'll tell Aunt Emma." Her gaze shifted back to his, worry crinkling her brow. "What will we do?"

He longed to soothe away her concern, but he didn't know how. "Ma said to tell you that you can stay with us for as long as you need to. So, don't worry about that for now."

Her lower lip wobbled, and she gasped a sob. "This is all my fault. If I hadn't encouraged Uncle Harvey to go against your counsel, then he'd probably still be alive."

Ethan took hold of her shoulders again. "You don't know that. The other wagon might have broken down, too."

"I sincerely doubt it." She shook her head and sucked in another gasp. "It's my fault that my uncle is dead." She buried her face in her hands.

He patted her shoulder, feeling awkward as a witness to her grief. He'd never known how to handle a woman's tears, especially since Della would wield hers like a weapon. Miss Marshall leaned toward him, and he gently pulled her against his chest, hoping to comfort her. "Things will work out, you'll see." He patted her back, realizing just how slight she was. The top of her head barely reached his chin. "I've learned to seek God during hard times. He brings us a comfort and peace that no man can. Trust Him, Miss Marshall. He will work things out."

She stiffened and pushed away. "God has never helped me before. Why would He now?" She turned and walked toward the wagon, wiping her eyes with the backs of her hands. "I need to tell Aunt Emma."

It saddened him that she felt the way she did about God, but maybe that was just her hurt talking. People said things they didn't mean when they were upset. He wished he'd been better able to comfort her, but he knew little about women. He glanced back at the horses and realized the mules weren't with them. "Where's your other wagon? Did it continue on?"

She hung her head. "Mr. Blake stole it during the night." Without commenting further, she trudged toward the wagon.

Ethan approached the horses, feeling lower than a frog's belly. He hated seeing the fire dim in Miss Marshall's eyes and wished there was something he could do to ease her pain, but he felt bad himself. Maybe if he'd been more adamant about advising her uncle against buying the pink wagon, the man might still be alive. He picked up a rock and flung it as far as he could. He couldn't help feeling that he was partly to blame. Now the women had lost not only a husband and an uncle but also the other wagon and all its merchandise. And, if he hadn't come along when he did, they would have lost the stock horses, too—and maybe even their lives. He hoped Mrs. Stone had some money stashed somewhere in the pink wagon, because she and her niece would surely need it when they were ready to leave the stage stop.

❧

Two days later, Sarah stood in the small graveyard on the Harpers' property. Beside her was her aunt, seated in a chair Aaron Harper had brought from the house. A minister she had just met—Pastor Bishop—read Scriptures from the Bible that she supposed were meant to comfort. Her uncle had already been buried because of the heat, but, for her aunt's sake, the Harper family had organized the small funeral service. Wildflowers lay across the fresh mound of dirt in the small cemetery, where only four other graves marred the grass. One was marked by a freshly painted cross bearing the name of Josiah Thomas; an engraved head stone with scrolling flowers bore the name Della Jane Harper—Aaron's wife; and the other two buried there also had the Harper surname. Were they children who had died, or some other family members?

A canopy of trees sheltered them from the sun, their leaves rustling overhead in the light breeze. A black iron fence had been erected around the small cemetery, probably to keep wandering cattle and horses from trampling the graves. Someone had gone to a lot of trouble to clip the grass, leaving the area tidy. The minister's voice droned on, but she couldn't focus on his words. If it wasn't for her, none of them would be here now. Uncle Harvey would still be alive, Aunt Emma wouldn't be a widow, and they'd still be on their way to Santa Fe. The only advantage Sarah could see was that they were no longer on the trail.

On the other side of the grave stood the three Harper brothers, cleaned up with their hair slicked down, as if ready to go to Sunday service. Aaron was the oldest and tallest of the three, standing only an inch taller than Ethan. The two favored each other in eye and hair color, although Ethan was leaner. Josh, the middle brother, had blue eyes and stood at least two inches shorter than Ethan. His build was slimmer than his brothers', and the few times she'd seen him since coming back to the stage stop, he'd had a book with him.

Aaron's two children stood between their grandparents on Emma's far side. Karen Harper had been very charitable in giving them the only bedroom downstairs, which was normally reserved for ill or injured people. Mr. Harper was a strong leader, issuing orders in a kind way but expecting them to be followed. Aaron and Ethan favored him, while Josh resembled his mother. They were a handsome family. Sarah let out a sigh. She shouldn't be jealous of the generous people who'd taken them in, but she'd always longed for a big family. Siblings. Parents. Still, she was grateful that her aunt and uncle had let her come live with them. She would have hated being raised in an orphanage, even one as nice as Mrs. Rayburn's.

"Let us pray."

Sarah bowed her head, ashamed that she'd missed most of the minister's message. He'd ridden a long way just to perform the service.

"Dear heavenly Father, comfort this family in the loss of their loved one. O God, whose blessed Son was laid in a tomb in a garden, we ask that You would console this grieving family. Grant that him whose body is buried in this grave may enter into Thy heavenly kingdom and dwell with Christ in paradise. In the name of Thy Son Jesus Christ our Lord, amen."

A subdued chorus of "Amens" rounded the grave. Aunt Emma reached for Sarah's hand and clung to it. Tears ran down her aunt's face as she gazed upon her husband's resting place. Sarah wished she felt more sorrow than she did, but she didn't miss Uncle Harvey. He'd never been kind to her. Still, she hurt because her aunt did. Emma laid atop the grave a trio of peach-colored roses that Mrs. Harper had tied together with a white ribbon, and Sarah helped her back up. This was the first time she'd been out of bed since their return to the Harpers' yesterday. Her husband's death seemed to have taken away her will to live.

Sarah was determined to help restore it somehow. Her aunt was all she had left in this world.

"Can I help you back into the wagon, Mrs. Stone?" Ethan held his hat in his hands, and his thick brown hair, which had been combed back and slicked down, looked much darker. He stood tall and handsome, with the glow of the morning sun radiating around him. She couldn't explain the relief she'd felt when he'd ridden to her rescue the other day, gun blazing. He was like the heroes of the romance novels she had borrowed from Abigail.

"I would appreciate that, young man."

A short while later, Sarah tucked her aunt into bed again. The room they shared was cozy, with two single beds, a small desk and chair in between them. One wall was lined with shelves holding a variety of medicines and bandages, and a rocking chair sat in one corner.

The two men the Harpers had hired to retrieve the supplies from their wagon were to arrive today. Good thing, because Sarah and her aunt both needed a change of clothes, and Aunt Emma wanted her black dress—widow's weeds. Wearing black may have been the custom when a family member died, but Sarah no longer owned a black dress. She hoped her aunt wouldn't insist she make one to wear.

Delicious aromas drew her to the kitchen. Mrs. Harper opened the oven door, bent down, and slid a tray of biscuits inside. Corrie was setting the table, which stood in front of a wide window with a view of the ranch. The rural scene whispered to Sarah, and she walked over to look out. In spite of all she'd been through, she had to admit there was a serenity to the prairie that one didn't find in the noisy, fast-moving city.

"Oh, Sarah. Is your aunt resting?" Mrs. Harper pulled out a chair at the table. "Come and have a seat. Lunch will be ready soon."

"May I do anything to help?"

"Mercy, no. We just buried your uncle, and besides, you're a guest in our home."

"We may be imposing on your hospitality for a while, so, please, put me to work."

Mrs. Harper studied her for a moment, then smiled, her brown eyes twinkling. "All right. There's a dinner bell out on the porch. If you don't mind, would you ring it so the men know to start heading this way?"

Sarah nodded. "Sure."

"I can show you where the bell is." Corrie dropped the last spoon onto the table and rushed toward her.

"Cora, go back and put that spoon in its proper place, and then you may show her."

"Aww! Yes, Grandma." The girl quickly did as told, then hurried back and took Sarah's hand. "C'mon."

They passed through the washroom and onto the back porch. A trio of rockers faced the barn and corral, where several horses were grazing.

"We don't really have a bell. It's a triangle—that's a three-sided shape." Corrie dragged one of the rockers over to the porch railing and climbed up on the seat, then she shinnied onto the wooden rail, heedless that she was wearing a dress, and stretched her arm toward the iron triangle.

Sarah reached out, ready to catch her if she fell. Standing on tiptoe, the girl just barely managed to remove the clangor from its hook, and then she handed it to Sarah. "Just run the clangor around the inside of the triangle."

Sarah did so, and the loud clang echoed in her ears. It seemed a rather barbaric way to summon people to dinner, but she supposed it was the easiest option, since the men were often far from the house. Corrie hung the clangor back, climbed down from the rail to the rocker, then jumped to the floor. Shaking her head, Sarah reached out to stop the rocker's gyration. Someone needed to teach this little girl how to be a proper young lady.

"You got any young'uns?"

Warmth rushed to Sarah's cheeks. "Um…no. I'm not married."

"Pa's not married, but he's got kids." Corrie ducked under the rail and spit like a cowboy. Sarah worked hard to stifle a gasp. "Grandma says Pa and my uncles all need to get married. Maybe you could marry one of 'em." Corrie stared up at her with wide, innocent eyes. The girl wore her hair in twin braids that hung over her shoulders and down her chest. One of the blue ribbons had come undone, and Sarah bent to tie it.

"Your father and uncles are fine men, but I plan to return to Chicago, just as soon as my aunt and I can make arrangements."

The girl frowned and stuck out her lower lip, as if the thought of Sarah leaving displeased her. "My mama died. She fell off her horse."

Sarah's heart lurched. She sat in the rocker so she could look Corrie in the face. "My mother died when I was a young girl, too."

"She did?" Corrie leaned against Sarah's leg with obvious interest. "How did she die?"

Corrie seemed smarter and more aware of things than most of the youngsters at the orphanage back in Chicago, but Sarah wasn't sure how much to tell her. "They had a carriage accident."

"They?" The girl's thin brown eyebrows dipped.

"Yes, my mother and father were both killed when their carriage slipped off a bridge."

"Your pa died, too?"

Sarah nodded. Aaron and Josh strode out of the barn, playfully pushing and shoving each other. She could hear their laughter and good-natured banter clear across the yard.

"Pa!" Corrie jumped off the porch and ran to meet her father, her short legs pumping hard. He caught her up and swung her in a circle. The girl squealed with laughter.

"You're good with Corrie."

Sarah spun around, her hand on her chest. Ethan stood at the end of the porch, leaning on the railing. He'd changed back into his work clothes—dusty denim pants and a light blue shirt with the sleeves rolled up, revealing his deeply tanned arms.

"Where did you come from?"

He grinned. "I do live here, you know."

"Well, you shouldn't eavesdrop."

"I'm just watching out for my niece's welfare."

Sarah lifted her chin. "What does that mean?"

"She misses her mother, and she latches on to any woman who stays more than a day. I'm just asking that you be careful and to not hurt her."

"I would never hurt a child."

"Not intentionally, I'm sure."

She gazed into his eyes, but this time there was no hint of laughter. Sarah spun around and rushed back into the house, not stopping when Mrs. Harper called her name. She shut the door to her room, tears stinging her eyes. Just what kind of a person did he take her for?

Chapter Ten

Ethan strode out to the paddock where Aaron was exercising a green broke mare while Josh and Toby watched. Twenty-four hours after his last encounter with Miss Marshall, he still couldn't decide if he'd been too harsh with her. He hadn't meant to be, but his attraction to her both flustered and riled him. He'd meant merely to caution her about getting too close to Corrie; but instead, he'd nearly bitten the woman's head off. He blew out a sigh. Ever since Della's death, he'd been overprotective of Corrie and Toby—and his ma. She'd told him many times that she was a grown woman and didn't need him hovering all the time.

He clenched his jaw. How was he supposed to find a balance between protecting his family and hovering?

"Uncle E'tan! Pa's riding a horsey!" Toby grabbed hold of the fence rail and stuck his head through the bars. Josh fumbled to keep from dropping the wiggly boy.

"Hold on there, pardner." Josh wrapped an arm around his nephew's waist and hauled him back through the bars.

Aaron trotted the mare around the paddock, then reined her around to go in the other direction. "She's coming along nicely, don't you think?"

Both Josh and Ethan grunted their agreement.

After a final time around, Aaron reined the mare to a stop in front of them and dismounted. He opened the gate and led her out, nodding. "Yes, she's smart and seems eager to please. She'll make a fine saddle horse."

Ethan followed his brothers and nephew into the barn. "Has Pa said if he wants to keep her or sell her?"

"Nah." Aaron unfastened the cinch and dragged the saddle off her back. "She's a mite small, though, for a man, unless he was real short."

"Maybe someone will buy her for a lady," Josh offered, snatching up a brush.

"Toby!"

All three men turned at the sound of their mother's voice. Only the boy ignored her, bent on wrestling the brush from his uncle's hand.

"He's in here, Ma." Josh lifted Toby up and carried him to the barn entrance.

"Send him in, and you guys come, too. Supper's ready."

"I'm starved!" Toby kicked his feet, already forgetting about currying the horse. Josh set him down, and the boy ran toward the house.

"He's gettin' big." Josh tossed the brush to Ethan, then laced his fingers and stretched his arms over his head, nearly knocking his hat off.

Ethan walked out of the stall long enough to make sure Toby had made it into the house, then went back and began brushing the mare. "Won't be too long before he'll be old enough to start his schoolin', like Corrie." He glanced sideways at his oldest brother. "Have you thought any more about what you'll do?"

"Some. Ma offered to teach them, but she's got so much to do already that I hate to ask." Aaron curried the other side of the horse, then set his brush on the shelf. "C'mon. Ma will be hoppin' mad if we're late for supper." They exited the stall, Aaron securing the gate behind them, and then headed out of the barn. Aaron stopped at the well, dropped the bucket in with a loud splash, and then began drawing it up.

"Have you thought about hiring an older girl from town who's finished her schooling?" Josh asked. "I'm sure there's someone who could use the extra money, and maybe she could even help Ma out."

Aaron shrugged as he drew the bucket up and set it on the edge of the well. "I don't know as any young gal would want to live here for months."

"Maybe Miss Marshall could teach them," Ethan offered.

Josh and Aaron both stopped and stared at him like he'd gone crazy.

"Are you dumb as a fence post?" Josh shook his head. "She just lost her uncle. She's in mourning."

Ethan bit back the words that came to mind. They didn't need to know that her uncle wouldn't be missed—at least not by her. "Well, she will be here for a while, so Ma says."

"And she's real pretty." Josh grinned and nudged Aaron in the side. "I bet you didn't know that *Sarah* is Hebrew for 'princess.'"

Aaron scowled. "What's that got to do with anything?"

"Nothing. But don't you think she's pretty?" Josh waggled his eyebrows.

"Sure." Aaron poured water into one hand, rubbed both palms together, and washed his face.

Ethan followed suit, preferring to keep quiet when his brothers were talking about Miss Marshall. If they suspected he was attracted to her—not that he was—they would tease him mercilessly.

Aaron shook off the excess water and headed toward the house.

"Does she remind you of Della?" Josh splashed water onto his face.

Aaron turned and stormed back, opening and closing his fist, as if he meant to punch Josh. "No, she doesn't. Why would you say such a thing?"

"Because she's got the same color hair and eyes."

"No, she doesn't. And she's much shorter."

"Don't go getting your spurs tangled. I'm just curious. It's been a long time since we had a pretty gal stay here more than a night or two." Josh stuck his hat back on and glanced at Ethan. "You're awful quiet, little brother."

"Stop calling me that." He was tired of their picking on him for being last in the birth order. It wasn't as if he'd had any say in the matter.

"Calling you what, little brother?" Josh asked with feigned innocence.

"Stop it." He ground his back teeth together.

Aaron stood with his hands loosely on his hips, a bemused smirk on his lips. "Maybe *little brother* is attracted to our visitor. He did come to her rescue, after all."

Josh clasped his hands together and pressed them under his chin, batting his eyes. "My hero!" he gushed in falsetto. "My knight in shining armor."

"I said stop." Ethan shoved his brother's shoulder.

"I think we've hit the nail on the head." Aaron folded his arms and grinned.

Ethan crossed his arms to keep from throwing a punch. The more he denied having feelings for Miss Marshall, the more they'd think they were right. He narrowed his gaze. "Maybe you just want her for yourself."

"Maybe so." Aaron smiled at Josh and then wiggled his eyebrows at Ethan. "What of it, *little brother?*"

Fed up, Ethan balled his fist and took a swing at his eldest brother.

Aaron laughed and jumped back, out of reach. He bumped into Josh, and they both fell backward, legs tangling, then landed with a loud thud on the ground. Both men shot right back up and tackled Ethan before he could react. He bucked like a mustang, trying to get his brothers off of him. Grunts and other sounds of scuffle echoed around him.

A sudden shot rent the air, and they all froze. Aaron glanced at his fist, lifted and ready to plunge into Ethan's face, and his expression shifted from anger to surprise. He lowered his arm, moved away, and dusted off his pants.

Josh rolled off of Ethan's leg and sat up. "Uh-oh."

Pushing up on his elbows, Ethan looked at the house.

Ma stood on the back porch, rifle in hand. "Just what's going on out here?" Her expression mirrored one he hadn't seen since they were adolescents.

Miss Marshall stepped outside after Ma, and her eyes widened at the sight of them. She spun around and hurried back through the door, obviously not wanting to get involved in a family squabble.

Galloping hooves announced Pa's arrival. He reined his horse to a stop and stared down with arched eyebrows at his three sons. "What's this all about?" He dismounted and strode toward them.

Aaron offered both brothers a hand and pulled them up. Ethan dusted off his backside, avoiding his pa's stern gaze. Not since he'd overturned the outhouse with Josh inside it had he felt his father's disappointment so severely.

"You are grown men, far too old to be fighting with one another. I expect more from you than this. We're a family, and families support one other." He looked each son in the eye, with his gaze lingering a bit longer on his eldest. Then, he shook his head, turned, and snatched up his reins. "We don't have a pretty gal on the property two whole days, and already you're carrying on like a bunch of cocks in a henhouse."

Ethan was glad Miss Marshall had gone back inside and hadn't heard his pa's remark. Maybe he *was* attracted to the pretty woman, and his protective nature had risen up because she seemed so needy, but that was all. He didn't want to marry a city gal who'd be whining all the time to go back to Chicago.

Sarah sat on the back porch with her aunt, having finally coaxed her from their bedroom. "It sure is quiet here, isn't it?"

Emma nodded but stared off with a sad, faraway expression on her face.

Sarah wished she could say something to make her feel better—to make her smile. "I've never been anyplace with so few people or such wide open spaces. It was frightening out there on the prairie. No buildings. Nothing but grass and insects...and wind."

"It was windy in Chicago, too."

Swiveling her head, she looked at her aunt. That was the first thing she'd said, other than comments about food and responses to direct questions Sarah had asked. "That's true. But don't you miss the buildings? All the people coming and going? City life?"

Emma shrugged. "Kansas is peaceful, and life here seems far less hectic."

Sarah's heart clenched. What if her aunt became so comfortable here that she never wanted to go back? "I miss the children at the orphanage. Did I ever tell you that Mrs. Rayburn asked me to come live with her?"

"She did?" Emma turned her head toward Sarah, but her eyes were not focused. What was wrong with her? Sarah had never seen her this way before.

"Yes, but I told her I couldn't. I didn't want to leave you."

"You're a dear, but you shouldn't let me hold you back like I did Harvey."

She took hold of Emma's hand. "Don't say that. He sold your house without even asking you and forced us both to go with him on this ridiculous journey. We didn't hold him back. He did just what he wanted." And look where it had gotten him.

"Shh, don't speak ill of the dead."

Sarah snapped her mouth shut so that she wouldn't say anything else. As guilty as it made her feel, she couldn't help it; she was not sorry her uncle was gone. Her life, and her aunt's, would be easier in many ways because he no longer controlled things. But their foremost problem was deciding what to do next and how to get along without an income. Sarah thought about writing Walt to see if he would send money to pay their way home, but it stuck in her craw to ask a favor of him after the blunt letter of dismissal she'd sent him. He probably didn't care to hear from her ever again, much less help her.

Maybe Mrs. Rayburn would allow both of them to live with her. Once Aunt Emma was feeling better, the children would surely give her a reason to smile again. She just needed time to grieve and get well. Sarah would pen another letter to Mrs. Rayburn that evening.

The sound of galloping hoofbeats yanked her from her thoughts. She stood just as Aaron raced around the corner. He reined his horse to a fast stop. "Get Ma. We've got an injured man comin' in."

Not Ethan. Sarah clutched the front of her dress and spun around to do as ordered. She hoped the injured person wasn't any of the Harper men. She hurried into the house and searched each room, but she couldn't find Mrs. Harper. She spied Corrie sitting with Toby on the settee in the parlor, looking at pictures in a book. "Where's your grandmother?"

Corrie pointed upstairs.

Sarah hurried to the bottom of the steps and clutched the banister, her whole body trembling. What if Mr. Harper was injured?

Sarah despised yelling, but she wouldn't venture up to the Harpers' private quarters uninvited. "Mrs. Harper?"

"I'm up here, Sarah," she called. "You're welcome to come on up. I've been meaning to show you the rest of the house."

"Aaron rode in quite fast and said they were bringing in a wounded man and to tell you."

"Oh." Something banged against the floor, like a broom being dropped, and Mrs. Harper appeared in a doorway at the top of the stairs. She all but ran down the steps, her face whiter than Sarah had ever seen it. "Did he say who was hurt?"

Sarah shook her head, imagining the concern that must be flooding the mind of her kind hostess. Did injuries happen often? It must be dreadful knowing someone you cared about was injured and in pain when the closest doctor was nearly a day's ride away.

"Is Pa all right?" Corrie slipped off the settee, and Toby followed like a little shadow.

"He's fine." Sarah rubbed her hand across the girl's head, hoping to reassure her. "He's the one who rode in and told me that someone was wounded, so don't worry." The girl's relief was obvious. Did she worry all the time that something might happen to her father? That was probably natural, considering the way in which she had lost her mother.

Mrs. Harper stepped into the room. "You two sit back on that settee and stay out of the way until I tell you, you hear?"

Both children nodded and didn't argue. Evidently, they knew their grandma's serious tone.

Sarah followed Mrs. Harper into the kitchen. "How may I help?"

"You can clear off the table and wipe it down." Mrs. Harper snatched up an empty bucket and stuck her head out the door. "Aaron, fill this up. How much longer before they're here?"

"Anytime," Sarah heard him say.

When Mrs. Harper stepped back inside, Sarah asked, "You mean, you want me to wash the kitchen table?" It sounded like a silly question, since that was the only table she'd seen in the house. But, surely, they didn't plan to doctor the man on the very table where they ate. She lifted her hand to her throat, her stomach whirling.

"Yes." Mrs. Harper nodded and dashed past her. "And I'm sorry, but I'll need to get in your room. Is your aunt napping?"

"No, she's out on the porch."

"Oh. I didn't see her. It's good we won't have to disturb her. I just hope all the commotion won't upset her." She opened the door to the room Sarah and Emma had been sharing and entered. Sarah heard bottles clink and a chair scoot across the floor, and then Karen returned, arms full.

Taking a clean cloth from the stack on a shelf, Sarah dipped it in the bucket of water used for cleaning and wiped off the table. Mrs. Harper deposited the bottles on the counter nearest the table, then bustled back to the bedroom, this time returning with rolls of bandages and several more bottles. She set them on the counter and nodded. "Good. We're ready."

Ready for what? Sarah wanted to ask, but Mrs. Harper didn't know any more than she did. A fast-moving wagon passed by the kitchen window, and Sarah followed Mrs. Harper to the door and out onto the porch. The woman reached out and clutched Sarah's hand as if needing support. She hadn't considered that Mrs. Harper might be vulnerable. The woman always seemed so self-assured and confident in her abilities, but now she was a wife—a mother—worried that one of her family members might be seriously wounded.

Mr. Harper rode around the corner, and the wagon followed, driven by one of the workers, who slowed it to a stop. Sarah was sure he was one of the men she'd seen leave here a few days ago to retrieve their belongings from the broken-down wagon. There were pitiful few things in back. And where was the other man who'd gone with him?

Aaron hurried to the back of the wagon, as did Mrs. Harper. Sarah stayed on the porch and glanced at her aunt, who was watching the wagon closely. How did Mrs. Harper bear the constant worry that one of her family could be killed as easily as Uncle Harvey? Sarah wrapped one trembling hand over the other and pressed them against her lips, hoping it wasn't Ethan who lay in the back of the wagon. But then, she didn't want kindhearted Josh to have been injured, either. But it had to be one of them—and whoever it was wasn't moving.

Chapter Eleven

Aaron and his pa slid the wounded man off the back of the wagon and, each of them supporting one of the man's arms over his shoulders, turned him toward the house. The side of his white shirt was stained crimson.

Sarah clutched the fence rail, weak with relief that the wounded man was neither Ethan nor his brother, but rather the other man who'd gone to retrieve her aunt's belongings. She felt bad enough that one of their hired hands had been hurt, but she couldn't face Mrs. Harper if she'd been responsible for the injury or, worse, death of a member of her family. Emma came to her side and watched as they juggled the man, having to turn sideways to get him through the doorway. Mrs. Harper followed them inside after assuring Sarah that her help was not needed.

"I'd like to see what's in the wagon," Emma said.

Sarah assisted her aunt down the stairs and over to the wagon, where the driver walked around the pawing, snorting horses, murmuring to them. She struggled to recall his name—Mr. Brown, or something like that. Sweat covered the animals' sides, evidence of their speedy run to save a man's life.

"Uh, excuse me, sir, but could you tell me what happened?" she asked.

"Thieves." He shook his head. "I went out hunting, hoping for a rabbit or prairie hen for breakfast. While I was gone, a bunch of robbers shot Fred." His expression changed. He ducked his head and began fiddling with his hat. "I'm right sorry, ma'am, but those thieves had already stolen many of your things by the time I got back. I ran them off, but they'd ransacked much of it."

Emma reached out and grabbed hold of the wagon wheel for support. She wobbled a moment, then proceeded to the back of the wagon, her head held high. As she turned and looked at the cargo, Sarah saw her face go white and her eyelids bat wildly, wet with tears.

She hurried to her aunt's side and wrapped an arm around her shoulder. And then, bracing herself, she looked in the wagon bed. Four crates were all that was left of her aunt's life. There were none of the sacks of food, which had been filled to the brim; none of their clothing or personal belongings, as far as she could tell; none of her aunt's beautiful furniture. Sarah's heart ached for her. She knew what it was like to lose everything, but her aunt didn't.

Emma trembled. "There's so little." She turned to the driver, one hand pressed over her heart. "Did they take everything else? My family heirlooms? My clothes?"

The man nodded. "There was two pieces of furniture still left in the wagon, but with Fred shot, I just grabbed him and tossed in the closest crates. We left before the bandits returned."

"So, you're saying some of our things are still out there?"

He shook his head. "Not much. There may be a small box or two, and maybe a couple of larger pieces of furniture, but the thieves must have been prepared. They had a buckboard, and they loaded things fast, because I'd been gone less than an hour when I heard the shots.

Emma turned toward Sarah and collapsed against her, soft sobs shaking her shoulders. Sarah patted her back. After a few moments, Emma sucked in a breath and pushed up. She spun around and leaned over the tailgate. "Did you see a black hatbox in any of these crates?"

Sarah hurried to her side, wondering about the frantic tone in her aunt's voice.

The man shook his head. "I don't think so, but we can look. Two of the crates are nailed shut, which is probably why the thieves didn't mess with them." He pulled one forward, careful to avoid the trail of blood on the floor of the wagon, and dragged it to the tailgate.

Sarah recognized the image of a watch her uncle had painted on the box. Her heart sank. Watchmaker's tools wouldn't help either of them.

Emma pointed to the other crate that was nailed shut. "See that 'W'? That one contains winter things, like my wool cloak and muff, H-Harvey's wool trousers, flannel shirts...."

The driver hauled the other two crates out of the back of the wagon and set them on the ground. Sarah saw her aunt's sewing basket and writing desk, as well as two small sacks of coffee, several bags of nuts and spices, and a few other supplies. The final container held an extra harness and some leather polish and rags. Not much left of forty-some-odd years of life.

Emma reached for Sarah. "I think I need to lie down again."

"Of course, Auntie." Sarah wrapped her arm around Emma's thin shoulders. How would she endure in the face of such a loss? So many cherished belongings and memories—gone. She could only hope her aunt would find a reason to keep going. Sarah couldn't lose her.

To avoid passing through the kitchen, she guided Emma around to the side door and then down the hall. She paused outside their bedroom. "I wonder if they will need the room for the wounded man."

Emma sucked in a sob, and her knees buckled, as if the thought of losing their borrowed room was the last straw. Sarah tightened her grasp and helped her aunt to the bed. "They'll just have to find another place for him."

Once Emma's shoes were off and she was tucked in bed, Sarah gazed down at her. Would she be strong enough to overcome all these tragedies? What would happen if she just gave up? Sarah blinked away the sting in her eyes. *I'll be all alone.*

She started to tiptoe from the room but turned when she remembered the black hatbox. Her aunt's eyes were already dipping down. Maybe she should wait.

"What is it, dear? I can hear you thinking clear over here."

She nibbled her lip, hoping her question wouldn't bring her aunt more dismay, but her curiosity was killing her. "What was in the black hatbox that was so important?"

Emma furrowed her brow and puckered her lips. "Our marriage certificate, Harvey's important papers, a-and all of our…m-money. We're destitute, dear." She sucked in a loud sob and rolled over, showing Sarah her frail back.

Destitute?

Numb, Sarah wandered down the hall to the parlor, where she found Corrie and Toby peering through the crack where the kitchen door met the jamb, watching the proceedings. She snapped her fingers, and they both jumped. "Your grandmother wouldn't want you to spy on her."

Corrie frowned. "We're not spying, just…uh…watching."

"Is Fred gonna die?" Toby asked, his brown eyes wide. "We had a cat that died. Never saw him again."

Sarah took the children by the hand and tugged them over toward the couch, where she sat down, keeping an arm around each youngster. "I don't think so, but I'm not sure. Fred had to lie in the wagon for a long time after he was shot, and he lost a lot of blood." She shuddered at the memory of the red streak in the wagon bed.

"We should pray for him," Corrie said, then bowed her head, as if expecting everyone to agree.

Sarah ducked her head, and Toby did the same, but when he peeked up at her, she closed her eyes.

"Dear God, please help Fred. Don't take him to heaven. Grandpa and Daddy need him. We want him here with us. Amen."

Sarah was duly impressed, and not a little convicted, by the young girl's prayer. She'd once had a childlike faith like Corrie's, but, after the death of her parents, and in the face of her uncle's cruelty, she'd lost faith in God. He'd never answered her prayers, anyway. Now, she didn't even know what to pray.

～

Ethan was so upset with Miss Priss, he could have spit. If she'd just listened to him in the first place, rather than being so stubborn, her uncle might still be alive, and Fred wouldn't be suffering from a gunshot wound and possibly dying. Or was he already dead?

Following Pa's orders, he walked with Josh out to the barn to groom and ready the switch team for the stage, which would be coming in any time. "How do you think Fred's doing?"

"Don't know, but I hope he makes it. Hate to lose a good man." Josh ran his brush across the back of a tall sorrel gelding.

"I don't think I'm going to offer help to any more city folks. Half of them don't take my advice, anyway."

Josh huffed a laugh. "Fine by me. We could use you around here more."

Ethan halted the brush in midair. The black mare turned her head, as if checking to see why he'd stopped grooming her. "Are you saying I'm not pulling my own weight?"

Josh swiped a brush over the sorrel's rump several times, then set it on the shelf and led the horse from the stall. "No, that's not what I'm saying. We all understand how hard a time you've had since Della's death."

Bristling, Ethan ran his hand over the back of the mare and then strode out of the stall, glaring at his brother. No one knew the pain he'd endured. No one knew how it felt to be at fault for someone else's death.

Josh dropped the horse's lead rope and held up his hands in surrender. "Now, hold on. Don't go gettin' riled up, little brother. I'm not complaining, just pointing out a fact."

"Quit calling me that," Ethan grated through clenched teeth.

Grinning, Josh patted his horse and led him toward the barn door. He called back over his shoulder, "You never minded until Miss Marshall came around."

"I'm twenty-one, for heaven's sake. Just stop calling me that."

Josh chuckled. "I think I'll give her that book I made, the one about prairie flowers. It might give her something to think about besides her problems." He stopped the horse in the doorway and looked back at Ethan. "You think she'd like that?"

Ethan shrugged, more irritated at his reaction to the thought of his brother giving Miss Marshall a gift than he was at the name-calling. Why should it bother him? He blew out a sigh. It did, though, as much as he might argue the fact. He scowled, half mad at himself. "How would I know what she likes?" He untied the horse and led him from the stall, scowling at his brother's back as he left the barn. "She's not staying, you know, so you might as well keep your dumb flower book."

He led the horse out of the barn and put it in the paddock to await the stage, then followed Josh back inside for another pair of horses.

"It's not a *dumb* book." Josh flashed him a wounded look. "I've worked years drawing all those pictures in that journal and researching their names and classifications."

"I know. Sorry." Ethan regretted his juvenile comment. He hadn't meant to hurt his brother. What was it about the presence of a woman that caused grown men to turn on those they cared about?

Ethan finished with the other horse, secured him in the paddock, and then strode over to the wagon still sitting in the yard. "Go ahead and unhitch those horses, Randy. No sense in them standing around."

"You don't think your ma'll need the wagon to get Fred to town?" Randy stood, keeping one hand on the back of the nearest horse, and eyed the house.

"We'd need a fresh team even if they do."

Randy nodded, then started unhitching the team. Ethan looked in the back of the wagon and winced at the amount of blood he saw. He sent up a prayer for Fred. The men hadn't brought back much of the Stones' belongings. How would they get by on so little, and without a man to provide for them, especially since they had no home to go back to? He supposed they might be able to go to Kansas City and stay with Bob Stone, but that might be awkward. And besides, Bob and his wife were to head down the trail soon, too. Would their plans change when they learned of Harvey's death? Had anyone written to them about it?

"You're sure doing a lot of sighing over there." Josh approached the other side of the wagon. "What are you thinking about?"

"Nothing."

"Doesn't sound like nothing." Josh rested his arms on the wagon's side boards. "Precious little in there."

"Yeah." Ethan blew out another sigh.

Josh turned around and leaned back against the wagon. "I've been thinking."

"So, what's new about that?" Ethan chuckled. Josh was studious—the thinker of the three brothers. Aaron could be quiet, too, but Josh was the smartest and the most educated. Most of the time, that didn't bother Ethan. It was just a matter of fact, and Josh wasn't bigheaded about his intelligence. But would Miss Marshall prefer a learned man to a dirty rancher? Weren't most Chicagoans highly literate?

"It looks like Mrs. Stone and her niece have lost most of their things. They could be here a long while." Josh looked up and caught Ethan's eye. "I don't know if they have other family or people who will take them in, but we sure could use a couple of women around here to help Ma." He glanced at the back door of the house and then peeked over his shoulder at Randy before stepping around the back of the wagon to move closer to Ethan. "What say we try to get Aaron and Miss Marshall together? That way, she and her aunt wouldn't have to worry about a place to live."

"I thought you wanted to impress her with your flower book and win her for yourself."

Josh shrugged and picked at the dirt under one of his fingernails. "Just because I might give her my book—if I do—doesn't mean I'm interested in her for myself."

"You're not?"

Josh exhaled a loud breath. "I don't think so."

His brother's response rolled some of the tension from Ethan's shoulders, but the thought of Aaron and Miss Marshall together buzzed in his head like a pesky fly. The idea both intrigued him and turned his stomach. "That woman is trouble. She knows nothing about country life."

"No…but she could learn. We could teach her, and, at the same time, expound her virtues to Aaron."

Ethan snorted. "What virtues?" The moment the words had left his mouth, he remembered the beguiling pair of blue eyes staring in shock from a mud-splattered face. The same eyes that had flashed victory when her uncle had purchased the pink wagon.

Well, she wasn't gloating now.

"She's pretty, for one thing, and she takes good care of her aunt. But I can see you're not convinced." Josh rubbed his hand across his chin, then shrugged. "What have we got to lose? I say we should do it."

As if that had settled everything, he pushed away from the wagon and headed toward the house. Ethan followed suit, thinking on his brother's crazy plan. There was one thing that made sense, at least—if he could find Aaron another wife, maybe the terrible burden of guilt would lift off his shoulders.

Josh paused and glanced back. "And if Aaron isn't interested in Miss Marshall, I just might change my mind and go after her myself."

⤸

With her aunt resting again, and the children gone outside with their father, Sarah ventured back into the kitchen to see if she could borrow some paper for writing letters. Aunt Emma sure wasn't in any condition to write to Bob and Lydia. Sarah paused in the hall just outside the kitchen door. No voices sounded inside, only splashing and some heavy breathing. She peered around the corner and found Mrs. Harper scrubbing down the table with soapy water.

The woman glanced up, smiled, and swept a loose strand of hair away from her face with the back of her hand. "Come on in."

"How is that man? Will he be all right?" *Will he live?* she wanted to ask.

"I think so, but time will tell." Mrs. Harper pressed a fist against the small of her back.

Sarah couldn't tear her gaze away from her blood-stained apron. Mrs. Harper looked down and gasped. She quickly untied the garment and shed it, then rolled it up and dropped it into a basket in the corner. "Mercy sakes, I should have changed aprons before cleaning the table. I'm just in a hurry. The stage is due through soon, and I've got to feed the passengers."

"Tell me what to do. I can help."

"I hate to ask, but tending Fred sure threw me off my schedule."

Sarah crossed the room. "You didn't ask. I offered."

Mrs. Harper nodded her thanks and dipped a cloth in the bucket. "I'm about done here, but if you wouldn't mind running downstairs and washing off the table nearest the outside door, I'd be grateful. We should only need that one. Aaron and the young'uns went to fetch water. Toby and Corrie can set the table when they get back. Oh, and use the inside stairs." She waved her hand toward a door Sarah hadn't noticed before. "Just go through there and down the steps."

"Yes, Mrs. Harper." Sarah pushed in a chair at the table and turned toward the door.

"Call me Karen. We don't cotton to formality much out here."

"Oh, I couldn't."

Mrs. Harper caught her eye. "I'll be offended if you don't."

Sarah offered a small smile and started for the door, but then she stopped. "Are you certain Fred will be all right?"

Karen nodded, but her eyes remained serious. "Only God knows for sure, but I believe so. The shot skimmed his side, leaving a nasty gash, but, thank the good Lord, it doesn't look like it damaged anything critical."

"That's good." She flashed a smile and then dashed down the steps. They were the same stairs she'd seen Ethan running up and down when she had eaten with the other travelers that night before heading down the trail—before so many things had happened. Though the room was a bit stuffy, the temperature was definitely cooler than the upstairs. She walked around the line of tables, waiting for the water to arrive, and found a stack of neatly folded cloths on a shelf. She stuffed one inside her apron pocket and ambled around, looking at the few pictures on the stone walls.

As nice as the Harpers had been, she still felt like an intruder. Living in someone else's home, especially a person who wasn't a relative, was awkward. She always felt the need to pause before going into a room, to make certain the family wasn't in the middle of a private conversation. And then, there were the three Harper sons, all of them older than she—and a marriageable age.

Something thumped against the door, and it flew open. Aaron entered, with Corrie and Toby close on his heels.

"I wanna help change out the horsies, Pa." Toby gazed up at his father with pleading eyes.

Aaron set the bucket on the table and squeezed his son's shoulder. "Sorry, champ, you're a mite too small yet. You know that."

"Howdy, Miss Marshall." Corrie waved hello with the bouquet of wildflowers in her hand.

Aaron's head jerked up, and he yanked off his hat, revealing his smashed-down, sweat-stained dark brown hair. His coffee-colored eyes reminded her so much of Ethan's. "Sorry, ma'am. I didn't expect to see you down here."

Heat rushed to her cheeks, and she held up the cloth. "Your mother asked me to come and wash the table. She said the stage was due soon."

He nodded, tucked his hat under his armpit, and then crossed his arms. "Uh...all right."

His discomfort was evident, and it only added to Sarah's. Aaron Harper was a handsome man, just like his brothers, and he was the largest one, with the shoulders of a man who'd worked hard all his life. The top of his hat—when it had been on, and not crammed under his arm—had nearly touched the basement ceiling.

"Uh...." He bent and tugged the flowers from Corrie's hand, then held them out to Sarah. "I'm real sorry about your loss, Miss Marshall."

Corrie frowned. "But, Pa, those flowers were for the—"

"Shh! You can pick some more. I'm giving these to our guest."

"Um...thank you." Sarah accepted them, because refusing would have caused even more awkwardness. Why had Aaron felt the need to offer her flowers Corrie had obviously picked for the table? And yet, his gesture was touching. "I have an idea. Why don't we put these in a vase, or cup, and set them on the table? Then, once the guests leave, I can take them to my room, so Aunt Emma can enjoy them, too."

Admiration brightened Aaron's eyes and softened his stoic expression. He seemed to be wound tighter than his brothers—less able to relax. Was that because he was the eldest and bore more responsibility? Because he was a father? Or maybe because of the hardship he'd endured after losing his wife?

Corrie nodded. "All right. I'll get a vase."

A gentle smile lifted Aaron's lips, and he hoisted Toby into his arms. "I'll take this rascal with me."

Footsteps pounded down the outside steps, and Ethan hurried in. "The stage is—" He scowled as he looked at the flowers in Sarah's hand, then at Aaron and back again. "What's going on?"

Crimson darkened Aaron's ears. "Just…uh…fetching water so Miss Marshall could clean the table." He pushed his way past his brother and up the stairs.

Ethan's gaze dropped to the flowers again, his disapproval evident.

"Pa gave those to Miss Marshall," Corrie stated matter-of-factly before disappearing up the stairs after her father.

Pursing his lips together, Ethan blew a loud breath out his nose. "You'd best get the table set. The passengers are washin' up now and will be down any second." He spun around and trotted up the steps.

Sarah set to scrubbing the table, glad both men were gone. What had Ethan thought when he'd come upon her alone with Aaron and holding a bouquet? He hadn't been happy, that much was evident. There was no point in admiring Ethan or his brothers. She'd never measure up.

Ethan Harper didn't want her here, disrupting his life. And that was fine with her.

She sloshed far too much water on the table, and it ran off the sides. She hurried to mop it up before the stage crew arrived.

Chicago.

That's what she needed to think about.

She must stay focused on getting back to Chicago.

Chapter Twelve

Ethan attached the harness to the last relief horse. His jaw ached from being clenched so tight. Aaron had given flowers to Miss Marshall, and Josh was talking about giving her a book—a collection of years' worth of writings and sketches. Were they already battling for her attention? They didn't know what he knew about her—how she'd done all she could to convince her uncle to go against his advice. He patted the horse and checked the gear, then headed toward the paddock. If he'd been more insistent that Mr. Stone buy the better wagon, the man would still be alive.

"Hey, Harper."

He spun around.

Jasper Biggs, the stage driver, strode toward him, rubbing his stomach. "Your ma sure knows how to wield a spatula. My belly's about to bust my buckle off." His eyes sparked as he wagged his brows. "Who's that looker in there helpin' her?"

Ethan scrambled for a response. He hadn't considered what to say to explain the presence of their female guests, and he sure didn't want to divulge any personal business of Mrs. Stone or Miss Marshall. "She and her aunt are Ma's guests for a time." That was true enough.

"Long time, I hope." Jasper pulled a small metal tin from his pocket, removed a toothpick, and shoved it in the side of his mouth. "She married?"

Great. Just what they needed—bachelors coming from all around to get a look at one of the few unmarried women in the area. "She's in mourning."

"For who?" Jasper straightened and looked concerned. "She ain't a widow, or she'd be wearin' black."

"Maybe she doesn't have a black dress. The horses are ready."

Jasper nodded and checked the team. He glanced back at the house. "You'll tell her I asked about her?"

"Get in line."

The driver narrowed his eyes. "What's that mean?"

"Just that you're not the first to notice her."

"So, you've got your eye on her yourself?" He yanked a pair of dusty leather gloves from his waistband and stuffed his hands inside. "Guess you Harpers have already staked a claim."

"Miss Marshall plans to return to Chicago with her aunt, so there's no point in staking a claim." Ethan nodded good day and then headed for the house.

Langston Barlow, the shotgun rider, ushered the trio of passengers over to the stage like one might herd cattle into a stockyard. They had a schedule to keep, and Barlow was pickier about it than Jasper. Barlow passed Ethan with a nod, but then he circled back and fell into pace with him. "Who's yer new help? She married?"

Resisting the urge to roll his eyes, Ethan shook his head. "She's just temporary. Leaving here once her aunt is well enough to travel."

Langston pursed his lips. "Too bad. She'd make someone around here a good wife."

"Why would you say that?" Ethan cast him a sidelong glance. "You don't know anything about her."

He shook his head. "Don't have ta. I'd just sit all day and look at her. She shore is purty." He strode toward the stage, checking to make sure everyone was inside and the door was secure.

Ethan waved as the stage rolled out of the yard. Thank goodness it didn't come through but twice a week. He couldn't stand a daily dose of men ogling Miss Marshall. Maybe he should offer to take the two women back to Bob Stone's in Kansas City so things could get back to normal.

"I don't want to return to Bob and Lydia's, even if they offer." Emma sat up in her bed, looking more determined than Sarah had seen her in days.

Sarah paused from her writing. "Why not? I'm sure they would be happy to take us in."

Emma's lips puckered like fabric with the thread pulled too tight. "As kind as he is, I won't be beholden to Harvey's brother. And, besides, they plan to head down the trail. We'd only cause them further delay."

Sarah laid the pen down on her aunt's writing desk. "So, what should I say to them?"

Her aunt lowered her head, and Sarah noticed the fingers of gray hair spreading out from the part down the middle of her scalp. "I'm sorry, dear. It's not your place to have to write and tell them about Harvey. I can do it."

"Are you certain you feel up to it?"

Emma blew out a huff. "It doesn't take much effort to write a letter."

Smiling, Sarah set the ink pot on the desk next to the bed, within reach of her aunt. She then slid off of the mattress and carried the writing desk to her aunt's bedside. "I have to admit I'm relieved to not have to pen another letter about what happened. If only there were some way to make a copy and send it to all of our friends."

"I suppose you could get a newspaper publisher to print off duplicate copies, but that wouldn't be very personal, would it?"

"No, I guess it wouldn't."

Emma waved her hand. "Go on. You shouldn't be cooped up in this room just because I am."

"I don't mind." Staying in the room meant she could avoid Ethan Harper and his censuring looks.

"No, you go on. I need some quiet to compose my thoughts. Telling Bob that his brother has passed will be difficult." She rubbed a tear off her cheek. "They had such plans."

Sarah touched her aunt's arm. "I'm really sorry about Uncle Harvey. I know you loved him."

Emma picked up the handkerchief that lay beside her on the bed and dabbed her eyes. She'd cried less today, but any mention of Harvey brought fresh tears.

Sarah left the room and wandered through the empty kitchen. Everything was in its place, neat and tidy. The faint aromas of freshly baked bread and pie still hung in the air. Mrs. Harper sure was a hard worker, cooking for and cleaning up after four grown men and two youngsters, besides feeding stage passengers and guests from the wagon trains. Sarah had never known anyone so industrious.

She pushed open the back door, walked out onto the porch, and looked around. Maybe Mrs. Harper was taking a much-deserved rest. The ranch yard was empty, except for the two horses that stood in the paddock, their heads hanging, their tails swatting flies. Shading her eyes, she looked to the northern side of the barn, where the lush garden grew. Several men were weeding or tending it, while another man poured a bucket of water over a partial row of plants.

She meandered to the end of the porch, wishing she had something to do. She wasn't one to while away the day. A loud snap drew her attention to the right, and she found Mrs. Harper out in the yard on the far side of the house, hanging the laundry she'd washed before lunch. Sarah pushed off the porch and hurried toward her. "I would have been happy to hang those for you."

Karen smiled over her shoulder. "Guess I'm just used to doing things myself."

Sarah took several of Toby's small shirts, shook them out, and draped them over the line.

Smiling, Karen handed her a fistful of clothespins, then shook out a pair of pants belonging to one of her sons or her husband. "How is Emma doing this afternoon?"

"Better, I think. She's been sitting up since lunch and even wanted to write a letter to my uncle's brother."

"That's good. I'm glad she's starting to do things. I can't pretend to know what it's like to lose a husband, but I did lose two young'uns, and Della."

A light breeze cooled Sarah, and strands of hair that had broken loose from her bun tickled her cheek. The quiet of the prairie wasn't nearly as intimidating when other people were around, and it was a nice difference from the noise of the city. As she thought about it, she was surprised to realize that she didn't miss Chicago as much as she had at first, although she did miss her friends and the children at the orphanage.

"It's sure nice to have other women around for more than a day."

Sarah shook out several towels and carried them to an empty space on the line. "How do you manage so much work all by yourself?"

"Oh, I'm used to it, I suppose. And if I get behind, I holler, and one of the boys comes and helps—usually Ethan, since he's the youngest. Corrie is getting to be more of a help, too."

Sarah glanced around when she realized neither child was nearby. "Where are the children?"

"Toby is napping, and Corrie is supposed to be resting, but I imagine she's probably drawing or practicing her letters. She's pretty much outgrown a nap, but I still make her rest each afternoon." Karen chuckled and shook her head. "That girl wants to read so bad, but she has a hard time of it. I just wish I had more time to teach her."

"I wouldn't mind helping her. Back home, I worked with some children in a small orphanage. Most of them were very young, but a few were old enough to learn their alphabet and simple words."

Karen clapped her hands as a wide smile lifted her lips. "That would be wonderful. I know Aaron would appreciate that. He worries about her not getting a good education since we live so far from town. I worried about the same thing when we first came here, but my boys turned out well, if I do say so myself."

Sarah had never considered the challenges people living on the prairie faced, not having access to schools for their children's education or a doctor for medical treatment. Not having a church close enough to attend on Sundays. Not being able to run down the street to the market when you ran out of something you needed.

"I talked with Emma last night when you and the young'uns went to see the kittens in the barn." Karen stopped her labors and turned to face Sarah, one hand still on the clothesline. "You're welcome to stay here as long as you want. God has blessed us with that extra room and plenty of food. Besides, I miss having women to talk to." She ducked her head, as if embarrassed by her need for companionship. "I know things are difficult right now, and you have a lot of worries, but I don't want you fretting about wearing out your welcome. We're happy to have you for as long as you need to stay."

Ashamed of her situation and the need to beg help from strangers, Sarah stared at the ground. A patch of tiny white flowers with bright yellow centers snagged her attention. That was one thing she liked about the prairie—the abundance of wildflowers. Mrs. Harper cleared her throat, and Sarah looked up.

"I'm not one for preaching, but I've learned that when things seem their darkest, God is often moving the most. You may not believe it now, Sarah, but God has a plan for your life. The safest place you can be is in His hands." She rested her palm on Sarah's shoulder and squeezed. "Things will work out. You'll see."

Sarah offered her a weak smile. "Thank you." No one had ever told her that God had a plan for her life, and she didn't know how to respond. Could it be true? Did God actually care what became of her? It didn't seem that way. If He did, then why had He allowed so many bad things to happen to her?

With no garments left to hang up, Sarah surveyed the stage stop. The Harpers' white clapboard house rose up before her, proud and inviting. Past it stood the barn, which housed stock, tack, tools, and feed for winter. She'd learned that the small stone building was the icehouse, although she couldn't imagine how they kept the ice from melting during the long, hot summers. Further away sat a bunkhouse and several small outbuildings, but she didn't know their purpose. And off to the right a ways sat a small, two-story house. Had the Harpers lived there before building the bigger one? She tried to imagine what life had been like when the family had first arrived—when there was nothing but prairie. Had things worked out like Mrs. Harper had hoped and prayed they would?

Karen picked up her basket and headed for the house, and Sarah followed. The older woman glanced back over her shoulder and slowed her pace. "I always try to do my washing on days when we have a south wind. That way, we're upwind of the cattle, and my clean laundry doesn't reek of them. Nothing worse than lying down for bed and having the sheets smelling like a barn."

Sarah laughed. "I can honestly say I've never had to worry about that. With the breeze off of Lake Michigan, our sheets always smelled fresh."

"That must be nice." Karen shifted the basket to her other arm.

Sarah glanced at her out of the corner of her eye. "I'm a decent cook. I often helped out in the kitchen…b-back h-home." She hated how her voice caught.

"Well then, maybe you can share some new recipes with me. I'm sure the men would love to eat something different for a change." Karen smiled, "There's my Corrie-girl. I've instructed her to always wait in the parlor or on the porch if I'm not in the house when she gets up from her nap."

"It must be hard raising children out here." *There are so many dangers.*

"I'm just thankful Nick and the boys help so much. Aaron is a great father, but, being the oldest, he can be a bit overbearing and stubborn at times. He doesn't always understand that young'uns need cuddling. He calls it 'coddling.'" Karen shook her head. "I do what I can, but those poor children need a mother. I keep praying God will send them one."

Sarah swallowed the lump in her throat. She hoped Karen's generous invitation to stay at her home wasn't her way of trying to find a wife for Aaron. While Sarah was becoming less afraid of the rougher life on the prairie, Chicago would always be her home.

"Grandma!" Corrie jumped from the rocker and dashed down the porch stairs. She closed the distance between the house and Karen with her arms raised in the air, then fell against her grandma and wrapped her arms around her skirts.

Sarah couldn't remember ever acting with such abandon as a child. She'd walked on eggshells in her uncle's home, always afraid she'd do something wrong to earn his ire. She dipped her head, hoping her jealousy didn't show. Corrie was such a sweet girl. She'd never know what it was like to live in a place she wasn't wanted, and Sarah was glad for that, but she still couldn't help wishing her own life had been different. Maybe if she married the right man, her future could be.

"Miss Marshall offered to help you with your reading." Karen beamed at the girl.

Corrie scowled. "I'm not good at it."

Sarah smiled. "Maybe I can help. I worked with other children back in Chicago."

"Can they read?" Corrie glanced up, her eyes hopeful.

"Well, both of them were older, but they were still just learning."

"I know all my letters."

"That's quite an accomplishment for a six-year-old." Sarah brushed a hand across the girl's head. "I know a trick or two that might make things easier."

"Truly?"

"Truly."

"Why don't you get your slate and chalk?" Karen suggested. "It's a nice day, so maybe you two can have your lesson on the porch. I think I'll get my mending basket and join you."

Five minutes later, Sarah was seated on the porch steps with Corrie, watching the girl print her alphabet. The letters were squiggly, but Corrie knew each one and worked hard to write as correctly as possible.

"Z. That's the last one."

"That's very good. Many six-years-olds don't know even half of their letters."

Corrie's eyes twinkled, and a wide grin curved her lips. She looked up at Sarah, then glanced back at her grandma, as if seeking her approval.

Karen nodded. "That's my girl."

"Now," Sarah said, "are there any words you can spell?"

The child shrugged. "I can spell 'horse' and my name."

"Horse?"

Corrie gazed up with serious eyes. "Pa said a girl who lives on a ranch has got to know how to spell that."

"I see." Sarah turned her head so that Corrie wouldn't see her grin. What odd priorities these country folk had. "Well, let's see if we can't get you spelling some other words. Would you clean off your slate, please?"

She did as asked. "Now what?"

"Let's turn the slate so that it's taller than wider and write an *a* and a *t* at the top, but start in the middle of the slate and not up against the left side." She waited until Corrie had completed the last letter. "Now, can you write the same thing again, three more times?"

Corrie scowled but complied.

"Keep them toward the middle, because I want to show you a trick."

After several long minutes, Corrie was done, and a crooked column of *a*'s and *t*'s lined the slate.

"Now, do you know what *a* and *t* squeezed together spells?"

Corrie shook her head, looking a bit perplexed.

"That's all right. I'll teach you." Sarah patted the girl's back and glanced up at Karen, who was concentrating on repairing the hem in a pair of pants. She had little doubt the woman was listening closely, though.

Sarah sounded out the two letters, exaggerating the sound of each one to give Corrie a hint as to what the word was. Finally, the girl cried, "At! It says *at*."

"Very good. So, tell me, what is your favorite animal?" Sarah hoped the child would respond as she expected.

"A kitten."

Oops. Not quite the answer she was hoping for. "And what does a kitten grow up to be?"

"A cat."

"That's right. Now, I want you to write a *c* in front of the first *a* and then see if you can tell me what it is, and don't forget what *a* and *t* spell."

"At." With the new letter in place, Corrie struggled to sound out the word, but finally her eyes lit up and she sat straighter. "It spells *cat*!" She clapped her hands. "Grandma, I wrote *cat*."

Karen smiled, her eyes beaming with pride. "Very good."

Sarah continued to work with Corrie, adding the letters *r*, *h*, and *s* to spell three more words. Delight soared through her at seeing the child so excited. Corrie was a bright and eager learner, which made things easier.

Hoofbeats sounded to her left. Sarah glanced up and saw the three brothers riding up to the house. They reined their horses to a stop, and Sarah caught a pungent whiff of the big animals, paired with manly sweat.

Corrie jumped up and bounced on the step. "I can read, Pa! Miss Sarah taught me. Cat, rat, hat, and sat."

"That's wonderful." Aaron dismounted and strode to his daughter, catching her up in his arms. His warm eyes captured Sarah's, his gratitude evident. He held her gaze a bit too long to be proper, making Sarah squirm.

Josh cleared his throat. She hadn't even noticed that he'd dismounted, too. He tipped his hat at her, then took the stairs in two steps and hurried inside the house. Ethan still sat atop his horse, the brim of his hat shading his eyes, his expression unreadable. A queasy sensation swished in her stomach. Maybe the heat of the afternoon was getting to her. He reached down, gathering the reins of Aaron's horse, then turned and headed toward the barn, with Josh's horse following on its own. Sarah stared at her lap. Was he uncomfortable with her staying at his home? She could hardly blame him if he was.

"Let me show you how I can read, Pa." Corrie kicked until he'd set her down, and then she picked up her slate and held it up to him. "See the words I wrote?"

Quick footsteps sounded behind Sarah, just before Josh plopped down beside her. The action was so unexpected that she jumped and scooted sideways, putting a distance of a foot in between them. She was certain Karen had chuckled.

Josh held a worn journal out to her. "I thought you might enjoy this book, Miss Marshall. It's one I started years ago. It contains pictures of the wildflowers native to this area, with a description of their color, what time of year they grow, and other important information."

She took the book and opened it, astonished at the rich detail of each sketch. Thumbing through the first few pages, she recognized several of the flowers. "Why, these are amazing! I saw this one when we were out on the trail. Rose verbena. I loved the beautiful purple of the petals." She smiled at him. "You're very talented."

Josh beamed, and his blue eyes—kind like his mother's—roved her face. "You can keep the book."

A blush heated Sarah's cheeks, and she glanced up at Aaron. Corrie was still talking, but her father was no longer smiling. He was scowling at Sarah. Behind her, Karen made a strange sound, rather like a cat coughing up a hairball.

Sarah scrambled to ease the situation. "Oh, no. I couldn't keep it, when you've put so much effort into it. But I would like to spend more time looking at your book, if you're sure you don't mind." She turned another page, admiring the expert drawings and avoiding Aaron's foul glare. She didn't want to cause conflict between brothers, but she didn't understand why her looking at Josh's book had upset Aaron so much.

"I wouldn't have given it to you if I minded." The intense look in Josh's eyes made her squirm again.

"I need to tend to my horse, sweetheart." Aaron set Corrie down and tweaked her cheek. "I'm proud of you learning to read and write those words." Lifting his gaze to Sarah's, he tipped his hat. "Thank you, Miss Marshall. I appreciate you helping Corrie." He gave his brother a wounded glance, sharing it with Sarah, too, before pivoting and striding with purpose, his long legs eating up the distance.

Saddened and confused, Sarah watched him go. He'd seemed to appreciate her helping his daughter, but now something else was bothering him. Had she done something wrong?

Chapter Thirteen

In the washroom, Ethan rinsed the day's dust from his hands and face, then dried off and slung the towel back on the hook. He'd gotten so busy tending the corn that he'd lost track of time, even though he'd heard the supper bell clang. His thoughts, as so often of late, had been centered on Miss Marshall. Corrie was captivated by her—and would be devastated when she left them. Still, he had to face the truth. No one else had had much luck getting his niece to read. She didn't like sitting long enough to work at it. What was Miss Marshall's trick?

He hurried into the kitchen, preparing himself for his ma's scowl. She didn't like her men to be late for mealtime. Right away, something seemed off. Everyone was seated at the table, but the serving bowls were still being passed around, so he wasn't too late. Then, it hit him—Aaron and Josh both wore clean, white shirts, with their hair slicked down, as if they were going to church or attending a town social. He glanced down at his dusty pants and gave them a good swat.

"Ethan, don't do that in the house," Ma scolded. "And take your seat. We've already prayed."

"Yes, Ma." He slid into his chair, properly chastised, and looked around the table, relieved to see that Pa was still wearing his work shirt. Ethan had begun to think he'd forgotten someone's birthday. Across the table, Miss Marshall glanced at him, then looked away, her cheeks pink. At least she was still wearing the same dress he'd seen her in earlier. But then, he didn't think she had much choice in the matter. He'd seen her wearing just a few different ones—the dark blue silk she'd had on back in Kansas City, a calico she'd bought at the mercantile there, and whatever she'd been wearing when she'd taken that spill in the mud. At least her dresses hadn't been stolen along with the rest of their belongings. He winced at the magnitude of their misfortune, but he realized he'd never heard her complain. He ought to round up some men and go fetch Mrs. Stone's furniture—if it was still there. Why hadn't he thought to do that earlier? Too busy, he supposed. The task would take several days. What if they went and found that everything was gone? Everything but that broken-down pink wagon.

Josh passed him a series of bowls, and he filled his plate with potatoes, peas, and stewed chicken. When Josh tapped his shoulder with the basket of biscuits, Ethan glanced at him and followed his gaze—it was latched onto Miss Marshall. A sick feeling washed through him, similar to the one he'd felt after tasting whiskey that a boy in town had snitched from his pa's collection. Josh was infatuated with Miss Marshall. That was why he'd cleaned up.

Ethan bowed his head for a quick prayer, then forked a piece of chicken into his mouth and glanced at Aaron. His eldest brother was cutting up Toby's meat, but he wasn't watching what he was doing. Instead, his gaze, too, was pointed in their guest's direction. Ethan scowled. Pa shoveled food into his mouth as if he were engaged in an eating contest, while Ma sat at the other end of the table, looking pleased as a cat that had caught the biggest mouse in the barn.

Ethan smelled trouble, and it all centered around one petite city gal.

Sarah's disappointment weighed her down as she watched the stage pull away. Only a week had passed since she'd written to Walt and told him of her predicament. It was too soon to expect to hear back from him, but when the new stage had rolled in, she'd gotten her hopes up anyway.

Walt was a quiet, accepting man, but she knew she'd hurt him by writing that letter saying she couldn't marry him. But how could she have known things would turn out so badly?

She returned her attention to the almond cake batter she was mixing for tonight's dessert. Behind her, dishes rattled on the dumbwaiter as someone pulled the rope to raise it. She'd hurried upstairs once all the guests had been served, hoping to have the cake in the oven before Karen needed her help cleaning, but she'd had to go out to the icehouse and collect two more eggs, so it had taken longer than expected.

The cellar door opened, and Karen entered the kitchen. She spied Sarah and raised her eyebrows. "What's this?"

Sarah smiled. "A surprise. Since those extras passengers ate one of the pies you'd planned to serve after dinner tonight, I thought I'd whip up something else."

"What are you cooking?" Karen crossed the room and peered into the pot sitting on top of the stove. "Almonds?"

Sarah nodded. "I found a sack of them in one of the crates that was salvaged and thought I'd blanch some and make an almond cake."

"Are you out to win the heart of one of my sons?"

Heat rushed to her cheeks, though certainly not from the warmth of the stove. "No, just to make things a bit easier for you."

"A mother can hope." She hugged Sarah's shoulders. "I do appreciate your making another dessert. We'll all enjoy it."

While the cake baked, Sarah helped Karen wash the dishes. "Aunt Emma said she'd like to sit on the porch this afternoon, after she's had a nap."

"I noticed the men are usually gone when she comes out. Do they bother her?"

"No, it's not that." Sarah nibbled her lip, not sure how to explain. "My guess is that she has several reasons. She's not used to so many people. Back home, there were just the three of us and a couple of quiet servants. But I think part of it is that she's embarrassed because she's so frail. She never completely recovered from having scarlet fever."

"What was your uncle thinking, taking her down the Santa Fe Trail?" Karen gasped and then covered her mouth. "Forgive me. I shouldn't have said that."

"No, it's all right. I felt the same way, and even tried to argue that point, to no avail. Uncle Harvey was bound and determined to go to New Mexico." But he hadn't made it. And it was her fault.

"Men can be stubborn when it comes to achieving their dreams." Karen spoke as if she had experience in the matter.

Sarah nodded. "I also think Auntie is a bit bewildered at everything that's happened. She believes in God but is confused about why He would allow such tragedy to befall us."

"God's ways are greater than man's, and we don't always understand, but it sounds like Emma knows that." Karen wiped a damp cloth across the table. "Her faith will see her through. Still, she needs to grieve her husband, and that's hard to do when you're living in a house filled with strangers."

Mrs. Harper was a perceptive woman, and Sarah enjoyed talking to her. Other than Mrs. Rayburn, she'd never known an older woman whom she considered a friend. She found it comforting not to feel so alone. She dried her hands and checked the cake.

Karen grinned suddenly. "Jasper certainly is smitten with you."

"The stage driver?" She'd noticed the lithe man staring at her as she served lunch.

"Yes. Him and his shotgun rider."

Sarah's cheeks warmed again. "I did nothing to encourage them."

"You didn't have to. You're a pretty, unmarried woman, and in these parts, that counts for a lot." Karen surveyed the clean kitchen with a satisfied smile, then took off her apron and hung it on a peg near the door to the washroom. "Do you know how to quilt?"

"Yes, but my stitches aren't the tiniest or the straightest."

"I thought I might work on that one in the corner of the parlor and give my feet a rest. Would you care to help? I'd enjoy the company."

Sarah smiled. "I would be happy to, if you're certain you aren't sick of me."

"Never. It's a rare thing to have a woman visitor here—at least, one that stays any length of time." Karen looped her arm through Sarah's and led her to the parlor.

Sarah thought of all the friends she had back in Chicago and felt a bit guilty for having so many when Karen had so few—at least none who lived nearby. "It's too bad your daughter-in-law died. I'm sure you miss her."

Karen swiveled a side chair around, motioning for Sarah to sit, and then took a seat in the chair beside the quilt frame. She opened a box, pulled out a needle and some thread, and handed them to Sarah. Then, she stilled, staring at the quilt. Sarah had just about decided Karen hadn't heard her question about Della when she heaved a loud sigh and looked up. "I don't like to speak ill of the dead, but Della was never happy here. You've only been here a little over a week, yet I already feel closer to you than I ever felt to Della. I prayed for years for her to settle into being a wife and mother, but she was like a hummingbird, flitting from one thing to the next, never finding a place to settle." She pointed to a spot on the quilt. "You can stitch around those flowers, if you will."

They worked for the next hour, interrupted only when Sarah returned to the kitchen to take the cake out of the oven. Karen asked a few questions about her life in Chicago, and Sarah answered her, but her thoughts kept turning to Aaron. What had his marriage to Della been like? Had there been problems that caused her to be so flighty?

A thump sounded in the kitchen, and then Corrie ambled into the parlor. She moseyed over to the quilt, leaned against her grandma, and yawned. Karen stuck her needle into the quilt and tugged her granddaughter onto her lap. From the looks of Corrie's wrinkled dress and mussed hair, the girl had succumbed to a short nap today.

"How's my Cora-girl?"

"It's Corrie, Grandma. I told you that a thousand times."

Sarah bit back a grin, and Karen's eyes gleamed.

"What's that brown thing in the kitchen that smells so good?" the child asked.

"That's an almond cake that Sarah was so kind to make for after supper."

"Can I have some now?" Corrie glanced up at her grandma with hopeful eyes.

Karen tweaked the girl's nose. "Didn't I just say it's for supper?"

The girl shrugged, but a sly grin tugged at her mouth.

"You may have the half slice of bread and jam I left out on a plate for you, though."

"Oh, goodie." Corrie slid off her grandma's lap, and her bare feet slapped against the wood floor as she ran to the kitchen.

"I was thinking about gathering some flowers to take up to my uncle's grave." Sarah glanced up from the quilt. "I wondered if Corrie could show me where she found those lovely ones she gave me the other day."

"Pa gave those to you, not me." Corrie walked back into the parlor, holding her bread, a line of jam coloring her upper lip. "But I can show you where they are."

One of Karen's brows lifted, and Sarah knew she'd latched on to the comment about Aaron giving her flowers. She wanted to deny it, but she couldn't. Thankfully, Karen didn't ask about them.

"Gathering flowers is a good idea," Karen said. "And you can pick some for our supper table while you're at it. A pretty bouquet always brightens the room."

Eager to flee and not give Karen a chance to question her about Aaron's gift, Sarah stood, then bent to address Corrie. "I'll check on my aunt and get your uncle Josh's book of wildflowers while you finish your snack, all right?"

Corrie nodded.

Sarah tiptoed down the hall and quietly opened the bedroom door.

Emma glanced up from the book she was reading, her eyes free of pain for the first time in a long while. She sniffed. "What's that delicious smell?"

"Almond cake. There were extra passengers on the stage today, and they ate one of the pies Karen had made for supper, so I thought I'd surprise her and make a cake using the almonds we had packed in one of the crates. So, how are you feeling?"

"Better, thank you."

"I gave your letter for Bob and Lydia to the stage driver, and he put it in the mailbag."

"I hope Bob doesn't take the news too hard. He and Harvey were never very close. Their temperaments were far too different, and living such a distance from one another didn't help. Lydia told me Bob had hoped the move to Santa Fe would help their relationship." Her eyes fluttered, and she looked away, staring at the window.

Sarah sat on the end of the bed. "I'm so sorry. I can't help but feel Uncle Harvey's death is my fault."

"No!" Emma's stern look caught Sarah off guard. "Harvey made his choices. You had nothing to do with it."

"I encouraged him to buy that pink wagon."

Emma took Sarah's hand in hers. "And I should have fought harder to make him forget his harebrained plan altogether. This life is too short for regrets."

"But—"

"No buts, Sarah. I've spent a lot of time lying here thinking, and I realize now that I've been letting my anger at Harvey and my grief over his death stifle my faith. As difficult as it is to believe, I now see God's hand in all that's happened."

Sarah frowned. "That is difficult to believe. Are you saying God had a hand in Uncle's death?"

Her aunt shook her head. "I don't have all the answers. But what I do know is that God is a God of love. He cares for us. He has given me strength over the years when I didn't know how I could go on. And He'll do the same for you, if you'll let Him." She cupped Sarah's cheek with her hand. "I'm sorry again for not doing a better job of teaching you about God."

"It's all right." Sarah blinked away tears, uncomfortable witnessing her aunt's pain and remorse. "Would you like to go sit on the porch? Corrie and I are going to gather flowers to put on Uncle Harvey's grave."

A sweet smile graced Emma's face. "What a lovely thing to do. I hope to be able to walk up there soon, but for now, I believe I'll stay here and read from Karen's Bible. Maybe when you return we could sit a short while outside."

Sarah nodded, then retrieved Josh's book off the chest of drawers and went to find Corrie. Together they headed up the hill. Halfway to the top, Sarah spied a small, yellow star-shaped flower and paused to open the book. "Oh, look. That's yellow star grass."

Corrie pulled several of the flowers and clumped them together with some white daisies. The grass tugged at Sarah's skirts, and the sun warmed her shoulders, making her thankful she'd abandoned her silk for the cooler cotton dress. They entered the cemetery through the gate, and Corrie laid the flowers on Uncle Harvey's grave. Sarah considered what her aunt had said. Maybe what had happened wasn't her fault. But, if that were true, why did she still feel guilty?

A loud bellow drew her gaze beyond the fence, but she didn't see any animals. "What was that?"

"Just a cow. Down the hill."

She'd never seen a cow up close. "Could we take a look at them?"

"Yeah, sure."

Obviously, a cow held no interest for Corrie, but Sarah was intrigued. In Chicago, milk had been delivered to their door each day by a little man who drove a cart pulled by a mule. She left the small cemetery and closed the gate. "Do you know how to spell 'cow'?"

Corrie shook her head, but Sarah could see the wheels of her mind stirring. "It starts with a *k*, right?"

They topped the hill. Down in the valley below, Sarah saw a number of brown cows grazing in the tall grass. A creek split the valley in half, with trees lining either side of it. "Actually, it starts with a *c*, followed by *o* and *w*. Maybe we can study *-ow* words for today's spelling lesson." A patch of beautiful lavender flowers caught her eye, and she walked down the hill toward it. "Oh, how lovely. Do you know what these are called?"

"Cow slobbers," Corrie called from the top of the hill.

"Really?" Sarah tipped up the brim of her bonnet and glanced back at the girl to see if she was teasing.

Corrie nodded, her face serious. "That's what we call them. They're slimy when you cut them."

Surely, there had to be a more scientific name for the pretty, tri-petaled flower. She flipped through the pages of the book.

"Uncle Josh says the real name is spiderwort."

"Eww! That's not any better." Sarah laughed but quickly stopped, startled by a rustling sound to her right. Backing up, she saw a movement in the grass and then a small calf, peering up at her with big brown eyes. "Oh, look, a baby cow."

"You'd best get away from it," Corrie hollered.

"I just want a quick peek." She stuck Josh's book in her pocket and took a few more steps, trying to get a better look at the darling calf with the huge eyes. Suddenly, a big cow came lumbering out of the tall grass just a few yards downhill.

"Run!" The frightened pitch of Corrie's voice shot concern through Sarah as she turned, picked up her skirts, and hurried up the hill. The cow bellowed. Thick grass grabbed at her skirts, slowing her down.

"Hurry!" Corrie screamed.

"Get inside the fence!" Sarah yelled as she reached the top of the hill, not daring to take the time to look back. A loud snort sounded close behind her. She raced around the fence, and only when she'd rounded the corner did she finally look back. The cow had just topped the hill. Sarah slid through the gate, slammed it shut, and hurried to Corrie's side. The girl's eyes were wide with fright.

The cow rammed the fence, making a loud clatter. Corrie screamed again.

Sarah hoisted her up. "Quick, climb the tree."

Corrie clung to her. "But what about you?"

"Just go!"

Sarah lifted Corrie as high as she could, and the girl caught hold of the lowest branch and swung up. Sarah jumped, but she couldn't quite reach the branch. She tried again but failed. The fence creaked as the cow butted it again, and fear unlike any she'd ever known soared through her. She could only hope Corrie didn't witness her demise. *Please, God. Save us.*

Chapter Fourteen

Ethan rode into the yard, every muscle in his body aching after the fall he'd taken from a mustang he'd been breaking. He longed to go soak in the cool water of the swimming hole, but Pa wanted his ma to have a look at the cuts he'd gotten when the young stallion had bucked him off. The scrapes on the back of his shoulder had made his arm stiff, but he'd live. It wasn't the first time he'd been thrown, nor the last, most likely.

He started to dismount when a high-pitched scream rent the air. Reining his horse to the right, he scanned the barnyard.

Ma burst out the back door, her eyes wide. "That sounds like Corrie."

"Where is she?"

"Up at the cemetery with Sarah."

"Heyah!" Ethan kicked his horse with his heels and raced around the back of the house. The cemetery came into view, but Ethan couldn't yet tell what was wrong. He galloped up the hill and saw Sarah hugging the tree nearby. A movement on the far side of the fence caught his eye, and he saw a cow ram the pickets, then turn and trot over the hill. As he drew closer, his gaze collided with Sarah's terrified stare and held for a moment, until he yanked his eyes away from her hypnotic hold and refocused on the cow. He rode Alamo around behind the cemetery to make sure it didn't return. A frantic bawl pulled his attention to a spot in the grass where a young calf lay. Only one thing would make a docile mama cow go on a rampage like that—someone had approached her calf. And he knew just who that someone was.

He reined Alamo around, suddenly wondering where Corrie had gone. He searched the small cemetery, but she wasn't there. Could she have been run down by the cow? His heart thumped. "Where's Corrie?"

"Up here, Uncle Ethan."

Relief flooded him at the sound of Corrie's voice. He glanced up as he dismounted. If something had happened to his niece, he didn't know how he would manage to go on. "I'll get you down."

He glanced at Miss Marshall. She stood, sagging, against the tree, as if plastered there. Her face was white. "You're not going to faint, are you?"

She hiked up her chin and glowered at him, color returning to her cheeks. "Certainly not. I've never once fainted."

She was probably too stubborn to swoon. As he approached, she stepped aside with a flip of her head. He lifted his arms to Corrie. She backed down the tree to a place where he could reach her, and then he grasped her by the waist and spun her around, holding her tight. "Are you hurt?"

"No."

"How did you get up in that tree?" He brushed some hair from her face and checked to make sure she hadn't been harmed.

"Miss Sarah lifted me up when the cow was coming."

A smidgeon of Ethan's anger dissipated with Corrie's confession, but he was still upset enough to boil water without a pot at the notion of his niece getting hurt over such foolishness. Miss Marshall stood off to the side, arms crossed, with her back to him. Didn't she know that one or both of them could have been hurt or even killed? What if the cow had gored them? Trampled them? He ground down on his back teeth. "Just what did you do to upset that cow?"

Corrie lifted her chin. "I told her not to bother that calf." Immediately her eyes widened, and her lower lip quivered. She must have realized that her confession only incriminated Miss Marshall more.

Ethan spun toward Miss Marshall. "What did you do? Don't you know not to approach a newborn calf?"

She whirled around, her eyes bugging out. "No! How was I supposed to know that? I'm from the city, remember? We don't have cows running up and down the street." She stalked toward the gate, then stopped and looked back at the spot where the cow had rammed the fence. "Is it safe to leave here? That c-cow won't come back?"

He nodded, and she bolted through the gate, as if she couldn't get away from him fast enough. Fine by him. Although she was rather fetching, all riled up like that. He shook his head to rid it of that unwanted thought.

"I did tell her, Uncle Ethan. We were pickin' flowers just over the hill when Miss Sarah saw the calf. She'd never seen one before. The momma cow was down and hidden in the grass so she couldn't see it. That cow almost got her before she got inside the fence." Corrie's eyes filled with tears, and she chewed her lower lip, as if the memory still frightened her. "But she did save me."

"Why didn't she climb the tree with you?" As if he didn't know. He snorted a laugh. Little Miss Priss in a tree—now that was hard to imagine.

"She tried, but she couldn't reach the branch." Corrie hugged his neck, squeezing hard, and he could feel her tremble slightly. Closing his eyes, he held her close and heaved a sigh of relief. She was safe—and Miss Marshall had made sure of that, even though it might have meant getting injured herself. Her quick thinking to get inside the fence just may have saved them both. He shouldn't have been so hard on her, but she stirred up strange emotions in him. One minute she'd do something stupid and provoke his anger and prove she didn't belong here; the next minute, he would admire her comeliness, her patient solicitude toward her aunt, her willingness and creativity as she helped Corrie with her reading. And all that admiration only angered him more. She was a city gal and had no place at a busy stage stop.

Still, he owed her an apology. And as much as it galled him, he'd have to eat crow.

⌣

Sarah stomped most of the way to the house. She'd been so scared—both for Corrie and herself—and that mulish Ethan Harper had the nerve to yell at her. Couldn't he see she was just as frightened as Corrie, if not more? At least Corrie was safe in the tree. Yes, she should have listened to the girl, but that calf had been so small and darling. She'd been so intrigued with it, just as she had with the kittens in the barn, that she hadn't even given a thought to its mother when she'd approached.

Karen stood at the end of the porch, watching her with concerned eyes. Sarah should have realized she would be worried, considering she'd heard her granddaughter scream. "Corrie is fine. She's with Ethan. We had a run-in with a cow."

One of Karen's eyebrows lifted.

"It was all my fault," she said as she drew near. "I saw a young calf nearby and went for a closer look. Corrie warned me not to get too close." She ducked her head, ashamed that a six-year-old was wiser than she. "I should have listened to her."

Karen stepped off the porch and wrapped an arm around her shoulders. "It's a different world out here. I made mistakes early on, too. You'll learn."

The woman spoke as if she thought Sarah would be there a long while. Sarah wished she could argue the point, but right now, she had nowhere else to go. "Well, you can be certain I've learned that lesson and won't repeat it."

Chuckling, Karen stepped back. "Experience is the best teacher. Thank the good Lord that Ethan rode in just when you needed help." She walked to the end of the porch and looked toward the cemetery. "They're coming back. Ethan is leading Alamo, and Corrie is riding. Looks like he's limping." She turned to face Sarah again. "I wonder why he's home at this hour. The men were supposed to be breaking horses out at the north pasture today."

As Ethan approached, Sarah saw that Karen was right; he was limping. Had he gotten hurt somehow? She imagined many of the duties of ranch life could be hazardous. And how did one go about "breaking" a horse? It sounded painful—to both parties.

"What's wrong, son?"

Ethan glanced at Sarah instead of his mother and shrugged. "Just had a little fall off a horse."

Sarah's heart quickened.

"How bad are you hurt?" Karen stepped forward, looking him over.

"Not bad." He glanced down, as if her concern embarrassed him.

"Grandma, that cow nearly got us! I was really scared." Corrie held out her arms, and Ethan lifted her off the horse, wincing when he did.

"There's blood on the back of your shirt." Karen tugged on his arm, turning him around.

"Hold me, Grandma." Corrie pulled at Karen's skirt.

Karen picked up the girl and glanced at Sarah. "If you wouldn't mind tending Ethan's wound while I see to Corrie, I'd appreciate it."

"Me?"

"Her?"

Sarah peeked up at Ethan, who was obviously just as shocked as she by his mother's request.

Karen nodded. "I'll be out here on the porch with Corrie if you need me." She sat down in the nearest rocker, and it creaked as she pushed it into motion.

Ethan marched inside the house, and Sarah followed him into the kitchen. Her heart thundered. What did she know about doctoring wounds?

Ethan pulled out a chair and spun it around, then exhaled a loud sigh and started unbuttoning his shirt.

"W-what are you doing?"

His brown eyes captured hers and held them for a long moment, sending her body into turmoil. She'd never felt so odd when Walt looked at her. Why did this rough rancher affect her so?

His expression turned patronizing. "You can't doctor my scrapes unless I remove my shirt."

"Oh." She glanced down at the floor and noticed a piece of biscuit hiding behind the table leg.

He cleared his throat. "There's some salve on a shelf in your— uh—the spare bedroom. Just wash the cut and put some of the salve on it. I'd doctor it myself if I could reach the wound."

Glad to have an excuse to flee his presence, she opened the door and tiptoed into her bedroom—not hers, the spare one. He'd made it clear she wasn't to become a permanent fixture. And that hurt her more than she cared to contemplate.

Emma had fallen asleep with the Bible across her chest, so Sarah tiptoed across the room.

There were several bottles of medicine on the shelves, but only one jar of salve, so she took it, along with several bandages she found stacked behind the glass door of the cabinet. Back in the kitchen, Ethan sat sideways in the chair, his shirt hanging from one of the posts, with his muscled arm resting on the table. His bare, bronze back was to her, and his shoulders were wider than she'd imagined, tapering to a narrow waist. Her mouth went dry at seeing a man's shirtless back for the first time—this man's shirtless back. Several nasty gashes caked with dried blood creased his left shoulder.

He glanced back at her and scowled. "You comin'? I've got work to do."

She hurried to the table and set the supplies down, pushing aside her nervousness. She got a large bowl, filled it with clean water from the bucket, then carried it to the table. Her hand shook as she reached for one of the clean cloths on the shelf and dipped it in the water. "This might...uh...hurt."

"Just do it."

His shoulder twitched as she touched the cloth to it, and her heart pounded so hard, it made her whole body tremble. She had never touched a man, other than to accept his assistance, and it didn't seem appropriate. But, as he'd said, he couldn't very well tend the wounds himself. Taking a deep breath, she gently pressed the cloth against the largest gash. He hissed and straightened but said nothing. She held the cloth there, allowing it to soften the dried blood, and studied the man who'd come to her rescue more than once. His hair was not as dark a brown as his brothers' but more resembled the color of a pecan shell. The lighter shade only made his deep brown eyes look darker. A section of his hair had grass in it and, from the looks of it, blood. She leaned in for a closer look and ran her fingers through his hair, searching for a lump. Had he hit his head? She wasn't sure. Being this close to him caused her to become all discombobulated—and breathing was harder.

⌒

Ethan closed his eyes as Sarah ran her fingers through his hair, sending delicious chills down his back. Suddenly his eyes popped open, and he jerked away. "What are you doing?"

"It looks like you may have injured your head."

He sniffed a laugh. "Don't worry about that. It's so hard, nothing can hurt it, so says Ma."

"Well, there's some blood, so that means there's a cut that needs to be tended."

He gritted his teeth, determined to survive the ordeal. He knew Ma's games, knew that she'd purposely sent them in together, hoping an attraction would develop between them. Well, something had—and he wasn't happy about it. How could his body betray him with constant surges of sensations each time Sarah touched him or leaned against him? He didn't want to like her. She was stubborn. She was trouble. And yet he felt a shift within him. Something was changing. He didn't like it one bit.

She clutched his wrist, stuffed a damp cloth in his hand, and then lifted it to his head. "Hold that there." Then, she resumed tending to his back. Every touch, every brush of her skirt against his lower back, made him want to jump up and run out the door. He tensed. Maybe he'd do just that and take the risk of his wounds turning red and painful later.

She pressed a small, warm hand to his shoulder. "Just relax, Mr. Harper. I'll be done soon enough."

He cleared his voice. "You might as well call me Ethan. Things get confusing around here when you refer to us all as 'Mr. Harper.' It's kind of like pointing out one brown horse in a whole herd of them." He chuckled, hoping to relieve her of some of her nervousness, but it did little to help his. Distance from this woman was all that would help.

She trailed her fingertips along his shoulder, sending a cascade of tingles plunging down his back. The tops of his forearms tightened as goose skin formed. He clenched his teeth. She gently pulled up the cloth off his back, and shafts of burning pain drove away the pleasant feelings.

"Does it need sewing up?" he asked.

"No, I don't believe so. There are some nasty scrapes, but none looks very deep." She dabbed the cloth for several minutes, rinsed, and then started dabbing again. After that, she blew across the cuts, causing Ethan to suck in a sharp breath. She was driving him crazy with her ministrations.

"Just put the salve on and be done with it." He had to get out of there before he did or said something he'd regret.

"Be patient." She gently brushed the cream down his shoulder—three times—and then placed a patch of cloth over it. "I don't know how to secure this. It's in a hard place to wrap."

Ethan jumped up, and she stepped back. "The salve and my shirt will hold it in place." He reached for his top, but she grabbed one sleeve.

"You can't put that dirty thing back on. Besides, I need to soak it in cold water, or the bloodstain will set."

Her gaze fell to his chest, and her eyes widened.

Ethan brushed a hand across the dark brown hair, feeling oddly self-conscious. He released the shirt and stepped back.

She visibly swallowed, then glanced up and met his gaze, looking a bit addled. "Wait. I…uh…didn't doctor your head wound yet."

He tossed the cloth that he'd been holding against the cut onto the table, ran his finger through the salve, and swiped it across the sore spot on his scalp. "There. Doctored." He spun and headed out of the kitchen and upstairs to the safety of his room. It dawned on him that he hadn't thanked her—or apologized for his earlier gruffness. In his room, he placed both hands on the windowsill and stared out, allowing the breeze to cool his soaring body temperature. What in the world was wrong with him?

Gentle footsteps echoed on the stairs, and he swiveled. Surely, Miss Marshall wouldn't follow him up to his room. His ma stood in the doorway, an odd look on her face. "Guess you're goin' to live, huh?"

If he died right now, it wouldn't be from his wounds but from his heart racing so fast after Sarah's treatment. "I reckon."

She inhaled a long breath through her nose, and a smile tugged up one corner of her mouth. "Tonight, after our guests retire, I want to have a family meeting in the parlor."

They hadn't had one of those in several months. "Why tonight?"

"I have a feeling our guests will be around a long while. We need to make some plans to educate Sarah on life out here, so we don't have a repeat of today's events."

"What kind of plans?" Wariness clawed at him like a frantic fox trying to snatch a hen from the chicken coop.

"She needs to learn how to live on the prairie—what she can do, what she can't do. And you boys can teach her." His ma spun around and trotted down the stairs, obviously not wanting to hear his objection.

He stared at the spot she'd vacated. He didn't have time to educate Miss Marshall. Why would his ma even suggest such a thing? She thought Miss Priss would be here awhile, but he knew better. She would be leaving soon. Ma was up to no good—he could smell it. She was lonely for female companionship, and if she could get Sarah to stay and maybe marry one of her sons, then she would probably get to keep Sarah's aunt, too. She wasn't fooling him.

But he wouldn't marry a city gal, even though he had to admit there was more to Miss Marshall than his initial impression had allowed for. He shook his head. If his ma thought they could change Chicago-loving Sarah Marshall into a ranch woman, she was going to be sorely disappointed.

Chapter Fifteen

Sarah scooted the chair over to the bedroom window and sat down to gaze at the setting sun. She'd never paid much attention to sunsets back in Chicago, mainly because you couldn't see them unless you were high up in one of the tall buildings and there wasn't another structure blocking your view. She'd missed so much and had never known it. The sun had dipped behind the horizon, and its bright rays painted the underbellies of the clouds on the western horizon a vivid pink. The sky had darkened to a bluish gray color but was not yet the black that it would soon be.

Another wonder she hadn't noticed in the city were the thousands of stars that dotted the night sky. They were like beautiful gems scattered across the black velvet lining a jewelry store's display shelf. And when had the moon gotten so big, so bright? Nature came alive out here on the prairie.

Sighing, she pulled her brush through her long hair, keeping time with Emma's soft snores. A comfortable breeze fluttered the curtains and cooled her skin. Outside her window, crickets chirped a loud chorus—a symphony she was beginning to get used to. There were no creaks in the Harper home like those in the old Chicago house that had frightened her so at night when she'd first come to live there.

Thoughts of Ethan's masculine torso had invaded her mind all evening. If Walt were to stand beside him, he'd look pale, skinny, and almost effeminate. She cringed. It wasn't fair to compare the two men. Walt was a businessman, raised in the city, while Ethan had spent most of his life outside in the sun—and what a handsome tan he had developed as a result. She sighed again and leaned her arms on the windowsill.

She couldn't allow herself to develop feelings for Ethan, not when she would be leaving soon. At least, she hoped it was soon. Any day she should hear back from Walt. There might even be a letter on the next stage. Or maybe Mrs. Rayburn would write back with an offer of assistance. Would the woman consider allowing both Sarah and her aunt to live with her in exchange for help caring for the children? And did the children miss her? Would they even remember her by the time she got back to Chicago?

A door banged somewhere in the house. The men had hung around tonight after dinner instead of separating to their rooms or going outside to do chores, as they usually did. She wondered about that but had been so eager to get away from Ethan that she had taken to her room as soon as the kitchen had been cleaned up. She could still feel the warmth of his skin against her fingertips, skin that felt different from hers—smooth, but not nearly as soft. Touching him, even in such a practical manner, had awakened feelings in her she had never experienced before. She didn't want to be attracted to Ethan Harper—but she feared it might be too late.

❧

Ethan followed his brothers into the parlor after saying good night to Corrie and Toby. "I'm just saying…if you hadn't given her that book of yours, this whole thing probably wouldn't have happened."

"Me?" Josh gave Ethan a slight shove. "I was a mile away from here. How can you blame it on me?"

"I'm just thankful Corrie and Miss Marshall weren't hurt." Aaron, once again wearing a clean white shirt, squeezed past Josh, who'd stopped half in, half out of the room.

"And what's with this?" Ethan tugged on his oldest brother's sleeve. "Why are you dressing up for dinner all of a sudden?"

Aaron yanked his arm away and glanced down. "What's wrong with putting on a clean shirt? Ma appreciates it."

"Well, I'm sure the effort is lost on the other females in the room." Ethan plopped down into a side chair and crossed his arms over his chest, grimacing at the sting of the cut on his shoulder.

Josh strode in and stood in front of Ethan, glaring down at him with fire in his blue eyes. "You didn't answer me, *little brother*."

Ethan shot up, instantly sorry for his sudden movements. Pain spiraled through his bruised body, but he fought to keep from showing it. He clenched his teeth and tightened his fist, ready to slug Josh if he called him that again.

His ma and pa entered the room, and ma planted her fists on her waist. "What in the world is going on in here?" She looked at each of her sons, one at a time. Aaron slunk down onto one end of the settee, and Josh backed up. "What is all this bickering? You all sound like fussing children instead of grown men."

Ethan ducked his head, ashamed of his unchristian behavior. He relaxed his fist and dropped down into the chair again. He peeked up at his ma's stern glare, then glanced at his pa. His shoulders were bouncing with barely contained mirth. A snort slipped out, and Ma spun around.

"Nicholas James Harper. Just what is so funny?"

He worked to keep a straight face and finally gained some semblance of control. Ethan glanced at Aaron, who looked back at him and shrugged.

Ma smacked Pa on the sleeve. "Are you going to answer me?"

Pa swiped the back of his hand across his mouth as if wiping off his smile, but his eyes still glinted with mischief. "Well, what do you expect to happen if you put three stallions in a corral with just one mare?"

From the side, Ethan saw his ma scowl, and then her eyebrows lifted and her mouth dropped open. She spun around, eyeing each of her sons again. "Well, I can see I called this meeting just in time."

Pa wiped his mouth again, but his smile remained. He took a seat on the settee beside Aaron, giving him a playful nudge. Josh shot Ethan another scowl, then sat in the rocker beside him. Ma crossed the room to the empty fireplace and then turned around, looking like a stern schoolteacher, and yet there was an odd glimmer in her eyes. She always stood, rather than sat, when she had something to say that someone in the room wasn't going to like. Having the benefit of height must give her more confidence. Ethan had a feeling she was up to no good.

She cleared her throat. "In light of what happened to Corrie and Sarah today, I've made a decision. I want you boys to help her learn the ropes around here."

Ethan shot a glance at both of his brothers, who looked as confused as he was.

Ma pulled a piece of paper from her pocket and perused it. "Aaron, you can teach Sarah to ride and talk to her about animals and how to stay safe around them. Josh, you can explain about what all we do here, about the garden—what to pick and what to let grow, who our neighbors are and where they live, and so on."

Ma's gaze locked on Ethan next, and he slid down in his chair. He didn't want any job that put him in close proximity with that prissy troublemaker.

"Ethan, you can teach her to harness a horse and drive a buggy...and how to shoot."

"Shoot?" Ethan ran his hand through his hair. He'd already taught her about harnessing a team, but using a gun? "Given her ability to get in trouble, don't you think teaching her to shoot is dangerous?"

Ma shook her head. "Out here, a woman needs to know how to protect herself, especially one who has more than her share of problems. I trust you to be careful and teach her what she needs to know to stay safe."

"Why me?" He jumped up from his chair and paced to the parlor entrance.

"She's talking to all of us, not just you." Aaron leaned forward, his brow crinkled. He shook his head. "I don't think I'm the right person to teach her to ride, given what happened to Della."

Ma's lips tightened. "I can see where that might bother you."

Josh leaned forward. "I'll do it."

The thought of Sarah riding a horse was almost more than Ethan could stomach. What if...? "It's a mistake."

Josh jumped up and pushed out his chest. "Just 'cause I'm more bookish than you and Aaron doesn't mean I can't teach Miss Marshall to ride as well as either of you."

Ethan raised a hand. "Hang on, that's not what I meant. I just think it's a mistake to put that city girl on the back of a horse. Period."

"Oh." Josh took a step backward. "Sorry."

"I'm thinking we need to rustle up another pair of women before our boys take to fistfighting again." Pa covered his mouth, but his brown eyes danced.

Ma stuck out her chin. "God will provide a bride for each of our sons in His good time. However, Sarah is excellent with children, and she would be a wonderful match for Aaron."

"Me?"

"Aaron?" Josh said.

Ethan sucked in a sharp breath. Why should the thought of Aaron and Sarah together bother him so much? Because he didn't want her here at all? Or because he didn't want his brother to get her?

Ma nodded. "You need a wife worse than your brothers. You have two young'uns that need a mother. Sarah is kind, she can cook and sew, she takes excellent care of her aunt...and she's destitute."

"What's that got to do with anything?" Aaron asked.

"She needs us as much as we need her."

Ethan leaned against the wall and folded his arms across his chest. He didn't like the idea of either of his brothers spending time with Sarah, but why was that? He sure didn't want her.

"Any questions?"

Pa shook his head. "You're meddlin', Karen."

"I'm not, either. I'm organizing my boys to help someone in need."

Pa didn't comment further, which was probably wise, since Ma had her mind set. Ethan didn't want his parents arguing about Miss Marshall.

Ma's gaze swiveled between Josh and Ethan. "So, I think it would be nice if you two younger boys help Sarah see what a fine man your brother is."

Josh kicked at a table leg. "And what if one of us has already set his cap for her?"

Ma arched one eyebrow. "Have you?"

Josh shrugged. "I don't know. Maybe. But it doesn't seem fair to push her toward Aaron without giving me and Ethan a chance."

Ethan didn't like the idea, either, but he kept quiet. This whole thing bothered him, but what bothered him most was the fact that he wasn't sure *why* it bothered him. Furthermore, Ma could be sneaky when she wanted something bad. He wouldn't put it past her to deliberately suggest Sarah would be a good match for Aaron so that Ethan would have to decide to fight for her, if he wanted her.

Well, he didn't want her. But then, he didn't want his brothers to have her, either. He blew out a sigh. How could one woman set a whole family spinning like a twister? He just hoped that when Sarah left, she didn't leave behind a pile of broken hearts amid the debris.

Pa yawned, then stood and stretched. "I'm headed to bed." He gave Ma a peck on the cheek. As he passed Ethan, he rolled his eyes and muttered something about playing with fire.

"All right, then. You know what I expect of you." Ma didn't wait for an answer but followed Pa from the room. She paused in the doorway and glanced back. "Last one out turn down the lamps."

The fact that she'd referred to Aaron as a man and him and Josh as "younger boys" wasn't lost on Ethan. He glanced at his brothers, and they both looked as flummoxed as he felt.

Josh shook his head and walked out.

"What do you think about all this?" Ethan asked Aaron.

His brother rested his elbows on his knees and ran his fingertips through his dark hair. He blew out a loud breath "Sure didn't see this comin', did you?"

"No." Ethan worked his mouth, trying to get the next thought into the right words. "You ready to marry again?"

His brother shrugged. "I guess. Maybe." He shot up out of the chair. "I don't know. Hadn't thought all that much about it. I kind of thought maybe you had your eye on Miss Marshall."

It took a lot of effort not to wilt under his big brother's stare. Ethan barked a laugh. "Me? Whatever gave you that idea?"

Aaron moseyed toward the parlor door. "I guess it's the way you look at her. Like she's the sweetest piece of candy in the jar." He turned back. "If you really aren't interested in her, I might test the waters and see how things go. Corrie really likes her."

"Be my guest."

Aaron studied him, and Ethan stared back, hoping his gaze didn't give away his conflicting emotions. Finally, Aaron nodded. "Good night."

Ethan leaned his head back against the wall and stared up at the ceiling. If his brother set his cap for Sarah, then he should support him. So, why did the idea sit on his belly like a glass of soured milk?

If not for the children's steady stream of chatter, breakfast would have been a silent affair. Sarah figured the men must have something important on their minds, because they all kept their heads down as they shoveled food in their mouths, finishing the meal within minutes—a meal that had taken close to an hour to prepare. Sarah had cooked all the pancakes, while Karen had fried up a mess of bacon, scrambled several dozen eggs, and sliced a loaf of bread.

Men. They were so baffling. She shook her head, garnering an odd glance from Karen, then took a bite of pancake. The men had all been quite pleasant last night, complimenting her on her almond cake, but they were probably still upset with her this morning for having endangered Corrie yesterday. She certainly hadn't meant to put the girl's life in jeopardy. These Harper men were protective of their family, and that only made her feel like more of an outsider—an intruder. There was a part of her that wished to belong within the Harper circle—to know what it was to be loved by a big, happy family—but she knew that would never happen. She'd be gone soon. Gone and forgotten.

With little appetite, she excused herself. Karen sent her a worried look, but then Toby dropped his fork on his plate, making a clatter that drew his grandmother's attention. Sarah scraped off her dish and then placed it on the counter, thinking again how close she'd come to suffering a grave injury yesterday. It goaded her that a child was more knowledgeable about an issue than she, but that was logical, since Corrie had grown up here. On the other hand, the girl would be quite bewildered if she had to maneuver her way through the busy Chicago streets. At least Sarah had learned her lesson. Next time the child called out a warning, she would heed it.

Chair legs squeaked against the floor as the men mumbled their thanks. They paraded through the kitchen and into the washroom, where, one by one, they snatched their hats from hooks near the back door and smashed them on their heads. Sarah blew out a breath, then gathered up their plates and carried them to the counter, thinking again about how quiet they had been. She hoped they didn't stay that way, because it made things tense and awkward.

Karen wiped the children's hands and faces, then sent them to their room to make their beds. She carried their plates over and set them down for Sarah to scrape. "Guess you noticed things were rather subdued this morning."

Sarah nodded, wondering if an explanation was coming. She turned and leaned against the counter, waiting.

Working her mouth, Karen glanced in the direction her men had gone. "It's my fault."

"Yours?" That was the last thing Sarah had expected to hear. "What did you do?" The moment the question left her mouth, she realized how rude it was. "I'm sorry. I shouldn't have asked that."

"It's all right." The older woman caught her eye. "Last night after you retired, I suggested to my sons that they should educate you in the ways of prairie life, since you'd likely be staying for a while."

A chill crept over Sarah, in spite of the warmth of the room. Karen's suggestion had only served to make things more uncomfortable between her and the Harper men. "I'm guessing they weren't too enthused about the idea."

"No, I don't think that's the case. They're just very busy this time of year."

Karen's dispassionate response only reinforced Sarah's impression. The brothers didn't want to be around her, much less spend time teaching her how to live on the prairie. "I should check to see if Aunt Emma is ready for her breakfast. Excuse me."

Lest Karen see the hurt in her eyes, she hustled to her room—no, not hers but the borrowed room—and reached for the door handle. Pausing in the hallway, she wiped her stinging eyes. Maybe it would be best for everyone if she just stayed in the room with her aunt. But she would go crazy with boredom. One could read only so many books, and she'd written all of the letters she needed to. If only they would hear back from someone—Walt, Bob and Lydia, Mrs. Rayburn—anyone who'd be willing to take in two destitute women.

Chapter Sixteen

An hour after lunch, the stage rolled in, carrying four passengers. Sarah kept busy helping Karen serve their meal of stew and biscuits, with gingerbread for dessert. Mr. Biggs, the stage driver, watched Sarah closely and grinned every time she looked at him. He even winked once. What had gotten into him?

She hustled over to Karen, who was refilling the water glasses. "Since we're about done here, I think I'll go upstairs and start cleaning the kitchen."

Karen nodded. "Would you mind peeking in on Corrie and Toby and see if they're still napping?"

"I'd be happy to." Happy to do anything that got her away from Mr. Biggs. He seemed a friendly sort, but she didn't like how his gaze followed her around the room.

She hurried upstairs and checked on the children. Toby was asleep, lying sideways on his bed with his head and one arm hanging over the edge. Sarah turned him so that he wouldn't slide off and land on his head. The boy was such a darling. He wasn't as outgoing as Corrie, but he had those dark brown eyes of Ethan's and the quiet mannerisms shared by most of the Harper men. It was a shame he'd lost his mother at such a young age. He probably didn't even remember her.

Sarah tiptoed across the room. Corrie had fallen asleep today, too, which was a rare event. The pretty girl lay with her mouth partially open. Sarah smiled and left the room.

She grabbed the wooden bucket and was going to fetch some water when a knock sounded at the back door. Her heart sank when she saw it was Mr. Biggs. When he saw her approaching, he smiled and removed his hat.

"Afternoon, Miss Marshall," he said, as if he hadn't just seen her a few minutes ago.

"Mr. Biggs."

He twisted the brim of his hat. "You can call me Jasper, if you want."

Sarah's stomach churned. "I'm afraid I don't know you well enough for that, sir."

His face puckered up for a moment, then brightened. "I reckon you will before long. The stage comes through twice a week."

"I don't expect to be here for very much longer, Mr. Biggs. My aunt and I plan to return to Chicago soon." She set down the heavy bucket, wishing the man would leave. Didn't he have a schedule to keep? In the yard, she could see the stage all hitched with a fresh team of horses and ready to go. If he'd just go.

"I don't reckon there's any time to waste, then." He straightened to his full height. "I'm right attracted to you, Miss Marshall. I don't have a lot, but I do have a small house in town, and I…uh…." He swallowed, his large Adam's apple wobbling. "Would you care to…uh…marry up with me and share it?"

Her heart sank at his unconventional and unexpected proposal. She didn't want to hurt the man or cause friction between him and the Harpers, but she shook her head. "I'm sorry, Mr. Biggs. As I said before, I don't plan to stay in Kansas, but I thank you for your kind offer."

He frowned and stuck his hat back on his head. "You sure you won't change your mind? I'm right fond of you."

"I'm sorry, but I can't. I have my aunt to consider."

"She can come, too." His brow creased. "Might make things overly crowded, though."

She shook her head.

He pressed his lips together and gave her a quick nod. He started to walk away but then turned back. "I gave Ethan the mail. There was a letter for you."

This time, her heart jolted in a good way. A letter!

She stayed inside the house to avoid facing Mr. Biggs again, wishing the stage would hurry up and leave. Finally, with a loud "Heyah!" and amid the snorting of horses and jingling of harnesses, the stage rolled out of the yard, leaving behind a cloud of dust. Sarah burst out of the house, hiked up her skirts, and ran all the way to the barn before the dust had settled completely. She desperately hoped Ethan hadn't left for the afternoon to go work in one of the fields and taken the letters with him.

The pungent odor of hay, horses, and manure smacked her in the face as she hurried inside the barn. The back doors were open, and light filtered in, but the large building was still darker than the house. When her eyes adjusted, she saw Josh walking toward her, a concerned look on his face.

"Is something wrong?" he asked.

"No, I was...um...." She glanced around the barn. "Do you know where Ethan is?"

Josh frowned and nudged his chin in the direction of the barn entrance. "He's working in the garden."

"Oh, thank you. Mr. Biggs mentioned that he'd given Ethan a letter that arrived for me. I'm quite anxious to read it."

Josh scratched the back of his head. "I hope it contains the news you're wanting."

She offered him a smile. "Thank you." As she turned to walk away, he gently caught hold of her arm.

"Wait, please." He lowered his hand and stood there, shifting from foot to foot. "I...uh, well, Ma thought you might like to learn to ride. Horses, that is. Or, rather, one horse." He waved his hand toward a small black horse in one of the stalls. "That one, actually."

Sarah blinked, unsure of what to say. She'd ridden a time or two and had enjoyed it. Riding might be a nice diversion from her long days of waiting for news, but then, maybe her waiting was over.

"We could go this evening after dinner, if you'd like."

She didn't fancy the idea of riding, or being alone, with another Harper man, but she knew his mother had put him up to this, so she conceded. "All right." She glanced around the barn again. "Do you have a sidesaddle?"

Josh's jaw tightened, and he glanced at a door, behind which she supposed was the tack room. After a moment, he nodded. "Yes, we have one, although riding astride is easier and safer."

Maybe in Kansas, a woman might ride astride, but no Chicago woman would stoop to such an uncouth practice. "I'd prefer to stick with the sidesaddle."

He suddenly grinned, looking just as handsome as his brothers, although different. With his slighter build, he reminded her more of a man she might see in town rather on a ranch. "This evening, then."

She smiled at him, then spun around and went searching for his brother. She was dying to read her letter.

She walked out to the garden, impressed by the massive size of it. She passed rows of lettuce and other greens, carrots, onions, turnips, tomatoes, and potatoes. At the far end of the garden, rows and rows of cornstalks rose up almost to her shoulders, and tiny husks held corn that would mature in the next month or so—corn she would never taste, because she'd be gone.

Ethan was nowhere in sight. She looked behind her, back at the barn and the part of the yard she could see, but he wasn't there, either. Maybe Josh had been mistaken. She ventured out a bit further, thinking Ethan might be on the far side of the tall corn. She glanced at the low hill to her right, hoping there were no cows nearby. There wasn't a tree to hide behind. Maybe she shouldn't be wandering all alone out here. She started to turn back when a rustling in the corn jerked her attention that way. Her heart pounded faster. What if a cow was in there?

Suddenly, a deep moan rose up from the corn, and the rustling noise grew closer. Sarah sucked in a breath and backed up, ready to take off running, but her curiosity held her in place. The form of a hunched-over creature—no, a man—rushed toward her, and then Ethan burst out of the cornfield, laughing.

Relief made her knees weak, but then she marched up to the rascal, pulled her fist back, and slugged him in the shoulder.

He rubbed the spot, but his ornery grin didn't leave his face. "Did you think another cow was after you?"

She shoved her hands to her hips. "Ethan Harper, you should be ashamed of yourself." She spun around and stalked away to the sound of his chuckling, but then she remembered the letter. She strode back, and his smile dimmed as she drew close again. He lifted his arm, as if preparing to ward off another attack. She held out one hand. He eyed it warily and lowered his arm. "Give me my letter, please."

His forehead wrinkled in confusion before comprehension dawned. "Oh, the mail. I always put it on the secretary in the parlor. You had two letters. From Chicago."

Sarah lifted her chin. His sweat-stained hat shaded his eyes, making them look even darker. "Did you read them?"

He grinned. "I'll admit I was tempted, but I figured you'd be able to tell if I did, and the last thing I want to do is incur your wrath. It's painful." He rubbed his shoulder.

Sarah tried to stay angry with him, but a smile pulled at her lips. "You're a scoundrel, you know that?"

He tipped his hat. "Yes, ma'am. I've been told that before, and on more than one occasion."

Shaking her head, Sarah turned and headed back toward the house.

"If you'll wait until I grab the buckets, I'll walk with you. Got some vegetables to take to Ma. I always pick them for her on the days the stage comes in, since she's so busy."

After his antics, she was tempted to go on without him, but she felt safer with him than alone. He disappeared into the corn and came back out carrying a bucket in each hand, one full of carrots and onions, the other, larger bucket with greens. Sarah had been amazed at the stronger flavor of fresh-picked vegetables. The produce they bought in Chicago was usually several days old by the time it made it to the market.

Her heartbeat kicked up several notches again as Ethan fell into step with her. Why did this man affect her so much? Being near Walt had never caused her hands to sweat or her pulse to pound like she'd been running, except the times when he'd asked for her hand in marriage. But that wasn't the same thing. What would she say if Ethan asked her to marry him? Not that he would, but the thought alone made it hard to breathe.

"You broke Jasper's heart today."

"Jasper?" Sarah searched her mind. Who was that?

"The stage driver."

"Oh, Mr. Biggs." She stopped suddenly, and Ethan passed her before skidding to a halt. "He told you?"

Ethan nodded. "Jasper's not one to keep secrets."

"Evidently not."

They started walking again. "I reckon he just wanted to stake his claim before some other man did."

Sarah halted again. "I am nobody's claim, Mr. Harper."

"Ethan. Remember?"

She heaved a sigh and looked down, her eyes landing on his tanned forearms, his muscles tight from holding the buckets. She was afraid to call him by his name. Afraid it would make her like him even more than she already did. And, again, what would be the point in that?

"Are you afraid to use my Christian name?"

"No!" She responded far too quickly, hating the fact that she'd just lied to him.

"Then say it." He gave her a smug look, his right eyebrow arched in challenge.

She stuck out her chin. "No."

"Why not?"

"I don't want to."

He sighed. "Like I said, you're afraid."

"Why would I be?" She didn't like that he'd pegged her so quickly. Could he tell she was attracted to him?

"I don't know. I'm a likable fellow. You've no reason to be scared of me."

She squeaked out a sound that was part cough, part huff. "This coming from the rogue who just scared me half out of my wits?"

He grinned, as if proud of what he'd done. Why did he have to be so handsome when he smiled?

"I need to get back so I can read my letters."

"We'll never get back if you keep stopping."

She shoved him in the arm again. "You're such a bully."

He shook his head. "No, I just want to hear you say my name."

She glanced up and his eyes captured hers. Her knees wobbled. "Why?"

He shrugged and looked away, a muscle in his jaw flexing. "I don't know. I just do."

"All right."

He whipped his head around and looked at her expectantly.

"I want to read my letters…*Ethan*."

His gaze held hers, his eyes warm. A slow smile pulled at one corner of his mouth. "Thank you."

She nodded, then hurried away, her heart pounding faster than her feet. How could merely speaking a man's Christian name cause a person to be so completely out of sorts?

⌒

Ethan let her go this time, half sorry for goading her. At least she'd finally called him by his first name. He watched her scurry away, as if she were being pursued, her dress swishing from side to side. Why had she resisted saying his name? What had made him push her to say it?

He blew out a sigh. He didn't know why he'd pressured her, but he was glad he had.

He shouldn't tease her, but he liked seeing her riled up—enjoyed putting that spark in her pretty blue eyes after seeing them so dull for days on end.

But teasing her was dangerous, and if he was a smart man, he wouldn't do it again.

The problem was, he always had to learn things the hard way.

⌒

Sarah peeked over her shoulder, half sorry Ethan wasn't following her. She was half glad, though, too, considering the way he set her nerves on end with his teasing and his handsome grin. She'd never had a man kid around with her before, and she found it quite disarming—and not altogether unpleasant. But the thing she couldn't understand was why he did it. His attitude toward her seemed to be changing, softening. At least, some days it was.

She scurried up the porch steps and hastened through the house to the parlor. Sure enough, there were five letters resting on the top of the secretary. She leafed through them, and joy surged through her at the sight of her name. She started to set the stack down, but then, remembering that Ethan had mentioned two letters addressed to her, checked the others. Sure enough, she discovered a second envelope bearing her name. After returning the other letters to the secretary, she took a seat near a window.

The missive in the cream-colored envelope was from Mrs. Rayburn, the note on stark white from Walt. She held one in each hand, knowing either letter could hold the key to her future. Living with Mrs. Rayburn and the children was preferable to marrying Walt, so she opened that one first and scanned the short note. The first paragraph was filled with expressions of regret for all that Sarah and her aunt had been through and shock over her uncle's death. The second paragraph stole her breath away, and she dropped her hands to her lap. Mrs. Rayburn had closed the children's home and sent the boys and girls to another orphanage.

Sarah closed her eyes, letting the news wash over her. Without the assistance of her and Abigail, caring for so many children had become too difficult for the older woman. Abigail had not kept her promise to help Mrs. Rayburn, and the other girls hadn't, either. Where was little Mary now? What about the other children?

The pain of losing them again tore through her. She'd thought her first loss just temporary—that she would see them all again. But it wasn't to be. Poor Mrs. Rayburn. Sarah knew the decision to close had not been an easy one. Taking a breath to steel herself, she read the final paragraph.

Another shock slapped her in the face. Mrs. Rayburn had put her house up for sale and was moving to a warmer climate—to Texas, to live with her sister.

Sarah laid her head back against the chair, blinking away the sting in her eyes. So, that door was closed. There was no hope now that she and her aunt could live with Mrs. Rayburn. Her throat burned at the thought of marrying Walt, but what other option did she have? Ethan's teasing eyes blazed their way to the forefront of her mind, over the fading image of Walt. *Ethan may enjoy poking fun at you, but he certainly would never consider marrying the woman who ignored his advice and nearly got his niece killed.*

Swallowing back her disappointment, she picked up Walt's letter and opened it. She gazed up at the ceiling, not even knowing what she hoped he had written. She supposed she expected him to be all apologetic over the hardships she'd faced and to eagerly forward her the money she needed to return to Chicago. Bracing herself, she unfolded the single page.

Dear Sarah,

I'm dreadfully sorry to hear about your uncle's death and all the troubles that have come your way. It's hard to comprehend how much you and your aunt have suffered. Please give her my condolences on the loss of her husband.

As for the other matter, I regret that I cannot send you any money. Perhaps "will not" would be a better choice of words. You broke my heart with your constant refusals of my generous and, I might add, humbling offers of marriage. Remember, if you will, the last time we spoke; I mentioned that if you refused me, I would not ask again. I stand by my decision.

I wish you the best.

Regards,
Walter Swanson

Numb, Sarah stared at the letter in disbelief. *"I wish you the best"*? She'd felt certain that Walt would come to their aid and could not believe he had refused. He must not have loved her nearly as much as he'd claimed to.

With both doors closed, what were she and Aunt Emma to do now?

Chapter Seventeen

Sarah rolled the dough out on the pastry cloth while her aunt sat at the table cutting out the biscuits. The beef for tonight's supper was already cooking, its warmth heating the room, the aroma making her stomach growl. She pressed a hand to her abdomen and peeked at her aunt, hoping she hadn't heard. "I can't tell you how glad I am to see you up and about, Auntie."

Emma smiled as she dipped the rim of a drinking glass into the bowl of flour, then pressed it onto the dough. "It feels good to be up and doing something productive, although I don't have the strength I used to."

Sarah started measuring the flour and other ingredients for a second batch of dough. She couldn't remember her aunt ever showing much strength, especially after enduring such a difficult trip, on top of losing her husband and most of her belongings, which had weakened her even further. At least she had some color in her cheeks today.

Sarah lifted the pliant circle of dough and placed it on a platter, then carried it to the table.

Emma looked up from her work. "Where did you say Karen was?"

"She and Corrie are taking the laundry down. Clouds are building, and she thought we might get some rain tonight."

"That would be nice, although it has seemed cooler today than in past days."

"I thought so, too." Even though the day had felt plenty hot when she'd been sparring with Ethan. She leaned against the counter, hearing the crackle of the letters in her apron pocket. She needed to tell Aunt Emma the news she'd received today, but she felt it best to wait until they were in their room for the night.

"What are we having for dinner? It smells delicious."

"Karen called it 'baked beef.'" Sarah set the bowl of dough on the table, pulled out a chair, and sat. "It's rather like stew, only baked in the oven with mashed potatoes covering the top."

Her aunt's thin eyebrows lifted. "Sounds interesting. If it tastes anything like it smells, it will be delicious. But then, everything Karen makes is good."

Sarah nodded, then picked up the extra glass she'd set down earlier and began stamping out biscuits.

Emma moved them to the baking sheet, casting odd glances at her in between biscuits. "Why don't you tell me what's bothering you, dear?"

Sarah stared at her aunt, amazed by her perceptiveness. "I thought I would wait until this evening to tell you."

Emma shrugged. "You may, if you want. But I can see that whatever it is has upset you."

Heaving a loud sigh, she pulled the letters out of her pocket and handed them to her aunt. "Read these and you'll understand."

Emma's lips tightened, and she nodded.

Sarah set aside a piece of leftover dough, which she would use later to make tiny cinnamon rolls for the children and started rolling out the next batch.

As Emma read Mrs. Rayburn's letter and then Walt's, the furrows in her brow deepened. After half a minute, she lowered the papers into her lap. "Well, that's disappointing news, for sure, but it's not the end of the world."

Sarah's mouth dropped open at the unexpected response. "Don't you understand? That means we have no way of returning to Chicago now."

Emma smiled serenely. "Yes, but, as I said before, God will provide if He wants us to return."

"How can you be so sure, after all that's happened?"

Emma laid a floury hand on Sarah's arm. "I know that you haven't had many people in your life whom you could trust, but I believe we can trust the Harpers. They are good people. Karen has said we can stay here as long as we need to, so I'm going to wait and trust God to arrange a permanent place for us."

Sarah sat back in her chair, both surprised and gladdened by her aunt's determination. "All right, then. I will try to do the same. I just don't want to wear out our welcome."

"We won't." Emma winked. "We'll make ourselves so useful that those Harpers won't want to see us go."

⌒

After a day of wrestling cattle and branding them, Ethan was ready for a long soak in the creek to soothe his sore muscles and a good supper to fill his belly. He followed his pa and brothers down the path toward home, trailed by several of their ranch hands. As he reined his horse onto the path leading to the house, a sharp pain stabbed his forefinger where it pressed against the reins. He rubbed the side of it, remembering the burn he'd gotten when he'd reached for the wrong end of a cooling branding iron he'd dropped because he'd been thinking about Miss Priss.

Pa removed his hat and swiped his sleeve across his forehead. "Long day. I must be gettin' old."

"I feel old, and I'm only twenty-four." Josh stretched and rubbed his back. "Ugh."

"It's just the heat." Aaron yawned. "Last night's rain felt good, and we sure needed it, but the moisture in the air made working today miserable."

They rode past the house, and Ethan noticed two horses he didn't recognize at the hitching post. Voices pulled his gaze to the porch, where Roger and Greg Woodward, dressed in their Sunday best, sat on either side of Sarah. Ma and Mrs. Stone were seated on the far side. Corrie and Toby jumped off the porch and ran toward them.

"Pa, we got comp'ny!" Corrie bounced on her toes and held up her arms. Aaron lifted her up and situated her in front of him in the saddle.

"Me too! Me too!" Toby jumped in place.

"C'mere, Scamp." Josh leaned down and hoisted up his nephew in his arms, then handed the boy the reins. "Guide ol' Chester back to the barn."

Toby's wide grin warmed Ethan's heart, but the fervent gaze in the Woodward brothers' eyes as they gawked at Sarah doused cold water on his delight. What were they doing here, anyway?

"One of you guys had better get busy and lasso that pretty little filly before someone else does," Pa mumbled with a sideways glance.

Ethan dismounted with a glance at Aaron, who shrugged. The Woodward brothers finally peeled their eyes off Sarah long enough to greet them.

"Howdy, Ethan." Roger nodded, and Greg did the same.

Ethan nodded at the men, then tipped his hat to the women, making eye contact with Sarah. Her cheeks turned bright red, and she glanced down. He couldn't tell if she was enjoying the Woodwards' attention or not. Della certainly would have.

Pa was slower to dismount. He lumbered up the steps and greeted their guests, shaking hands with the men. Then he leaned back against the porch railing. "What brings you two out here today?"

Roger peeked at Sarah, then looked back at Pa. "We heard you had a new mare for sale."

Behind Ethan, Josh snorted, as if fighting hard not to laugh. Ethan narrowed his gaze. Surely, Roger wasn't referring to Sarah. "There aren't any horses up here at the house."

Ma swatted her hand in the air as if batting at a gnat. "Of course not. We were just having a neighborly visit and enjoying a little sit-down time."

And enjoying the dessert that was supposed to be served tonight, from the looks of things.

Greg stood and faced the women. "Thank you kindly for the pie and coffee, Mrs. Harper. Nice to meet you, Mrs. Stone." He turned to Sarah, stuck his hat back on, and touched the end of the brim. "A pleasure to meet you, Miss Marshall. We're the closest neighbors, just about five miles or so to the south, so I reckon we'll see you again before too long."

Roger all but shoved his brother aside in his efforts to get closer to Sarah. She leaned back in her chair, as if trying to put distance between herself and the two men. Ethan gritted his teeth. He didn't like them pestering her.

"It was a delightful pleasure to meet you, Miss Marshall." Roger reached for Sarah's hand, tugged it up off the arm of the chair, and kissed the back of it.

Sarah eyes widened. When he released her hand, she immediately tucked it under her skirt—to wipe it off, if Ethan wasn't mistaken. He couldn't help grinning. Maybe she didn't care for the Woodwards' attention. And just why did that thought make him happy?

Both of the short, wiry brothers bopped down the stairs, then ambled toward Ethan.

Aaron dismounted, leaving Corrie seated atop his horse. "We've got some green broke horses, and one small mare that's about ready to go, but that's it for now. Unless you're interested in the mare, you've wasted your time."

Both men peeked over their shoulders at Sarah. "Eh, I wouldn't say that." Greg turned back with a wide grin on his face.

Ethan took a step closer and leaned down, keeping his voice low. "Miss Marshall isn't sticking around here for long. She plans to go back to Chicago soon."

Roger straightened, as if to make himself taller, but the top of his head still came only as high as Ethan's nose. "Well then, maybe one of us can change her mind."

Greg nodded. "Would be a cryin' shame to let a purty gal like that one get away. So, where is this horse?"

"I'll show them." Josh handed Toby down to Ethan. "Follow me."

Ethan cradled Toby in his arms, like he'd held him when he was a baby, tugged up the boy's shirt, and blew on his belly, making a loud *pltt*. Toby giggled and rubbed his tummy. Ethan glanced up and saw Sarah staring at him, a soft smile tugging at her lips. A flock of butterflies was loosed in his own belly, and he swallowed hard.

Was he doing the wrong thing letting Aaron pursue her?

∽

Even though they weren't wearing work clothes, the Woodward brothers took turns riding the mare but quickly decided she didn't have the right gait for them. They rode off, casting long, forlorn looks at the empty porch.

Ethan gave Alamo a good brushing-down, followed by a bucket of feed and a pat on the rump. "You worked hard today, boy. Enjoy the evening off."

He dragged his saddle off the stall railing, carried it to the tack room, and set it on the wooden block. Then he hung up Alamo's bridle. His brothers were just finishing grooming their own horses, after being delayed by the Woodwards' visit. Ethan headed for the barn door, anxious to shed the layers of dust that had accumulated on him.

"Hold up, there." Aaron strode toward him, and Josh followed.

At least Aaron hadn't called him "little brother" this time. It was a ridiculous nickname, anyway, since he was taller than Josh. Ethan paused just inside the barn door and waited for his brothers.

"I told Aaron that I might be interested in Sarah, too." Josh frowned as he walked toward him. "But he said he thought *you* were."

Ethan rolled his eyes. Why did that question keep coming up? "I'll admit she's pretty, and that I'm attracted to her. But too much has gone on between us for me to be interested in her in…uh…." He waved his hand in the air. "You know…in a marrying way."

Aaron shut the tack room door, then strode toward him, pinning him with that big-brother stare that had made him squirm when he was younger. "Are you sure?"

"Why do you keep asking me that?" Couldn't they take the hint? He remembered Sarah's gentle touch as she'd doctored him and how it had stirred him up on the inside. But wasn't that natural? Wouldn't he have had a similar reaction if some other pretty gal had done the same thing? It didn't mean anything.

Aaron's mouth quirked up on one side, and he rested his hands on his hips, then glanced at Josh. "We need to do something before every unmarried man in the county comes visiting, and there's only one way I know to settle this."

Josh stared at him for a long minute. "All right, but whoever wins, wins. And us other two will bow out. Agreed?"

Aaron nodded, then both brothers looked at Ethan. He blew out a sigh and gave a curt nod. They'd settled more than one argument this way.

Josh spun around and kicked at the hay on the barn floor. After a few moments, he bent down, then stood and turned around, holding out three sprigs of hay. "Long one wins and gets the right to court Sarah."

Ethan wasn't even sure why he'd agreed to draw, since he already made it clear he wasn't interested. Josh held the sprigs out to him first, and he selected one, pulling out a short, stubby stalk. He didn't feel the relief he'd expected. Josh held the remaining two out to Aaron, and he touched one, then the other, finally picking the first one. He pulled slowly, and a long stem came loose from Josh's hand.

Josh held his piece of hay next to Aaron's. "Shucks, you win."

"Maybe it's not too late to get your book back." Ethan gave his brother a playful shove.

Josh glared at him, then turned to Aaron. "I'll go ahead and take Sarah riding tonight, since I promised her I would."

Ethan frowned. "I still think that's a mistake."

"Well, I don't. She'll do fine." Josh strode past Ethan. "You smell like cow dung."

He chuckled and headed toward the house. "So do you."

Aaron fell into step beside him. "If you're certain you're not interested in Sarah, you need to stop looking at her like you are. You'll give her the wrong impression."

Ethan skidded to a halt and stared at his brother, confused. "How do I look at her?"

"Like she's the prettiest thing you've ever seen." Aaron cocked his head and gazed, starry-eyed, at Ethan, in what he guessed was supposed to be a charming manner. "Like that. Sort of."

Ethan couldn't hold back his laughter. "I certainly hope I don't look as green around the gills as you just did."

Aaron's ears turned red, and he shrugged one shoulder. "Falling in love can make you feel that way sometimes. Just be careful how you look at Sarah. Women are emotional and tend to imagine things that aren't there."

What was that supposed to mean? "How about I just avoid looking at her from now on? Will that work?"

Aaron smiled and shook his head. "She'll probably think you're mad at her and wonder what she did."

"How's a guy supposed to know what to do around a woman?"

"You don't, but that's the fun of it—trying to figure it all out without making her cry or getting her angry." Aaron clapped a hand on his shoulder. "I can see we need to take you to Windmill for a town social or two."

"Trying to figure women out sounds like a lot of hard work to me."

"It is, but it's worth the effort, believe me."

"Even when things don't turn out as you hoped?"

Aaron was silent for a long moment, and Ethan wondered if he'd pushed him too far. He rarely talked about his relationship with Della.

Staring up at the sky, Aaron heaved a sigh. "Yeah, it's worth it." His gaze caught Ethan's. "I know what you're thinking. I'd hoped Della would come around and settle down, especially after Corrie was born. I guess she wasn't the settling type."

Feeling emboldened by his brother's rare willingness to talk, Ethan decided to voice a question he'd always wondered about. "If you could do it over—marry Della again—would you?"

Aaron pursed his lips for a moment, then nodded. "Of course. I wouldn't have Corrie and Toby if I hadn't married Della, and they're my world."

Ethan shifted his gaze to the tips of his dusty boots. "I'm sorry. You don't know how much I regret not keeping her safe. It was my fault she died."

"Don't say that."

Ethan jerked his head up at his brother's harsh tone. "You *know* it was my fault."

Gazing at him with somber eyes, Aaron shook his head. "No, it wasn't. Della was the one who decided to race that day. You tried to stop her. If it's anyone's fault, it's mine, for not escorting my own wife."

"But…that day she died, you said you'd never forgive me for what I'd done."

Aaron heaved a sigh. "I was wrong. I should have told you I forgave you a long time ago, but it's obviously taken me a while to be able to talk about it." Aaron's brown eyes begged him to believe him. "I let my anger and hurt rule me, and you're the one who's suffered for it. I'm sorry, Ethan. Forgive me."

"Of course." He grabbed his big brother and hugged him, feeling a tightness in his throat and the release of the burden he'd carried for so long.

Chapter Eighteen

The evening sun dipped toward the horizon and slipped behind a low-hanging cloud, shooting beams of sunlight across the sky. A light breeze blew several loose strands of Sarah's hair, tickling her cheek. She longed to scratch the itch but didn't dare lift her hand, for fear she'd fall off the horse as it circled the paddock and land in a pile of manure. The sidesaddle had to be one of the most uncomfortable contraptions ever made, second only to the corset. She'd become convinced that a man had designed both devices for the purpose of torturing women. The two previous times she'd ridden, Abigail had goaded her into it, and they hadn't gone any better than this. Why had she agreed to ride again?

As Josh led the horse around the corral, Sarah caught a glimpse of a man ducking inside the rear doors of the barn. Aaron had taken the children down to the creek for a swim, and the ranch hands had already gone back to the bunkhouse. Mr. Harper was sitting on the porch with Karen. That only left Ethan. Could he be spying on her?

As they rounded the corner, she quickly glanced over her shoulder. The action threw her off balance, and she flailed her arms in an effort to maintain her position.

Josh reached up and grabbed her forearm, steadying her. "Face forward. Keep your shoulders and hips square with the front of the horse."

"I'm not sure this is such a great idea."

"You're not going to chicken out on me, are you?"

"I'm seriously considering it."

Josh chuckled. "If you're going to live on a ranch, you need to know how to ride a horse."

"Does your mother ride?"

"She does." He glanced back at her, his blue eyes twinkling. "But she rides astride."

Sarah sucked in a breath. She'd never seen a woman ride like a man. It was improper. Unthinkable. Although it certainly must be easier than riding sidesaddle and sitting with one leg wrapped awkwardly around a hump.

"When we first moved here, there was much to be done, and we were all still pretty young. Ma had to help with the cattle and horses. Riding sidesaddle just wasn't practical, not to mention we didn't own one."

"I can't imagine how life must have been when you first arrived."

Josh lifted his hat, wiped his sleeve across his hairline, then slapped it on again. Looking down, Sarah could see the top of the sweat-stained hat. She'd opted not to wear a bonnet, since the sun was about to set, but she rarely saw the Harper men without their western hats, unless they were in the house.

"You sure are good with Aaron's kids. I know he appreciates how you're helping Corrie learn to read."

Heat rushed to her cheeks at the unexpected compliment. "Thank you. They are very pleasant children."

He nodded. "Yes, but they sure need a mother."

Sarah bristled. She decided to change the subject rather than step into that quagmire. "Do you like living on a ranch?"

He shrugged and peered back at her again. "Shoulders pointing straight ahead." He smiled, then faced forward again. "Yeah, I like it, for the most part. I'd like to live in town one day, though, and try my hand at some kind of business. There's talk of the train going through these parts, eventually. If that happens, we'll probably lose the stage contract, and we'll need some additional income."

Sarah didn't know quite how to respond to his surprising revelation. "What kind of business?"

"I don't know. I'm good with figures—numbers. I kind of thought I'd like working in a bank or keeping records for a business."

She knew he loved to read and study, but she couldn't have imagined him ever wanting to leave the ranch—and his family. "Wouldn't that be hard? Being so far from your folks and brothers?"

"Yeah, and I'd sure miss Ma's cooking." He paused at the gate, then pushed it open.

"Where are we going?"

"You're ready to ride outside the fence."

"No, inside is just fine. I mean, what if something startles the horse and you let go of the reins?"

He chuckled and shook his head. "Nothing will startle this old mare, and I promise not to let go."

He didn't give her much of a choice as he led her from the paddock. They walked toward the house, and Karen waved at her. Sarah dipped her chin in acknowledgment, afraid to wave back and risk losing her balance again. "How about heading back to the barn?"

"Ready to call it quits?"

"Yes. If I sit up here much longer, I won't be able to walk tomorrow."

"All right. You've done well for your first time."

"Thank you. Do you really think the train will come down this way someday?"

"Yeah, there's talk of connecting the towns in eastern Kansas with Colorado and possibly even going as far south and west as Santa Fe."

If only the railroad passed through here now, her uncle might still be alive, and they wouldn't have lost all their belongings. But that would also mean she'd be living in Santa Fe—or maybe she'd be back in Chicago. Strangely, neither place sounded as inviting as the idea of staying right where she was—at Harpers' Stage Stop. Sarah sucked in a sharp breath. When had her desires shifted so dramatically?

Josh turned the horse toward the barn, and Sarah spotted the same man she'd seen before. It *was* Ethan. Why was he spying on her? Did he think her incapable of riding a horse? She sat up straighter, determined to prove him wrong.

Outside the barn, Josh looped the reins over a hitching post rail, then reached up and helped her down. He studied her for a long moment, and she thought she saw regret in his eyes. "You're easy to talk to. You should try talking to Aaron. He's a good man, but he keeps to himself a lot. Losing Della was really hard on him." He gave her a tight-lipped smile before untying the horse and leading it into the barn.

Sarah watched him go. Given enough time, she thought she and Josh could become friends. But she wasn't attracted to him, and she hoped he wasn't looking for a romantic relationship. He was nice, but he didn't move her on the inside like Ethan did.

"Are you crazy?" Ethan's loud voice was unmistakable.

Curious, Sarah glanced over her shoulder at the porch, relieved to see that Mr. and Mrs. Harper had gone inside. She crept over to the barn door and cocked her head so that she could hear better.

"What's that mean?" Josh had raised his voice several notches from when he'd been talking to her.

"You put Sarah on Della's saddle?"

She clasped her throat with her hand. Why hadn't she stopped to question how Josh had produced a sidesaddle? She'd just assumed it belonged to Karen. After Josh's comment about her riding astride, she should have realized the saddle had belonged to Della.

"So? That saddle's not doing anyone any good sitting in the tack room. We might as well sell it as leave it in there for years."

"You know Aaron won't do that."

"Then it won't hurt to use it."

"Well, I don't like it."

"Quit trying to protect every woman that crosses your path, Ethan. You can't save everyone."

Sarah peeked around the corner and saw Ethan and Josh standing face-to-face, like two roosters preparing to have it out. "I know, but what if Sarah had fallen off and broken her neck, like Della?"

Sarah gasped, but her anger had already taken over. She marched into the barn, skirts swishing, and both men turned to gape at her. Ethan's eyes went wide.

Her chin jutted forward. "Stop comparing me to Della this instant. What happened to her was unfortunate, to be sure, but that doesn't mean the same thing will happen to me. Especially since I don't plan to be riding much. A buggy suits me just fine."

Ethan glanced at Josh. Neither man uttered a word.

Feeling as if she'd put Ethan Harper in his place, she turned and hurried from the barn, her heart pounding. Why did she have to fall for the wrong brother? Aaron was solid, responsible; Josh, smart and friendly. But Ethan was bossy and…and so handsome, she wanted to kiss him. She kicked at a rock, wishing it were Ethan instead. It hurt that he didn't think she could ride a horse in a paddock without getting hurt.

Why did he have to be the one who'd stolen her heart?

Especially since he didn't want it.

⌒

Josh narrowed his eyes. "You see how your overprotectiveness annoys people."

Ethan's emotions bounced off the barn walls. He wanted to chase after Sarah and explain how he couldn't stand the thought of anything happening to her. He wanted to take that sidesaddle to the trash heap and burn it. He wanted to slug his brother. But he wouldn't do any of those things. Instead, he hung his head. "I don't know how to be any other way."

"I know. It's just because you care so much." Josh blew out a breath and clapped a hand on Ethan's shoulder. "You've got to pray more and worry less. At some point, you've got to entrust those you love to God. He can protect them far better than we can."

"That's much easier said than done."

"Yep." Josh nodded. "But when you try to do God's job, you're telling Him that you don't trust Him to do it."

Ethan rolled that thought around in his mind. "I never really considered that before, but it makes sense. No matter how hard I try, I can't be with Ma, the kids, or Sarah all the time."

"Right. Aaron's had to learn the same thing. Remember how he didn't want to let the kids out of his sight after Della died?"

"Yeah."

"And what happened?"

"They became clingy and whiny and cried whenever he did leave them."

"Right. Even children need room to grow and develop into the people God made them to be. Adults need even more room."

Ethan gave Josh a gentle nudge. "When did you get to be so smart?"

"On the day I was born." Josh grinned, revealing his straight, white teeth.

He had always been a bit envious of his brother's smile, since his teeth weren't as straight, and he had a tiny gap between the top two in front. "You're humble, too."

"Don't I know it."

They shared a chuckle, then Josh sobered. "Have you considered that maybe God stranded Sarah here so that she and Aaron would meet and fall in love? I mean, it's not like we have lots of time or opportunities to meet marriageable women."

"No, I can't say that the thought ever crossed my mind. But, if it's true, God sure went to a lot of trouble to get her here." Ethan strode out of the barn, leaving Josh to groom the mare. He glanced toward the house, but Sarah must have already gone in. Sniffing a laugh, he shook his head, amazed at how effectively she'd put him in his place. Aaron would have his hands full if he succeeded in wooing her. Ethan's grin faded, and he gazed up at the darkening sky. Only a few stars were visible, peeking out between the indigo clouds. Could it be that God *had* brought Sarah here for Aaron?

On the porch, he dropped into a rocker, planted his elbows on his knees, and raked his fingers through his hair, knocking his hat off. Josh was right. He had to quit trying so hard to protect everyone he loved, but just how did one go about letting loose of the reins?

He had to start with Sarah. He'd told Aaron twice that he wasn't interested in her, and now he had to let her go—not that he'd ever really had her. The thought left a nasty taste in his mouth, but Aaron had drawn the long straw. He'd won the chance to woo Sarah, regardless of how Ethan felt about the matter.

The best thing to do would be to help Sarah fall in love with Aaron, so they could marry and she wouldn't have to worry about her future. Once that happened, he was sure he'd be free of the strange hold she had on him.

He hoped and prayed that was the case.

⟿

Sarah stared out the bedroom window, not bothering to wipe away the tears that wouldn't stop. Crickets chirped a happy chorus, as if to say that everything would be all right. But nothing would be right, not when she'd fallen in love with a man who didn't want her. Even worse, she'd fallen for his whole family, and now the thought of leaving them nearly broke her heart.

But she and her aunt were only guests; they couldn't stay here forever. When they left, where would they go? How would they survive?

She could probably find work of some sort, as a clerk—maybe. Or possibly as a nanny or a cook, but both of those positions usually required living with a family. Whatever salary she received beyond room and board would not be sufficient to provide for Aunt Emma, too. Tears burned her eyes. There was no easy answer, and mulling everything over had created an ache in her stomach that made her feel as weak as her aunt.

Emma had taken to reading the Bible more of late and had quoted a verse to Sarah tonight—something about trusting God and not leaning on your own understanding. If only that would help.

The problem was, she had no understanding. She didn't understand how anything good could come of a situation that seemed utterly hopeless. For a brief time, she'd hoped something could develop between her and Ethan, but it was clear that would never happen. She could never aspire to his standards in a woman.

She sniffed back a sob. Why couldn't Ethan notice her strengths instead of her mistakes?

She laid her head on her arm. "God, if You can make sense of this whole situation, I'll gladly give it over to You."

Tears spilled from her eyes, and she longed for her mother's embrace. Longed to see her father's teasing grin again. But that would never be. And she was beginning to think she would never see Chicago again, either.

Chapter Nineteen

*D*riving a buggy is a lot easier than driving a big wagon," Ethan explained. *Except when a man is seated next to the woman who makes his pulse race like a runaway horse.* He glanced sideways at Sarah.

"Easier because there's only one horse?"

"Yes, and only one set of reins." He smiled at her, enjoying the humorous glimmer in her blueberry eyes. Swallowing hard, he faced forward again, reminding himself that he was helping his brother. If Aaron married Sarah, she'd need to know how to drive a buggy.

"Tell me again why you're teaching me this." She angled a glance at him, then faced the front, her sunbonnet blocking his view of her pretty face.

"You need to learn." *And Ma said he had to teach her.* "It's good for a woman to know how to handle a horse. Take my ma, for example. There may be a time she'll need to ride for help if something happens when the men are gone. And you need to know in case you want to visit a neighbor, like Ma sometimes does."

"You let her go alone?"

She had him there. With the nearest ranch or farm miles away, one of the men accompanied her whenever she left home. "No, but she needs to know how, in case a problem comes up when we're all gone."

She breathed out a soft sigh. "Then, show me what to do."

"All right. First, hold your hands in front of you, with your wrists turned in slightly and your elbows nearly touching your sides."

He jiggled her arm. "Relax. Not so stiff."

She blew out another breath but did as told.

He held out the reins to her. "Take one in each hand, but don't pull them taut. Leave them relaxed a bit. You don't need much tension unless you're stopping."

Sarah nodded and took the reins from his hands. As she did, her fingers brushed across his, scattering his thoughts and sending his gut into turmoil. "Uh...."

The front door banged, and Ethan jumped.

Corrie trotted down the porch steps. "Can I go, too?"

His first inclination was to say no, because he wanted to spend some time alone with Sarah. But, on second thought, it might help to have her along. "Sure. C'mon."

Corrie smiled and skipped toward him. He caught her up and set her on the bench seat between him and Sarah. That was safer. Much safer.

Corrie hugged Sarah's arm and then sat back. Sarah smiled at his niece, then at him, but when he caught her gaze, her smile vanished and she turned away, as if she'd done something wrong. He probably confused her as much as she did him. One day, he treated her kindly; the next day, he acted grumpy and merely grunted in response to one of her questions. If only he knew what was wrong with himself.

"What next?" she asked.

Driving. Keep focused, Harper. "Release the brake and give the reins a gentle shake on the horse's back."

"Don't forget to cluck."

"Cluck?" Sarah peeked at Corrie.

The girl nodded and made a clicking noise out the side of her mouth.

"Ah. All right." Sarah smacked the reins, albeit a bit too hard, on the mare's back and made a feeble slurping sound, but the horse started off. Sarah squealed. "What do I do now?"

Ethan tamped down a smile. "Just tug in the direction you want the buggy to turn. Or, keep the reins straight, if that's the direction you want to go. And watch out for the barn."

His fingers itched to reach for the reins; but, at the last moment, Sarah pulled hard to the right, the horse turned, and they all breathed a unified sigh of relief. She steered the buggy out of the yard and down the road toward the Santa Fe Trail. Did she realize where she was going?

After they had jostled along in the buggy for several minutes, she smiled at him. "This isn't so bad. In fact, it's pretty easy—much easier than riding a horse."

"Well, I reckon that's a matter of opinion. I much prefer a horse."

"So, what do I do now?"

Corrie shot to her feet. "Pa! Pa! Look! I'm riding in the buggy."

Ethan grabbed her and pulled her onto his lap. "We don't stand and jump in a buggy. You might scare the horse or fall out."

"Sorry." She didn't look sorry. She waved again at her father, who rode across the pasture with Toby on his lap.

When Aaron reached the road, he reined his horse into step with the buggy. "Where are you off to?"

"Nowhere in particular." Ethan glanced at Sarah. "Pull up here."

"How?"

"Just pull back on the reins. Gently."

She did as requested, but her arms ended up in the air, as if a sheriff were pointing a gun at her. He shook his head and shifted Corrie back to the seat, then climbed out. Once on the ground, he positioned himself so that Sarah couldn't see his hands, then he motioned for Aaron to dismount. Aaron lifted one eyebrow but slid his leg over the back of the horse, carrying Toby down with him. Ethan relieved him of the reins, hopped up onto his brother's horse, and then winked at him.

Aaron wasn't taking the hint. Ethan nodded his head toward the buggy and held the reins as if he were driving one.

"Uncle Ethan wants you to finish Miss Sarah's driving lesson, Pa," Corrie volunteered.

"Oh. Oh!" Aaron frowned at him but set Toby in the buggy. "You two scrunch up for a minute." The buggy tilted as his big body weighted down the one side, and then he lifted Toby onto his lap.

Ethan rode back toward the house, feeling more than a little guilty. What would Sarah think about his sudden abandonment?

⟜

Ethan couldn't stand to be around her for any length of time. That had to be the reason he'd tricked his brother into finishing her driving lesson just when things had seemed to be going so well. If he felt that way, why had he even bothered to go to the trouble of teaching her in the first place?

She dared a glance at Aaron, who looked quite bewildered. "What do I do now?"

"Huh?"

"Ethan was teaching me to drive."

"Oh. Uh…just keep going down the road. Or turn around."

Sarah stared down the road, but she'd lost her heart to drive any further. If only she could load her aunt in this buggy with their measly stock of supplies and drive it all the way to Chicago. But then what?

Why hadn't Abigail replied to her letter? Did she no longer want to be friends, knowing how far down Sarah had sunk? They had never been considered people of great wealth, but they'd lived in a nice home and had everything they wanted and needed. At least, she and Aunt Emma had.

Corrie bumped her arm.

"Sarah?" Aaron's voice pulled her from her musings. "Would you like me to drive back?"

"No, I can do it." She wouldn't give Ethan the satisfaction of knowing she had failed. "Just tell me how to turn around."

"Get the buggy going again, then find a fairly smooth area, and tug the reins in the direction you want the horse to go."

"Can I drive, Pa?"

Aaron tweaked his daughter's nose. "Not this time, sweetheart. It's Sarah's turn."

With her heart pounding, Sarah clucked to the horse again, and it started walking. A mile or so down the road, she spied a fairly flat area, where she guided the horse to the right in a wide arc, then circled back to the left. The buggy creaked as it turned, but they made it around safely and started back toward the house. She blew out a breath of relief.

"Very good. I'd think you were an expert if I didn't know better."

Sarah glanced at Aaron and smiled. His warm brown eyes held a glimmer of humor and an offer of friendship. Maybe she'd been too focused on Ethan to even notice his brother. But that would change, starting now. Everyone kept saying she was good with Corrie and Toby. Maybe that was the answer. Maybe she and Aaron could make a match.

As she drove past the house, she noticed Aunt Emma sitting on the porch, stitching something. She waved. It was good to see her getting up and out of the room more and more.

"Just stop the buggy in front of the barn, and I'll take care of it." Aaron must have seen the panic in her eyes, because he added, "Pull back on the reins with a steady hand. It helps to brace your feet and wrap the reins around your hands."

Sarah followed his instructions, and the buggy came to a halt. The horse tugged at the reins, lifting its head, and she relaxed her hold. "Whew!"

Aaron grinned. "Aw, that wasn't so bad, was it?"

"I suppose not." The driving part, that is. The part where she'd been pawned off was another issue.

"Back already?" Ethan strode out of the barn.

Sarah ducked her head and climbed out of the buggy before either man could offer to help her. "You children want to come with me and see if we can find a snack?"

"Yeah!" they cried in unison. Aaron lifted Toby out of the buggy and swung him around in a circle before setting him on the ground.

Corrie bounced up and down, clapping her hands. "Me too!"

The girl squealed with delight as he spun her around, her braids flying out behind her. Sarah grinned at the sight, then glanced up and saw Ethan watching her. The smile on her face dimmed, and she looked down.

Aaron set Corrie on the ground, and she skipped over to Sarah, Toby running after her. Sarah took Corrie's hand and walked the children back to the house, her head held high. She wished things could be different, but they never would.

Aaron spun around to face Ethan. "Why did you do that?"

Ethan shrugged. "I don't know. I thought you might like to spend some time with Sarah, and when I saw the opportunity, I grabbed it."

"Well, don't do that again." Aaron rubbed a hand across his jaw. "I can't tell you how awkward that felt. I didn't have a clue as to what was going on. Did you two have an argument or something?"

"No. I'm just trying to help get the two of you together."

Aaron straightened and began unharnessing the horse. "I told you before that I don't need your help finding a wife. I'm capable of doing that on my own."

"I know. Sorry."

"Does this have anything to do with what we talked about before?"

Ethan kicked at a dirt clod. "If you're going to marry another city woman, she needs to learn the ways of ranch life beforehand."

Aaron closed his eyes and rubbed his forehead with his fingertips. "Stop trying to play matchmaker."

Pacing away, Ethan tried to put his feelings into words. "I don't think you understand that you only have a short time to woo Sarah. Sooner or later, one of the other men around here will snag her attention, or she'll get a letter and go back to Chicago—forever. Then it will be too late."

Aaron worked his mouth, as if preparing to say something, but merely nodded. "I see what you mean. Sarah is nice and pretty, and I like her. A man could do a lot worse."

"Good. I'm glad you're seeing the light."

He led the horse to a stall. "Just don't try to 'help' too much. Like I said, I know how to court a woman."

Ethan gave his brother a curt nod and then strode out of the barn. Had his brother meant that he knew how to woo a woman because he'd done it before, or did it have something to do with his being the oldest in the family? He wished he knew.

In the house, he crept to the kitchen door, hoping Ma had left a plate of gingerbread for an evening snack. Corrie and Toby both sat at the table, munching on some kind of cookie he hadn't seen before. He stepped into the room. "What are those?"

"Mmmumbles." Toby glanced up with sparkling eyes and sugar stuck to the sides of his mouth.

"Not mumbles, jumbles." Corrie rolled her eyes and shook her head.

Ethan pulled out a chair and helped himself to several of the golden cookies. Before tasting, he sniffed. Cinnamon? He bit into the cookie, the delicious sensation of sugar and spice exploding across his tongue. "Mmm, these are good. Why hasn't your grandma made them before?"

"Because Sarah made them, not Grandma." Corrie's voice held a tone that said, "Don't you know anything?"

"Cora Elizabeth Harper, that's no way to speak to your elders." Ma marched into the kitchen, from the direction of Sarah's room. Had they been talking?

"Sorry, Grandma."

Ma glanced at Ethan with narrowed eyes, then looked back at the children. "That's enough cookies, you two. Time for bed."

"Aww," they said in unison.

"No 'awws.'"

Both children slid from their chairs and then hugged their grandma and Ethan. At the doorway, Corrie paused. "When's Pa comin' in?"

Ethan swallowed a bite of cookie. "He's grooming a horse and should be in any minute."

Corrie nodded, then disappeared through the doorway.

Ethan reached for another cookie and held it up. "These are delicious."

Ma took hold of the top of a chair. "Which of you boys upset Sarah?"

He set the cookie down and sighed. "Probably me."

Ma pulled out the chair and dropped into it with a heavy sigh. "What did you do?"

"I don't know."

"Explain what happened." She reached for a cookie, took a bite, and closed her eyes as she savored it.

"I took her driving—to teach her, as you said." He went on and explained how he'd let Aaron take over when they'd stumbled across him and Toby.

Ma shook her head. "Did it ever occur to you that Sarah might rather be with you than Aaron?"

"Me?"

"You're the one who can't keep his eyes off of her. I thought at first, maybe Sarah would be a good fit for Aaron, but I've changed my mind."

All thoughts of cookies fled. He jumped up and started pacing the room. "Sarah can't like me. I just told Aaron he could have her."

Ma sighed. "Sarah's not a prize in a contest. She has feelings, and those feelings are rather fragile right now, with all that's happened. I taught you boys to be sensitive to women, and that's what I expect."

Wasn't he being sensitive in letting Aaron take over the driving lesson, when he would have liked nothing more than to slip his arm around Sarah and tug her to his side? If Corrie hadn't asked for a ride, he just might have. Sarah had been so brave, in spite of being so vulnerable. He hadn't meant to upset her, and it bothered him that he had. Too bad women didn't come with a set of instructions.

Chapter Twenty

It was a shame men didn't come with an instruction manual. Sarah shook her head as she pulled a crisp, clean sheet off the line. She folded it and laid it in the laundry basket. A distant hammering pulled her attention to the cemetery, where Aaron was repairing the fence that the cow had nearly demolished in its pursuit of her. He'd carried the laundry basket outside for her, given her a shy smile and a tip of his hat, and then headed up the hill with his hammer.

He had been friendlier to her of late—smiling more, pulling out her seat at mealtime—and Josh and Ethan couldn't talk about him enough. "Aaron's so good at this"; "Aaron's smart, even though he doesn't talk much"; "Aaron's a wonderful father." It was as if they were on a campaign to make her believe their eldest brother was the most capable man around. And yet, when Aaron paid attention to her, Ethan was usually frowning. He didn't want her, but it seemed he didn't want Aaron to have her, either. It was all so confusing.

She carried the heavy basket back to the house. The stage would be coming through today, hopefully with a letter from Bob Stone or Abigail—and hopefully with welcome news. As she came around the corner of the house, she noticed a buggy and a saddled horse stopped in front. Karen must have some more visitors. Sarah paused, hoping it wasn't another suitor. The high-pitched laughter of women drew her to the door.

"There's Sarah now." Karen hurried outside and relieved her of the basket. "Come on in and meet some of my closest friends."

Sarah leaned toward her and whispered, "'Closest' as in 'best friends' or 'nearest'?"

"Both." Karen set the basket down on the bench where the men usually sat to remove their muddy boots, then took her arm and all but dragged her to the parlor.

Two women—who must have been mother and daughter, given their close resemblance—sat on the settee, both wearing rose-colored calico dresses. Aunt Emma, looking quite perky, was seated across from them, and a tall man stood in the corner, holding his hat. He nodded at her and smiled, his blue-green eyes dancing. Sarah's stomach started swirling. Not another one.

"These are the Middletons," Karen said, gesturing to the group, "Louise, and her children, Stella and Jim. Their farm is to the north of ours."

The women smiled and nodded. Jim stepped forward, twisting his hat, and pinned her with a smoldering stare. "A pleasure to meet you, Miss Marshall."

"Nice to meet you, too." Panicking, Sarah turned to Karen. "Why don't you sit down and visit with your friends while I fix some tea and apple bread?"

"I've already got the water heating. Sit down with Emma and get to know them a little. I'll be right back."

For someone who seemed determined to promote her sons in hopes that one of them might catch her eye, Karen sure seemed eager for Sarah to meet other men. She swallowed hard and sat in the rocker near the fireplace and Aunt Emma—the furthest seat from Jim Middleton. She set the chair to rocking, until Emma reached across and stopped her.

"Mrs. Middleton and her husband own a large farm. They trade vegetables with the Harpers in exchange for beef. Isn't that innovative?" Emma smiled.

Sarah nodded. The Harpers' garden was large but not nearly big enough to grow enough vegetables to feed a family their size, as well as the stage passengers who came through. "That sounds like a smart partnership, beneficial to both sides."

Mrs. Middleton nodded. "We've all been quite happy with it. I just wish we lived closer to one another. A woman gets lonely out here."

An awkward silence stretched across the room. Sarah glanced at Stella Middleton, a pretty, green-eyed woman with light brown hair, and was disappointed to see her fidgeting. Sarah hadn't talked to a woman her age in weeks, and this one looked as if this was the last place she wanted to be.

Mrs. Middleton cleared her throat. "Karen said that you two are staying here for an extended visit. Are you family? Close friends?"

Sarah glanced at her aunt, unsure just how much to reveal.

"We've stumbled upon hard times," Emma said. "We had just started traveling the Santa Fe Trail when our wagon broke down. My husband, God rest his soul, rode back for help and was later found dead."

Though both women gasped, Mr. Middleton leaned forward, as if glad to finally hear something of interest.

"It's true. No one knows exactly what happened to Harvey, but we suspect his heart gave out. We're staying here until we can return to Chicago or make other arrangements."

"I'm so sorry for your loss." Mrs. Middleton nudged her daughter, who parroted her words. "My oldest son, Phillip, was killed by Quantrill—or Charles Hart, as that traitorous Bushwhacker was known here in Kansas."

"Ma." Jim pushed away from the wall and gave his mother a stern look.

She waved a hand dismissively. "I'm all right. These women have suffered a recent loss. They understand. Phillip was such a charming boy. But when the Bushwhackers—those blood-craving Missouri warriors—attacked Lawrence, Kansas, Phillip left in the night to join the Jayhawkers. We got a few letters but never saw him again."

"I'm so sorry," Emma said. "It must be terrible losing a boy in the prime of his life like that."

Mrs. Middleton nodded and wiped a tear with her fingertip. Stella rolled her eyes, as if she'd heard the story a thousand times. Sarah knew a little about the vicious battle that had been fought along the Kansas-Missouri border in the days surrounding the war. Kansas was an abolitionist state, while Missouri had fought to keep slavery, and a bloody fight had erupted, resulting in the deaths of many innocent people. She shuddered, glad those days were over.

Karen bustled into the room carrying a large tray, which she set the side table. Sarah rose to help her, but Karen shook her head and motioned for her to sit. "I can't tell you how delighted I am to have so many women in the house." She glanced to her right and smiled. "And another man."

Jim stepped forward, hat still in hand. "If you'll excuse me, Mrs. Harper, I'll go visit the menfolk."

"Of course, but wouldn't you like some tea first?"

He glanced at the tiny cup she held out to him and shook his head. "No thank you, ma'am."

"Are you certain you don't want to stay and get to know Karen's guests better?" Mrs. Middleton indiscreetly tilted her head toward Sarah.

Sarah felt like one of the Harpers' mares being surveyed by a potential buyer. If only she could crawl up the chimney and disappear. She lowered her head, knowing her cheeks must be ruby red.

"Maybe we can talk later, Miss Marshall." Jim smiled and set his hat on his head, then turned to Emma and tipped it. "A pleasure to meet you, too, Mrs. Stone. Please excuse me."

After he'd gone, Mrs. Middleton sighed. "That boy has such good manners."

Stella straightened her posture. "Mama, I'd like to go out and say hello to the Harper men, too."

"Let's have our tea and visit first. The men are probably busy, anyway."

Stella flopped back, obviously unhappy. Why did she want to see the men? Did she have designs on one of them?

Sarah didn't welcome the envy building within her. Why should she be jealous? Yes, Stella Middleton lived close enough to Harpers' Stage Stop to visit often, but what did that matter? Whether she wanted to or not, Sarah had no claim on any of the men.

As Karen handed her a teacup and a slice of apple bread, she raised an eyebrow, as if she'd read her mind.

With a shaky hand, Sarah lifted the cup to her mouth and took a sip. "Mmm, just how I like it."

Karen smiled. "I know." She served the other women and then took a seat.

Mrs. Middleton took a tiny bite of the apple bread. "This is delicious. I must get your recipe."

"I didn't make it." Karen nodded toward Sarah. "Sarah did."

"Well, I must say, it's scrumptious. I'm glad to know she's a good cook."

Sarah's head snapped in Mrs. Middleton's direction. Why should it matter to her if she could cook?

"Oh, she's a wonderful cook, and a fine seamstress, too," Aunt Emma offered.

Stella crossed her arms and rolled her eyes.

Instead of feeling irritated this time, Sarah bit back a smile. She finished off her apple bread, gulped down the last of her tea, then stood and crossed the room. "Thank you, Karen." She set the saucer on the tray. "I was thinking maybe Stella and I could go for a walk while you caught up with your friend."

"That's fine, dear. I suppose you young women don't care to hear the latest news."

"Auntie, are you all right, or do you need to lie down?"

"I'm perfectly fine and would enjoy getting to know Mrs. Middleton more."

Sarah nodded and glanced at Stella, who bounced to her feet and followed her from the room.

Once outside, Stella heaved a loud sigh. "Don't they make you feel like a cow at an auction?" She fanned her face. "Oh, my! She can cook. Blessed be, she can sew. What nice hips she has, perfect for childbearing. And would you look at those teeth!"

A giggle welled up within Sarah that she couldn't hold back. "Exactly. At least they didn't make me stand up and spin around."

Stella grabbed her arm. "Mama did that to me once when we visited a family in town who had a son looking to marry. I was mortified."

"I can imagine."

"How do you bear living here when Mrs. Harper has three sons of marrying age?"

Sarah shrugged. "It's not too hard, most of the time. Though things can get awkward on occasion."

"I envy you."

"What?" Sarah spun to face Stella. "Why?"

"*Why?* Are you daft? The Harper brothers are some of the most handsome men in three counties, not to mention their fine, upstanding character. What's not to like about them? I'd give the silk faille gown that Papa brought me from New York if I could trade places with you. Which brother have you set your cap for?"

Sarah didn't know how to respond. She could hardly mention that her heart pinged whenever Ethan came near or caught her gaze. "I…uh…we plan to return to Chicago."

"Well, all the marriageable women in these parts will be glad to hear that." She halted. "Oh, dear. That didn't come out right. I meant, with you being so pretty and refined, and a good cook to boot, it just seems certain one of the Harper men will want to marry you."

Sarah ducked her head, trying to hide the blush creeping into her cheeks. Surely, Stella was mistaken. No man had ever said she was pretty. Well, Walt may have, a time or two, but that had been when he was trying to get her to marry him. Ethan sure didn't think that.

⁓

"Jim Middleton's visit proves my point," Josh said as they finished the milking. "Word is getting out about Sarah."

Ethan nodded, although, with his head parked in the cow's side, his brothers couldn't see him. "That's right. You'd better get moving, Aaron. No letters came on today's stage, but they will sooner or later. And Jasper hasn't given up." He sat back and peeked around Josh. "Did you know he brought her a bag of lemon drops?"

Aaron scowled. "All right. Fine. I'll try to spend more time with her. It's just hard because I need to be with the children in the evenings and whenever I'm close by."

Ethan rested his cheek against the cow's warm hide and continued to squirt milk into the pail. Jim must have asked a hundred questions about Sarah, not that it was any of his business. He'd rather see Sarah end up with one of the Woodward brothers than Middleton, who was well-known to be a womanizer in Windmill. She deserved better. She deserved someone like Aaron. Or like him.

He shook that thought out of his mind. She couldn't be his.

But his mind and body still reacted every time she smiled at him or looked at him with the haunted expression that sometimes overcame her. He knew she was worried about her future, and he wished that he could offer her some security. But what did he have? He was twenty-one and still lived with his parents. Granted, his brothers were both older and did the same, but at least Aaron had a house on the property, even if he chose not to live in it right now.

If Aaron and Sarah married, it would be much easier on Ethan if they moved out to the small house. He couldn't stand the thought of seeing her blue eyes alight with love for his brother.

The cow bellowed an angry moo and nearly stomped on his foot. Ethan forced himself to relax. How could one tiny blonde woman send a man into such turmoil?

C'mon, Lord. I need some help. I've agreed to let Aaron pursue Sarah. He needs a wife and a mother for his children. Help me to stop thinking about her all the time. To stop being infatuated with her.

⟿

Sarah sat on the porch and watched Corrie and Toby run around the yard trying to trap fireflies in tin cups. Their antics made her laugh, and after a tiring day with the tension caused by the Middletons' visit, she needed something to lift her spirits. There had been little doubt that Jim Middleton was interested in her, but she couldn't understand why. She had neither money nor property, and the man didn't even know her.

"I got one!" Corrie placed her hand over the opening of her cup.

"Let me see!" Toby tugged her hand away. "I see it! Uh-oh, it got away."

"Toby!" She shoved his shoulder, and he skipped aside to keep from falling.

"Hey!"

"That's enough. Both of you." Aaron strode through the twilight, carrying a bucket of milk. "Time for bed."

Ethan followed, his appearance sending Sarah's heart into a tizzy. "If you'll take my bucket to the icehouse, I'll put these two yahoos to bed." His gaze latched on to Sarah's. "Nice evening, isn't it?"

She nodded, afraid that if she voiced her agreement, it would come out hoarse. She wondered why Ethan had offered to put the children to bed when Karen or Aaron usually did that task.

"Just set the bucket on the porch, and I'll get it after I put mine away." Josh took Aaron's pail and headed for the icehouse.

Ethan set his bucket down, then dashed out into the yard after Corrie and Toby, growling like a bear. Both children squealed and instantly forgot all about the fireflies.

"Save me, Pa!" Corrie ran toward Aaron, but, just before she reached him, Ethan grabbed her from behind and tossed her up into the air. A squeal filled the night, startling the crickets to silence.

Toby latched on to his father's leg, and Aaron hobbled around the yard, calling his son. "Toby? Has anyone seen Toby?"

The boy's delighted giggles warmed a cold spot in Sarah's heart.

"Down here, Pa. I'm riding on your leg."

"Ah, there you are." He peeled the boy off and tossed him up.

Sarah didn't understand how either child could sleep after such exertion. Evenings in the Stone house had always been a somber time, unless company had been present. Even during the day, she'd never played like these children did with their father and uncles. She hated to admit it, but she was jealous of Aaron's children—of the freedom they had to be young and to run and play. Of the love they enjoyed from their large family.

Aaron sat down on the porch step and gave each child a hug. "Go on in with your uncle Ethan, and I'll be in to check on you in a little while."

Toby followed Ethan inside, but Corrie danced over to Sarah and gave her a hug. "'Night."

"Good night, sweetie."

Josh returned for the final bucket and carried it to the icehouse, leaving Sarah alone on the porch with Aaron. She rose to go inside, but he moved to block the door.

He yanked his hat off, twisting the brim with his long fingers. "I was…uh…wondering, would you care to…uh…take a walk? It's a nice night."

A walk? That was the last thing she'd expected him to say. "Um…I guess."

He blew out a heavy breath, then smiled. "Good. C'mon, then."

At the steps, he held out his arm, and Sarah's heart all but stopped. Why was he doing this? She owed him and his family, so she forced her hand to lightly grasp his arm and then proceeded down the steps, stiff as a broom handle.

With his other hand, Aaron grabbed the last milk pail and headed toward the icehouse, with her in tow. Josh came out the door of the small stone building and nearly collided with them.

"Whoa! Good thing I wasn't wearing my gun, or you'd have another belly button, brother."

Sarah couldn't help giggling at Josh's silly comment, and the act helped her to relax a smidgeon.

Josh, barely visible in the fading light, tipped his hat. "Have a nice walk."

With the children inside, the crickets resumed their song. They strolled down the path toward the road leading to Windmill and then turned in that direction. The night was peaceful, quiet. So unlike the noisy streets of Chicago. Nature came alive on the prairie.

To her right, something flapped loudly—and far too close. Sarah squealed and jumped against Aaron's side. He stiffened the arm she clung to, and his other hand reached out to steady her. "What in the world was that?"

"A bat. They come out this time of night to eat insects. They're strange-looking but harmless."

"Are you certain?" She felt foolish, practically hanging on him as she was, but it seemed all the critters in Kansas had it in for her.

"I'm sure." He patted her arm, then lowered his hand, allowing her to continue clinging to his other arm.

"Things are so different here."

"Don't you have critters in Chicago?"

"Yes, we have some pretty birds—lots of pigeons—and cats and dogs. But nothing like bats or cows—at least, none that I know of. And there are many varieties of waterfowl around the lake." Talk of home set her at ease. "Of course, we have horrible creatures, like rats." She shuddered. "I hate those things, especially when they die inside the walls of the house. The stench lasts for weeks."

"That would be bad. Can't say that's ever happened here. We bury things fast, especially in the hotter months."

She thought of how fast her uncle had been buried—even before she and Aunt Emma had returned.

"It may seem crude to some to bury a family member so soon after death, but it's one way to control the spread of sickness."

Sarah decided to switch to a less morbid topic of conversation. "Do you like living here?"

"Yeah, for the most part. Summers can be hot and winters cold, but the rest of the year is usually nice. There's plenty of land out here for a man, and you aren't crawling over your neighbors."

"So, you think you'll stay here, even if the train comes through?"

"Someone told you about that, huh? I'd like to stay here if we can. Might be hard without the stage contract, but I reckon we'll manage somehow. God always takes care of His people, and He'll provide for us."

All of the Harpers seemed confident God would meet their needs. How had they come by such a stalwart faith? That was just another thing she envied.

Aaron stopped, released her arm, and removed his hat. "You're really good with my kids. Corrie is real excited about learning to read."

She smiled. "They're good children. Very pleasant to be with."

"How do you know so much about kids?"

"I volunteered at a children's home for orphans."

"Well, that explains it." He was silent for a long while. Soon he stopped walking and rubbed the back of his neck. "This is going to sound rather sudden, but I want you to know I've thought a lot about this. It's not as hasty as it sounds."

Sarah nodded but had no idea what he was referring to.

He cleared his throat and gazed down at her, the moonlight illuminating the lower part of his face, his hat hiding the rest. "Would you...uh...maybe...uh...consider marrying me?"

Chapter Twenty-one

Stupefied. That was the only word that described how Sarah felt at the moment. Her knees wobbled, and a multitude of thoughts bounced around in her mind like passengers in a carriage traveling a rocky road. There was a part of her that wanted to grasp at this chance to stay at the Harpers' and not go back to Chicago, but another part of her wasn't ready to let go of that desire just yet. Marrying Aaron would make her the mother of his children. Was she ready to become a wife *and* a mother at the same time? Marrying Aaron would also eliminate any hope of a life with Ethan, who stirred her heart and made her wish for something she'd never had.

Aaron shuffled his feet. He crossed his arms, then dropped them to his side, and then crossed them again. "I…uh…hope you're not completely repulsed by the idea."

She touched his arm. "No, not at all. In fact, I'm honored that you would ask. It's just that your proposal was so unexpected, and there are a number of things to consider, mainly my aunt."

"She would always be welcome here, I can assure you that. Our family would become hers, too. Ma treasures her companionship."

"That's very kind of you, and I know that would be the case."

"But?" He rubbed the back of his neck and heaved a sigh. "Maybe I'm not being fair to you. Obviously, this wouldn't be a love match but more of a business arrangement."

She knew that to be the truth, but hearing the words voiced out loud still stung.

221

"I'm not looking to marry for love, but I like you, and my family likes you. My children need a ma, and you're good to them. From what I understand, you and your aunt need a place to live. It seems like a workable arrangement to me."

She remained silent, unsure what to say. She'd had half a dozen proposals from men who didn't love her, and she ought to be used to hearing them by now, but this one had taken her completely by surprise.

"I'm sure you've seen the smaller house, past the barn a ways...."

Sarah nodded. She had seen the charming cottage and longed to peek inside but hadn't yet worked up her nerve to ask.

"That's where Della and I lived, before she...uh...." He kicked a rock, sending it skittering into the grass beside the road. A bird took wing and flew away. A whiff of Aaron's scent—far better than yesterday, when he and his brothers had been branding cattle—drifted her way. He must have bathed this evening, because the faint fragrance of Karen's soap still lingered on him, sweet yet masculine.

He was a man who would be easy to look at across the breakfast table every morning. She tried to imagine his hair scruffy from the previous night's sleep and his jaw shaded with whiskers when he first got up. All of the Harper men practiced their morning ablutions with diligence, so she had seen only the hint of a shade of whiskers, and that in the evenings. With his quiet manner and agreeable nature, Aaron was a man she was sure she could get along with. But should she marry out of desperation? Would it be fair to him? To her?

"You don't have to answer now. Take a few days to think about it."

"I'd like that."

"All right." He blew out another sigh, as if he'd just unloaded a heavy burden. "I would appreciate it if you'd keep this to yourself, though. I don't want my family knowing until you decide what you want to do."

"I'd like to tell my aunt, if you don't mind, since it affects her, too."

He nodded and cleared his throat. "I want you to know...if you...uh...want children of your own, I'd oblige you."

Sarah inhaled a sharp breath through her nose, forcing herself not to gasp. She'd never spoken of something so personal with a man, and she didn't want to think about it, either, but she supposed she had to. What if *he* wanted other children? "Um...that's good to know."

Her response seemed indifferent, she knew, but she'd been unprepared for his offer. She was certainly thankful for the darkness of night, obscuring the flaming red color her cheeks must definitely be. They were so warm, she wondered if he couldn't feel the heat radiating from them.

"I reckon we should head back, so I can kiss the children good night before they fall asleep."

"All right."

He held out his elbow again, and she took it, marveling at how much had changed since she'd stepped off the porch with him only minutes ago. Should she marry him? Did she really have a choice?

She remembered Stella's comment about how the marriageable women in the area would be happy to wed any one of the fine, upstanding Harper brothers. So would she, but she had a different brother in mind. If only Ethan had proposed to her. But he hadn't. And she didn't have the luxury of waiting much longer to make a decision regarding their circumstances. She was responsible for her aunt now, and marrying Aaron was the best offer she'd had. Both Emma and she could have a good life here. Not the one she'd always envisioned, in Chicago, but a satisfying one.

Was this God's provision for her and Aunt Emma? Since she'd arrived in Kansas, several people had told her that God would provide. Maybe He had.

But she wasn't ready to say yes to Aaron just yet.

⌒

"Aaron asked me to marry him."

Seated on the edge of her bed, Aunt Emma held her hairbrush held in midair, her eyes as wide as Sarah had ever seen them. "He did? When?"

"Last night."

"And what did you tell him?"

"I thanked him and asked for some time to think about it."

"Maybe this is the answer to our prayers. Maybe this is why God brought us here—for you to marry Aaron and mother those sweet children."

Sarah picked a piece of lint off of the navy skirt Karen had given her. "I've thought of that. I just hate to make a decision when I haven't heard from Abigail yet. Maybe her family would take us in."

Emma stared at her lap and fingered her hairbrush for a moment, then looked up. "I haven't said anything, but, even if they offered, I don't think I'd feel comfortable accepting such an invitation. I don't even know Abigail's family."

Sarah had been so desperate to find them a place, she hadn't considered that her aunt might not want to live with one of her friends. The more she thought about it, she didn't think she'd like being beholden to Abigail and her family, either. Abigail was a good enough friend, but she had a way of expecting some kind of payment for every favor she granted. Sarah shook her head. "I don't know what to do. I like Aaron, but is that enough to build a marriage on?"

Her aunt rose and came to sit beside her on her bed. She wrapped an arm around Sarah's shoulders. "I've been praying more and more. Praying about our situation. About you. And I keep feeling that God is going to do something wonderful for us."

"But *how* do you know? What if He doesn't?"

"Then we'll be no worse off than we are now, will we?"

Sarah smiled and laid her head on her aunt's shoulder. "How did you get to be so wise?"

"Age and experience, dear." Emma squeezed her arm. "Now, we need to hurry so we don't miss Sunday service again."

"If you'll turn around, I'll braid your hair for you." She scooped up her aunt's thick tresses and separated them into three sections. "There's not a speck of gray back here."

Emma's shoulders bounced in laughter. "Was that a back-handed compliment?"

"Oh, I'm sorry. I don't suppose that sounded very nice."

"It's all right, I'm just teasing. So, how long will you keep Mr. Harper waiting?"

She crossed one long section of hair over the middle one. "I don't know. Until I decide, I guess."

"He seems a kind man, and he's very patient with his children. And he treats his mother with respect—that's always important. A man who treats his mother well will usually treat his wife the same."

Emma could have been talking about any of the Harper brothers. Sarah couldn't help wishing again that Ethan had been the one to ask for her hand in marriage. She could have joyfully agreed without hesitation. She blew out a sigh. "There, you're ready."

A few minutes later, she and her aunt walked through the house and out to the yard. The family was already gathered under the tall oak, the only tree nearby, except for the one at the cemetery. Several men were heading that way from the bunkhouse, including Fred, who had fully recovered from the gunshot wound he'd sustained while trying to retrieve their belongings. Sarah was happy to see him up and about.

Someone had brought several chairs from the kitchen, and Karen, Mr. Harper, and the children were seated, leaving two chairs for her and Emma. The three brothers stood shoulder to shoulder. When she glanced at Aaron, he tipped his hat. Her gaze slid to Ethan, who did the same, only he held her gaze. Her cheeks heated, and she turned and took her seat, glad to put them out of sight.

She expected Nick Harper to lead the service, but Aaron was the first to head to the front. He opened his Bible and began reading one of the Psalms. Sarah couldn't help but study him, since everyone else was looking at him. He'd removed his hat, and his dark brown hair had been slicked back; it glistened in the morning sunlight. There was no doubt he was a handsome man, one any woman would be proud to have for a husband. When he finished his reading, he looked up, right at her. She returned his ever-so-brief smile, then studied her lap, embarrassed half to death when she remembered his talk about having children.

Josh strode forward next. "Please join me in singing 'What a Friend We Have in Jesus.'"

As he began signing the hymn, one Sarah had never heard before, she was amazed at his beautiful baritone voice. The music at the church in Chicago they had occasionally attended had been far more somber. And what a novel idea that Jesus could be your friend.

"Oh, what needless pain we bear, all because we do not carry, everything to God in prayer," those around her sang. Had she borne needless pain because she had tried to solve her problems on her own? Would God actually help her if she asked Him to?

As Josh started the second verse, Sarah felt certain the song had been penned just for her. "Have we trials and temptations? Is there trouble anywhere? We should never be discouraged—take it to the Lord in prayer."

She had many trials, yes, but not so many temptations. In fact, there was only one that she could think of. She glanced over her shoulder to see if Ethan was singing. He was looking right at her. Sarah snapped her head back to the front, her heart pounding.

Why did he have to look at her like that? If she didn't know better, she'd think he cared. He looked so handsome in his white shirt, so vivid against his deeply tanned skin—and those dark eyes, the color of fresh coffee.

She forced her thoughts back to the hymn, sorry for missing part of it.

Josh continued the lovely song: "Are we weak and heavy laden, cumbered with a load of care? Precious Savior, still our refuge—take it to the Lord in prayer."

Had Josh purposely picked this song because he thought it would encourage her? Or had God's hand guided him? The thought was almost more than she could comprehend.

Josh walked back to his seat, behind her, and an older ranch hand took his place at the front—Chester? No, that was Josh's horse. Charley, maybe? She hadn't spent any time around the Harpers' work hands, so she was unsure of his name, but he had a kind face, and one of the biggest mustaches she'd ever seen. Ever since she'd first seen him, she'd wondered how he managed to eat with those whiskers always getting in the way.

Kind blue eyes locked on her. "We're thankful to have two additions to our group. You ladies enjoy our service this morning. I'm Chet, by the way." He nodded to her and her aunt, then scanned the rest of the group. "I reckon everyone here knows God is a gardener. One of the first things He made was a beautiful garden. But did you know that God likes to work in the dirt? Genesis two, verse seven says, '*And the LORD God formed man of the dust of the ground, and breathed into his nostrils the breath of life; and man became a living soul.*'" Chet bent down and scooped up a handful of soil, then let it sift through his fingers. "Ain't that somethin'? We're made from dirt. No wonder we can't keep you cowpokes clean."

Sarah smiled, and soft chuckles tittered behind her. This sermon was unlike any she'd ever heard before.

Chet continued, "When God sees the dirt—us—He looks for a seed. He looks for something in you that can be fed, watered—something that can bear fruit. Oftentimes, we look at ourselves, and all we see is the dirt. We can't see the small seeds inside us in various stages of growth, but they are there, anyhow. What you need to do is to make your dirt as fertile as possible. Read your Bible. Spend time in prayer. Fellowship with other Christians. Fertilize your dirt, so that, when God plants a seed, you'll be ready. God can use anyone, even an unbeliever, but how much more so a man or woman that loves Him? Don't leave here today without making Jesus Lord of your life—your friend. If anyone wants to pray with me, I'll wait over yonder." Chet ambled off to the side, a short ways from the group.

What a novel idea, having God as a friend. Sarah tried to imagine talking to him as she might Abigail—or a true best friend who actually cared about you and the problems you faced. Truth be told, her aunt was probably her best friend, and they'd grown even closer since her uncle had died.

Ethan walked to the front, and his gaze grazed hers as he pulled a piece of paper from his pocket. "I'd like to read a couple of verses from Isaiah forty-three, then I'll close in prayer. '*Thus saith the LORD that created thee, O Jacob, and he that formed you, O Israel, Fear not: for I have redeemed thee, I have called thee by thy name; thou art mine.*'" He looked up and smiled. "I believe that confirms Chet's message—that God loves us, dirt and all. Now, if you will all bow your heads, we'll close with a word of prayer." He lowered his head and closed his eyes.

Sarah ducked her head, too, but kept watching him. His long, dark lashes fanned his cheeks, and his hair—not lacquered down with pomade, but thick and full—lifted on the slight breeze.

"Dear Lord, thank You for this beautiful day and for our family and friends who are gathered here. I ask that You keep each one of us safe this coming week and that You would allow good seeds to grow in each of us. Thank You for bringing Mrs. Stone and Miss Marshall to stay with us for a time. I pray that You will bless them and work out their situation according to Your will. In Jesus' name, amen."

Tears burned Sarah's eyes. She wanted to be a friend of Jesus. Wanted to grow good seed. But she didn't know how to go about doing that. She stood with the others, then helped her aunt to the porch, so she could enjoy the cool of the morning.

"That was an interesting message, wasn't it?" Aunt Emma sat in a rocker and adjusted her skirt to cover her ankles. "Simple but very thought-provoking."

Karen held hands with her grandchildren as they walked up the steps. "Well, what did you think of our service? It's not too fancy, but we find it an encouragement."

Emma bobbed her head. "That Josh sure can sing, can't he?"

Sarah felt a bit raw and didn't want to talk about the service. "Do you need help in the kitchen?"

"Always. Just let me get changed out of my fancy clothes. They're too tight, and they itch."

Sarah smiled and shook her head. "I suppose I should change, too. I wouldn't want to spill anything on this nice skirt you gave me."

"It looks good. My boys couldn't take their eyes off of you." Karen gave her a satisfied grin.

But what Sarah wanted to know was, why were they looking at her?

⌒

Ethan hadn't been able to take his eyes off Sarah all morning. Her waist-long blonde hair flowed freely in soft waves down her back like ripened wheat rustling on the light breeze. He'd never seen anything like it. Della's hair hadn't been half as long, and she'd rarely worn it down. But Sarah's hair was like the expertly combed mane of a prized palomino he'd once seen at the county fair. Beautiful. Perfect.

His fingers longed to trail down the length of her hair—to test its softness—but he curled his hands into fists. He didn't want to be attracted to Sarah. Aaron had started pursuing her by taking her for a walk last night, and it looked like something might develop. His fists tightened more, until he realized he was clenching them and then forced his fingers to relax. He needed to find out how that walk had gone. He grabbed a kitchen chair in each hand and hurried to catch up to Aaron.

"So, how did it go last night?"

Aaron shot a sideways glance at him, then flicked his eyes to the porch, where Mrs. Stone was sitting. "Not here."

"Where, then?"

"Out front, after the chairs are put up."

In the kitchen, Corrie and Toby sat beneath the table, pretending, as they sometimes did, that it was a playhouse. Corrie held up one hand. "No, Pa, we don't want those back yet."

"Yeah," Toby said. "No chairs." Then he looked at his sister. "How come?"

"They get in the way, silly."

"Cora, don't call your brother names." Aaron set one chair along the wall, then placed the other one beside it.

Ethan did the same, but his gaze was drawn to the stove by the delicious aroma that teased his senses. It smelled as if Ma was making his favorite—chicken and dumplings. His stomach rumbled in anticipation.

"I'm going back outside to talk to your uncle," Aaron told his children, "so stay here till Grandma comes back."

Ethan followed Aaron as he clomped through the house, out the front door, and across the lawn, away from anyone who might overhear them.

Finally, Aaron stopped and turned to face him. "What do you want to know?"

Ethan shrugged. "I'm just curious, what happened with you and Sarah?"

"Nothing. We just talked."

"About what?"

Aaron shook his head. "Nothing in particular. Home. The kids. Chicago."

"And?"

"And what?" Aaron narrowed his eyes, obviously losing his patience. "What did you think was going to happen?"

"I don't know." Ethan looked away. Why was this bothering him so much? He gritted his teeth, but curiosity wouldn't allow him to stay silent. "Did you kiss her?"

Aaron stiffened. "What if I did? It's none of your business, so why all the questions?"

"I just don't want to see you make another mistake."

"Another?" Aaron stepped closer, his gaze narrowed. "Are you saying Della was a mistake?"

Even though Ethan thought that to be the case, he couldn't tell his brother. "We're not talking about Della. But Miss Marshall is a city gal, through and through. Remember what happened with that mama cow. She could have gotten Corrie killed."

"But she didn't. She made sure Corrie was safe, even though she was still in danger. I believe we can trust her, Ethan." He tapped his chest. "I feel it in here."

"I hope you're right." Ethan scowled, then turned and headed toward the cemetery. What did Aaron feel in his chest? That he could trust Sarah? Or did he mean something else? Had he already fallen in love with the beguiling woman?

Ethan opened the cemetery fence and then slammed it shut, making a loud, satisfying bang. He opened it once more and then closed it hard again, to let off some steam before he exploded. Why couldn't he be happy for Aaron? If he ended up with Sarah, then the children would have a mother, and Aaron wouldn't be alone anymore.

But Ethan would.

He walked around the cemetery and down the hill toward the creek, stopping partway to sit in the warm grass among the wildflowers. Soon a bee hovered nearby, then dropped onto a red flower whose name he couldn't remember. Josh would certainly know, but he could enjoy a flower just as well without knowing its name. Three feet away, a bright yellow butterfly flittered from blossom to blossom. The color reminded him of Sarah's hair. Aaron would be a lucky man if they married.

He closed his eyes. The thought of Aaron and Sarah together sent a sharp, hot pain slicing through his gut, like the trail of a bullet. It hurt—bad—and yet, hadn't he stepped aside to make it happen? Even *encouraged* Aaron to stake his claim to her?

Ethan clenched his teeth and blew out a sharp breath. He was a fool.

No, he was sacrificing something he might want in order to make his brother's life better.

And he would stand by his decision, no matter how much it pained him.

He just couldn't let himself think of them kissing. That thought made him want to hit the trail and never return.

Chapter Twenty-two

Sarah set a pot of potatoes on the stove to boil, then moved to the sink to rinse her hands in the basin. She stared out the window, which offered a faraway view of the beginnings of the Santa Fe Trail. How far had the wagon train traveled? Were the travelers still in Kansas? Had they encountered any Indians? She rubbed her arms, in spite of the heat from the stove, and had to admit she was thankful to not still be making that rugged journey.

She'd barely slept last night, her mind occupied with Aaron's unconventional marriage proposal. He'd promised to take her to see the small house this afternoon when the children were resting. She was leaning more and more toward accepting his offer, especially after Walt's harsh rejection and Ethan's obvious disinterest. What other alternative did she have?

Karen set a pot of peas and carrots on the stove. "You care to tell me what all that heavy sighing is about?"

Sarah jerked her head toward her. "What sighing?"

Karen grinned and shook her head. "C'mon. Let's go sit in the parlor. Everything here will be all right for a few minutes."

Her heart pounded so hard, she was certain Karen would hear it as she followed her into the other room. Had she accidently muttered something out loud?

Karen sat on the settee and patted the other side. Sarah joined her, turning so that they were sitting knee to knee. The older woman's face was flushed red from the heat of the stove, and several wisps of her graying auburn hair that had come loose flew around her face in an almost comical manner, but the seriousness of her blue eyes kept Sarah from smiling. Out the nearest window, she could hear Corrie squealing in play.

"Don't get too far from the house," Aunt Emma hollered from the porch.

"Now," Karen said, "tell me what's wrong. Did one of my boys say something that upset you? They're good boys, but they're men, and men don't always think before they speak or react to things."

"You know that I've been worrying about what to do." She looked down and stared at her hands. Hands that had been soft just a few weeks ago but now were red and rough. "I wrote to Walt, the man who asked me a number of times to marry him, but he refused to help us. He said I made my choice that last time I declined his offer."

Karen covered Sarah's hands with one of hers. "I know his refusal must have been a blow, but maybe it was God's way of protecting you from marrying the wrong man."

She hadn't thought of it quite that way.

"I hope you know that you're welcome to stay here indefinitely. Maybe at some point, I could even pay you and your aunt a small wage, to supplement room and board, in exchange for helping me. Since you've come, I've been able to get so much more done, and I've spent more time with the children. They so need the attention."

"I'm glad we've been helpful. I don't know what we would have done, if it weren't for you and your family." Sarah pursed her lips and blew a breath out her nose. The Harpers were good people, but she didn't want to take advantage of them. She admired almost everything about them, especially their deep faith in God. She wanted answers about her spiritual questions as much as she needed to know what to do about Aaron. "That message Chet shared this morning really touched me. I need God's help, but I don't know how to get it."

Karen squeezed her hand, a warm smile on her soft cheeks. "I can't tell you how happy it makes me to hear that. All you have to do is ask God to come into your heart, to forgive you of your sins, and to make you His child. And He will."

"Can I do that now?"

"Of course." Karen ran a hand down Sarah's cheek, like a mother might, making her feel loved and cherished.

"What do I do?"

"Just close your eyes and say what I said."

"Um...." Sarah squeezed her eyes shut. "Jesus, forgive me of my sins, and make me Your child. Please. Help me with the decisions I must make." She sucked in a breath, feeling fresher—cleaner—than she could ever remember. Her eyelids fluttered open. "Anything else?"

"That's it." Karen beamed, her eyes moist. "Welcome to the family of God."

"I think I actually feel different."

Karen nodded. "Some people do right off, and others don't. Now, you need to read that Bible I loaned your aunt, and make sure to pray about the things that are troubling you."

"I see a difference in your faith, compared to those in the church we sometimes attended. Yours seems real."

"I'm glad you're attracted to our faith. We try hard to live according to God's Word and treat others kindly."

"You do. I think part of the reason I distanced myself from God and the church was my parents' death. For years, I blamed Him."

"I did that, too, for a spell. I struggled a lot both times I lost my baby girls, shortly after they were born. You have to grieve a loss, but there comes a time when you have to let go of the pain and trust that God knows best."

Sarah smiled. "I think I understand. I'll read your Bible, if I can get it away from Auntie."

Karen looked at her as if she had something else to say, but then she turned her gaze to the window.

Sarah could hear the pots bubbling in the kitchen. "I should probably stir the vegetables and start the biscuits." She stood.

Karen jumped to her feet and pulled her into a hug. "I want you to know I'd be honored to have you marry one of my sons."

Gasping, Sarah stepped back and stared at her. "Aaron told you?"

"Told me what?"

"Um…I can't say if he didn't."

Karen cupped her cheek again, a warm glint twinkling in her eyes. "That's fine, dear. You don't have to tell me anything before you're ready." She lowered her hand and started to leave, then turned. "I'd be delighted to have you for a daughter-in-law, Sarah, as long as you marry the son that's right for you."

Stunned to silence, Sarah gaped at her as she watched her leave, her dark green dress swaying side to side.

What did she mean? Did she think Aaron was the right son for her?

Or the wrong one?

⌒

"You did *what*?" Ethan couldn't believe what he'd just heard.

"I asked Sarah to marry me."

A familiar panic, like he'd felt when he'd first realized Della was dead, squeezed his heart and cut off his breath. "W-when?"

Aaron frowned. "When did I ask her? Or when are we getting married?"

Ethan fell back against the stall railing and held on. Why was he reacting this way? He'd sorted it out yesterday: he had encouraged his brother to pursue Sarah, and he wasn't going to be upset if he succeeded. So much for that. "What did she say?"

Aaron shrugged and studied his boots. "She didn't seem appalled by the idea, but she wanted some time to think it over."

"Well, she'll probably come around. She doesn't have many other options."

Scowling, Aaron pushed off of the post he'd been leaning against. "You make it sound as if I'm her last resort."

"Sorry. I didn't mean it that way." But how did he mean it? He tightened his grip on the railing. "You're acting awful strange. You're not getting sick, are you?"

Ethan shook his head, but he wasn't altogether sure his brother hadn't hit the nail on the head. The thought of his brother and Sarah together made him nauseous. He took hold of Alamo's halter and backed the horse out of his stall.

"Where you going?"

"Riding."

"Well, don't forget I'm headed into Windmill soon with Ma and the kids. Corrie and Toby need some new shoes. We'll be back tomorrow evening. Sarah will do the cooking."

Ethan nodded and went to retrieve his gear from the tack room. When he'd saddled and bridled his horse, he trotted toward the road. Sarah was sweeping the back porch, and he tipped his hat at her. When she waved back, his heart kicked into a canter. He reined Alamo down the trail and nudged him to a full gallop, reveling in the warm wind whipping at his clothes and the sound of rapid hoofbeats. Maybe if he rode fast enough, he could outrun his attraction to Sarah.

He never wanted to like her. Never wanted to care. And he certainly never wanted to fall in love.

He stiffened and reined Alamo to a trot then a walk. The horse tugged on the reins, wanting to run some more, but Ethan held him back, stunned at the sudden revelation. He loved Sarah Marshall.

Nothing could have shocked him more, unless Della came walking across the wide open prairie.

He loved Sarah.

And his brother planned to marry her.

That sick sensation swirled in his belly again. He had to stop them. But how?

Would Sarah even consider marrying him rather than Aaron, after all that had happened between them?

Aaron was responsible, smart, and honest to the core; Ethan was a joker and an overprotective grouch. But he would do anything for the woman he loved. And he loved Sarah.

He inhaled a cleansing breath through his nose, then exhaled. How could he hope to win Sarah's heart, when he'd been so mean to her at times?

He'd found a precious jewel—and let her slip from his fingers before he'd realized her value.

⁓

Sarah watched as Aaron tied the mare she'd seen him working with to the back of the wagon he was about to drive to Windmill. He'd sent Corrie and Toby to the privy so they'd be ready for the long trip to town. Sarah's stomach swirled like a tornado, and her knees wobbled. If she didn't tell him her answer now, she'd have to wait two more days, till his return from Windmill.

"Yes."

Aaron rechecked the mare's lead rope, then patted her. He glanced at Sarah with eyebrows raised. "Yes, what?"

"Yes, I'll marry you. That is, if you still want me to."

"Oh." His eyes widened, but he didn't look all that elated. Had he hoped she'd turn him down? "Good. I still want to, as long as you're sure."

"I'm sure, but could we wait to tell the others until we know each other a bit better?"

He seemed to contemplate that thought for a moment, and then he nodded. "I don't see how that will hurt anything. At least you can stop worrying about what you'll do."

She nodded, disappointed that he didn't seem more enthusiastic. But what did she expect? This was a business deal, after all. She picked up the picnic basket she'd carried outside. "We've packed plenty of food for your trip."

"Thanks. Is there anything you need from town?"

She thought of a long list of things, but she shook her head. She wouldn't ask him to buy her anything she couldn't afford on her own, at least not yet. Sarah shook her head. "Thank you for asking, though."

Karen and the children met at the wagon at the same time, and they all piled in. "Help yourself to whatever you need for supper," Karen told her, "and take care of Nick and Ethan."

Josh rode out of the barn and reined his horse into step behind the wagon. "I decided to go, too." He tipped his hat at her. "Got word there's a new stack of books at the general store."

Sarah smiled and waved to the group as they pulled out of the yard. Because of the distance, they would stay the night at the boardinghouse and start back after breakfast tomorrow. The place would be lonely without them.

Mr. Harper was out with the ranch hands, spending all day moving the cattle from one pasture to another. Aaron had said that Ethan had ridden off, but she had no idea where he'd gone or when he'd be back. She swallowed hard, thinking of being alone with her aunt on the big farm. The place was too quiet, especially with Aunt Emma resting after the exertion of helping prepare breakfast and pack food for the trip.

As the wagon rounded the corner, Aaron glanced back at her and smiled. She wished she felt less anxious about marrying him, but she supposed all brides were nervous.

She started back to the house, planning to look through some recipe books for something new to cook for supper, when she spied Aaron's house out of the corner of her eye. She glanced around, though she knew no one was there, and pushed her feet into motion. After the short walk, she paced around the small, two-story house, which was painted a pale yellow. When she married Aaron, this would be her home.

She reached for the doorknob, paused, then turned it. The house was unlocked. What would it hurt for her to have a peek around? She pushed the door open and stepped inside. Directly in front of her, a staircase led to the second floor. To her right was a charming kitchen with a black and silver stove, not as large as Karen's but plenty big enough for a small family. A square table was situated in front of the window with yellow gingham curtains, offering a view of the barn and part of the yard and the big house. She could easily see herself baking in the kitchen and helping children with their schoolwork at the table.

In the parlor, there were several pieces of furniture covered with sheets. She lifted the corner of one to find a black horsehair settee with walnut trim legs. Under another sheet were a matching armchair and a rocker. A fireplace with a carved wood mantel was the focal point of the room.

She ventured upstairs next. As expected, there were two bedrooms, both with large windows. It was quite a charming house—one in which she could be comfortable. Maybe down the road, she could talk Aaron into adding a room for Aunt Emma.

Footsteps sounded below, and Sarah sucked in a gasp. Who could that be? Wasn't everyone gone for the day? What if an ill-meaning drifter had noticed everyone leaving and had decided to poke his nose around?

Holding her breath, she tiptoed to the stairway and peered down. Her heart pounded in her ears. She longed to run downstairs but feared encountering the intruder. Glancing around, she spied a door in the bedroom to her right and headed for it, walking as softly as possible. She turned the handle, slipped outside, and found herself on a balcony with no way down. She quietly closed the door and backed up against the house, hopefully out of sight, should the person inside peek through the window. She thought her heart would explode from her chest. *Please, Lord, protect me.*

The vibration of footsteps came her way, and the door opened. The barrel of a gun emerged. Sarah gasped and closed her eyes. She would have screamed, but even if someone heard her, help wouldn't reach her fast enough. Oh, how would Aunt Emma endure if something happened to her?

"Sarah?"

Relief charged through her with the force of a stampede. "Ethan! You scared me half out of my wits."

He holstered his gun and chuckled. "Then, you must not have any wits left, since I already scared the other half out of you down at the garden."

"Oh, you." She gave him a shove and hoped to slip past him, but the solid brute refused to move out of the doorway. She glanced up and saw that all humor had fled his face.

"What are you doing in here?"

She shrugged, knowing she couldn't very well tell him the whole truth. "I was curious to see what this house looked like inside."

"I suppose that's fitting, since you'll soon be living here with my brother," he said, his voice thick with disdain.

Sarah stepped back. "How do you know that?"

"Aaron told me."

She glanced down, upset that Aaron had told Ethan, when she'd asked him to wait to tell his family.

"Is it true? Are you going to marry him?"

She lifted her chin. Why did he seem upset about it? "Yes, I am, and I'm sorry if that bothers you. I'm trying hard to adapt and learn to live on the prairie. You might give me some credit for that, at least."

She pushed against his rock-solid chest, and this time, he moved aside. She hurried to the top of the stairs, then glanced back. His sad expression tore at her heart.

"Do you love him, Sarah?"

Chapter Twenty-three

Ethan held his breath and watched all manner of expressions race across Sarah's pretty face. Aaron deserved to marry a woman who loved him, but if Sarah said she did, it would gut Ethan.

"Why do you want to know?"

"Because he's my brother, and he's been hurt deeply once. I don't want to see that happen again."

Her eyes blinked, as if holding back a flood. "I like him, and I'll be good to him. I'm sure that, in time, I'll come to love him."

A savage hope burst in Ethan's chest, like the first rays of morning sunlight, but it was dashed just as fast. What if Aaron loved her?

"I need to go check on Aunt Emma." She scurried down the steps, her feet making quick taps on the wood.

He secured the door to the balcony and then went after her, his long legs quickly closing the distance between them. "Sarah, wait. I don't want you to marry Aaron."

She halted in the yard and spun around, a mess of skirts and fury. "I've never been good enough for you, have I?" Tears glistened in her eyes and ran down her cheeks. "I'm sorry for going against your counsel with that pink wagon and the horses. You'll never know how sorry. I just wish I could measure up to your standard." She dabbed her red nose with an embroidered handkerchief she'd tugged from her sleeve. "I'm sorry if you don't approve of me marrying your brother."

She turned and fled again.

"Sarah, wait." She'd completely misunderstood him.

"Ethan, let her go."

He turned and saw his pa sitting on his horse, just inside the barn door. "You can't rationalize with a woman when she's that upset." Pa dismounted and walked toward him.

Ethan wasn't sure a man could ever rationalize with a woman, upset or not.

"Wanna tell me what that was all about?"

He shook his head. Aaron had confided in him about his plan to marry Sarah, but Ethan didn't want to be the one to spill the beans. That was Aaron's place.

Pa clapped a hand on Ethan's shoulder. "Son, it's not your job to find a bride for your brother. And even if you did, it wouldn't ease your guilt over Della. Only God can do that, and only God can bring Aaron another wife. You can't force things. You've got to forgive yourself for what happened and move on."

"I'm trying, Pa." The burden had been much lighter ever since Aaron had told him he didn't blame him for Della's death, but it was still there, nagging him.

"Let me pray for you, all right, son?"

Ethan nodded and closed his eyes, grateful he had a godly father.

"Dear Lord, take this burden from Ethan. You know he's not responsible for Della's death, and so does everyone else, except him. He's a good boy who loves a lot, which is why this bothers him so much. Help him to put what happened behind him and move on to what You have for his future. And if that future includes a pretty blonde with blue eyes, I ask that You would make that very clear to him. Amen."

Ethan's eyelids flew open. He stared at his father. "How...how did you know that I care for Sarah?"

With his forefinger, Pa drew a circle in the air around Ethan's face. "It's written right here."

He closed his eyes, thinking of Aaron. Thinking of Sarah. Then he opened them again. "What should I do, Pa?"

"I can't answer that. It's between you and God...and that pretty little lady you upset so much."

"And what about Aaron? I don't want to see him hurt again."

Pa took hold of both of Ethan's shoulders and gave him a gentle shake. "Have some faith in your brother. He's tougher than he looks. And he's a man of God. He'll realize that he's making a mistake, if that's the case."

Ethan nodded. "You're a wise man, Pa."

His father grinned, brown eyes dancing. "Don't forget that next time we have a disagreement." He snagged his horse's reins and tossed them at Ethan. "Here, help out your ol' man and groom his horse."

"Yes, sir." Ethan led the horse into its stall, then removed the saddle and took it to the tack room. Pa was right. He needed to forgive himself once and for all for Della's death, and he had to accept the fact that it wasn't his responsibility to find Aaron another wife. God didn't want him to be beaten down with guilt forever. And he needed to seek God about a future with Sarah—before he lost her altogether. Right there, in the warm tack room, he dropped to his knees. "Help me, Lord."

~

Sarah sat at the table, futilely trying to avoid Ethan's frequent glances. Nick droned on and on about ranching on the prairie, while Aunt Emma listened with rapt attention. The few bites of beans and cornbread Sarah had eaten felt like rocks in her stomach.

Could she marry Aaron when Ethan seemed so opposed to it? Yes, they could eat their meals at the little house, so she wouldn't be confronted continually by Ethan's scowl, but there were bound to be many family meals, and those would be horribly awkward if Ethan never gave his blessing to the marriage. But what other choice did she have?

She excused herself from the table and stood. The men hopped to their feet as she crossed the room and set her plate on the counter. She grabbed the bucket to ladle some hot water out of the stove's reservoir, but Ethan hurried to her side.

"Here, let me do that."

She handed him the bucket, avoiding his gaze. "Thank you." She removed the butter dish and salt bowl from the table and carried them to the counter, setting them down at the same time Ethan put down the filled bucket.

"What else do you need help with?"

"Nothing, but thank you." She forced herself not to look up at him. Doing so, with him so close, would surely make her dizzy, considering how conflicted she felt.

"I want you to hurry and get done. There's somewhere I want to take you."

"What?" Her gaze shot up to meet his, in spite of her efforts at avoidance. "Where?"

The intensity of his beautiful eyes captured her.

"You need to learn to shoot," Nick said.

"Shoot?" she said in unison with Emma.

"Yep." Ethan nodded. "Every woman that lives in these parts needs to be able to defend herself. What if that had been a robber in the house instead of me this morning?"

She scoffed. "It hardly mattered that I couldn't shoot, since I wasn't armed."

Ethan leaned in closer. "Wash the dishes, and then we're going to shoot some targets."

"I can't leave Aunt Emma alone."

A chair squeaked across the floor as Nick slid back from the table. "I'll stay with her. You won't be gone all that long."

Sarah blew out a breath. "Don't I have a say in the matter?"

Both Nick and Ethan shook their heads.

"It was Ma's idea, anyway." Ethan grinned, as if that were the clincher.

An hour later, Sarah sat in the buggy with Ethan Harper—the last person on earth she wanted to be with—riding down the road to who knows where. Would Aaron be upset with her for spending time alone with his brother? Most men who were promised to be married probably would.

Even though she wished Aaron would mind, she felt certain he wouldn't. Theirs wasn't a love match, after all.

She sat stiffly in the wagon, trying hard to not bounce against Ethan's shoulder whenever they hit a rut in the road. They were traveling down the Santa Fe Trail in the same direction she'd gone before. Who could have foreseen how much her life would change in a few short weeks?

And who could have dreamed she would fall in love with the man who'd left her sitting in the mud? She peeked sideways at him. He sat with his elbows on his knees, reins held loosely in his hands—a man confident with himself. He had a handsome profile, with a straight nose that was just the right size, a nice forehead, and a square jaw. His thick hair was beautiful, and she longed to touch it again. She blew out a shaky breath. She loved every inch of his face.

Maybe she should just tell him that she was in love with him. But all her life she'd bottled up her emotions and opinions. Uncle Harvey certainly had never wanted to hear them, and she was afraid of upsetting her aunt. So, she'd learned to keep quiet. And she would remain quiet now.

Ethan drove off the road and took a barely traveled path toward the creek. Up ahead was a line of trees—and trees on the prairie generally meant water. Soon, he pulled back on the reins, bringing the horse to a halt. He hopped down, then turned to help her. In the melancholy mood she was in, she didn't dare let him touch her. She ignored his inviting hands and climbed down her side of the buggy.

He didn't seem bothered in the least that she'd snubbed his gentlemanly offer of aid. He grabbed a crate out of the buggy's boot, carried it across the field, and then dumped out its contents. Sarah tried to keep her back to him, but the clatter stirred her curiosity. She peeked across the buggy. He'd flipped the crate on its side and was now setting up empty cans on top.

She walked a few feet away and plucked a pretty yellow flower with seven petals. She couldn't remember if she'd seen it in Josh's book or not, but it was lovely. Too small for a bouquet, though.

"I'm ready, Sarah. C'mon."

Well, she wasn't. She feared moving closer to him, lest he feel her trembling. Afraid to look him in the eye, lest he see her love for him. When she didn't move, he came for her, his boots crunching in the tall grass.

"Are you afraid? Is that what's wrong?"

Her heart took off running, just like she knew it would. What a ninny she was, loving a man who didn't even like her.

He reached out and took her hand, his warm and calloused palm stealing every whisper of breath from her lungs. She was too weak to fight back, so she allowed him to tow her along. He stopped her a short ways from the crate and turned her to face it. She might as well do as he wanted and get this over with as quickly as possible.

He took her shoulders and gave them a gentle squeeze. "Relax, Sarah."

Impossible, with him so close and touching her. He explained to her about gun safety and how she should never point a gun at a person unless she intended to shoot him. He also showed her how to load the pistol, but her brain was frozen, and if he'd asked her to repeat the process, she couldn't have done it. What was wrong with her?

She needed to get a different image in her mind—the picture of that cocky cowboy who'd left her muddied and embarrassed. That would keep her focused.

"Are you ready to try shooting?"

"I suppose."

He chuckled. "You sound so enthusiastic."

"This wasn't exactly my idea, you know."

He handed her the pistol, and she realized that she needed to concentrate on what she was doing so that neither of them would get hurt.

"Just pull the hammer back, aim, and fire the trigger. Go ahead and try."

She lifted her hand and realized just how heavy the weapon was. Her arm began to tremble as she attempted to hold up the gun long enough to shoot it.

"Here, let me help with that." Ethan stepped up behind her and stretched his arm out to support hers, his cheek nearly touching her cheek, as he lifted the gun, providing stability. "Go ahead, take a shot. And try closing one eye."

Using both thumbs, she worked until the hammer clicked into place. Concentrating on a target was hard with Ethan cocooned around her. She closed her left eye, tried to line up the gun with the middle can, and slowly squeezed the trigger. The gun boomed and jumped, knocking her back against Ethan. She squealed.

"I don't believe it! You hit one of the cans."

Her gaze jerked to the crate, and she saw the second can from the left lying on its side. Not the one she'd been aiming for, but a hit nonetheless. She spun around, a wide grin tugging at her mouth, and her gaze collided with his. Ethan's proud smile wobbled as he looked into her eyes. He tugged the gun from her hand, and suddenly his expression changed. He grabbed her and kissed her hard on the lips. Then he let her go.

She stood there, wavering from the shock of his kiss, as Ethan took aim at the target. The gun spit out five bullets in fast succession, a can pinging and jumping with each hit. Ethan marched toward the crate, kicked it several feet, then slammed each can inside it and carried it to the buggy.

He stalked back to her, all signs of affection gone. "Are you really going to marry my brother?"

With her eyes, she pleaded with him to understand. "I don't have any alternative."

He pursed his lips and scowled.

He helped her into the buggy, and they drove back in silence. Sarah's thoughts rambled around her mind. Ethan was the first man to kiss her—really kiss her. Walt had given her several pecks, but those had felt like kissing Uncle Harvey. But Ethan's kiss.... Her whole body felt afire. If she jumped in the creek just now, surely steam would rise up.

Why had he kissed her? She thought he despised her.

As the buggy drew to a stop behind the house, she started to rise, but Ethan grasped her arm. "Sarah, please don't marry Aaron."

"Why?" She held her breath, hoping, praying he'd say he loved her.

"Because you don't love him."

"How do you know?"

A soft grin lifted one corner of his mouth. "Because a woman in love doesn't kiss another man like you just kissed me."

The brute! She slugged him in the arm, then clambered out of the buggy and ran into the house, her heart breaking. Had that kiss been a test to prove she wasn't worthy of Aaron?

As if she didn't know that already.

Chapter Twenty-four

After supper the next evening, when the children were tucked in bed, Sarah followed Aaron outside for a walk. She'd dreaded this moment ever since Ethan had kissed her, but that kiss had sealed her fate.

"Corrie and Toby sure are proud of their new shoes and clothes."

"Yeah." Aaron chuckled. "I thought Toby would bust his britches over those boots."

"I've never seen any so small."

"Me, neither. It's something new that Gus Yeager is selling."

"I bet they'll sell well." Sarah glanced up and realized they were headed straight for the little house. She scanned the yard. Nobody else was around. She had to get this over with. She only prayed he wouldn't take the news too hard. "Aaron, I need to tell you something."

He turned and faced her, his eyes still squinting in delight at his son's happiness. She hated putting out that light.

"I'm sorry, but I…I can't marry you."

"What? Why not?" He ran his hand over the back of his neck.

She picked at a hangnail to avoid looking him as she spoke. "I did a lot of praying while you were away, and there are several reasons, but two main ones."

"What are they?" She heard disappointment in his voice, which threw her off guard. Had he been looking forward to marrying her? She sent a silent prayer heavenward that God would help her to say what needed to be said.

"The first reason is that I don't believe I'm the right woman for you. You're a fine man, Aaron, and I am deeply grateful for your offer of marriage, but you deserve someone much better." He opened his mouth, but she held up two fingers, silencing him. "The second reason is that we don't love each other, and it isn't fair to either of us to settle for a marriage without love. It would hurt us both in the long run, and it would hurt all of the people we love."

He was quiet for a long while. Finally, he heaved a loud sigh. "I'm not gonna lie; I'm disappointed. The children would have been thrilled, and so would Ma. I understand, but I'm still disappointed. I was just gettin' accustomed to the idea."

"I'm really sorry. You're a wonderful man, Aaron, and one day the right woman will come along and sweep you off your feet. But I'm not that woman."

He nodded, then turned and strode into the barn.

Tears stung Sarah's eyes. She hated causing him pain. She took one last look at the cottage, then walked back to the house. A huge burden lifted from her shoulders, but another weight remained: What were she and Aunt Emma to do now?

⌒

Ethan walked into the kitchen and looked around. "Where's Aaron? One of the kids sick?"

Ma shook her head. "No. Why?"

"He didn't show up for the milking. Josh is tending his cow."

Ma smashed down her bread dough, folded it, then smashed it again. "Aaron said he wanted to go hunting for a few days."

"Hunting? Now?" Ethan searched his mind. Game was often hard to come by in the heat of summer.

Ma stopped kneading the dough, wiped her hands, and faced him. "Sarah told me about his proposal, and how she accepted at first but then turned him down. Your brother is hurting right now, and you know he likes to be alone when he's hurting."

"I need to talk to him, Ma. Do you know where he went?"

"He asked me not to tell anyone, but I'd feel better if you went after him and talked to him. He's at the camp spot your father likes, near Olathe."

"Consider it done." He kissed her forehead and gave her a quick hug. "I'll pack a few things and head out."

~

Ethan rode into the camp just before sunset. Aaron sat leaning against a tree, nursing a cup of coffee. Ethan dismounted and touched the pot that sat in the ashes of the fire. Lukewarm, but it would do. He'd left home before the coffee had been made this morning.

"What are you doing here?" Aaron grumbled. "Can't a man have some privacy?"

"Not when there are things to be said."

"What things?" Aaron held out his cup for a refill.

Ethan topped off his brother's cup, filled the cup he'd brought for himself, and then squatted down. "I owe you an apology."

Aaron glared at him. "You're the reason Sarah turned me down, aren't you?"

"It wasn't intentional." Ethan gazed into his brother's eyes, praying his confession wouldn't harm their relationship. He loved Aaron. "I think I've been in love with Sarah since the first time I saw her neck-deep in mud on a Kansas City street."

Aaron cocked an eyebrow. "Neck-deep?"

"Well, knee-deep. I tried for so long to deny my attraction to her, but even you saw it. So did Ma and Pa."

"I wish you'd made a move instead of encouraging me to. When Sarah said yes, I got to thinking maybe our marriage could work out."

"I'm sorry, Aaron. I didn't know for sure until yesterday."

Aaron swished around the coffee in his cup. "What happened yesterday?"

"I kissed her."

His brother stiffened. "When?"

"When I took her shooting. And it just happened. I didn't expect it, and I sure didn't plan it."

Aaron plucked a nearby dandelion and twirled it in his fingers. "Did she kiss you back?"

He nodded, ashamed to admit it.

"Well then, there's only one thing to do." Resignation laced Aaron's voice, and Ethan braced himself for his brother's fist in his jaw.

"Don't let her get away."

Ethan let the tension flow from his body. "I won't. I'm sorry, again." He hated seeing Aaron disappointed. All his life, he'd looked up to his brothers, especially Aaron, because they were the most alike.

"Stop saying you're sorry and get me some more coffee."

He hopped up, grabbed the coffeepot, and filled Aaron's cup again, then poured the last little bit into his own.

"So, how long do you plan to hang around here?"

"Long enough to help you track down a turkey for Ma."

One corner of his brother's mouth lifted, sending cascades of relief through him. If Aaron could smile now, that meant he'd be okay. Life was looking up, and tomorrow, Ethan would confess his love to Sarah and ask her to be *his* wife.

～

Sarah scanned the basement, satisfied that everything was in order. She'd heard the stage pull in just as she'd headed downstairs with a tray of fresh bread. She moved the bouquet of wildflowers that Corrie had picked so that it was situated more in the center of the table.

The dumbwaiter creaked, and she hurried over to retrieve the crock of soup.

Footsteps sounded upstairs, and a shadow filled the doorway. Sarah's heart lurched to see Jasper Biggs descending the steps. He tipped his hat to her.

She glanced past him. "No passengers?"

"Just one, and he's here to see you. I left him at the back door."

"I have a guest? Who is he?"

Jasper shrugged. "Some fancy dandy."

She set the soup on the table just as the shotgun rider came in, his face still wet from a recent scrubbing. She smiled at him. "You two help yourselves while I run upstairs and see what that fellow wants."

For the life of her, she couldn't imagine who would have come to see her. She hurried up the steps, hoping the man wasn't another would-be suitor, and nearly collided with Karen.

"I was just coming to get you. There's a visitor waiting in the parlor. Emma's talking with him." The gleam that normally lit her eyes had dimmed. "This fellow introduced himself as your fiancé."

"What?" She rushed passed Karen and through the doorway, then skidded to a halt. Aunt Emma sat on the settee with Toby and Corrie. A man sat across from them. "Walt?"

He rose and hurried toward her, looking thinner and paler than she'd ever seen him.

"Have you been ill?"

He halted for a moment, then continued to her side. "That's hardly the greeting I expected."

Sarah scrambled for a response. "Why are you here? You made it clear in your letter that you'd washed your hands of me."

She felt Karen standing behind her, and she turned, holding out her hand. "Please excuse my poor manners. This is Mrs. Harper. She runs this stage shop with her husband and sons." She faced Karen. "This is Walter Swanson, and we were never officially betrothed."

The relief in Karen's eyes piled heaps of guilt on her for having worried her friend.

"Walt is the only passenger today," Sarah told her. "I set the soup out for Mr. Biggs and Mr. Barlow and told them to help themselves."

Karen nodded. "I'd better go set a bowl aside for your guest, or he won't get any. Nice to meet you, Mr. Swanson. As soon as your business is done, Sarah can show you where to come for your meal. The stage doesn't tarry long, so you'll need to hurry if you plan to eat."

Sarah bit back a smile at Karen's effort to shoo Walt on down the road.

"Actually, I won't be continuing on with the stage."

Her heart lurched. The last thing she wanted was for Ethan to meet Walt and think there was a fire smoldering between them. She realized her initial impression of Walt being sick was wrong. He merely looked that way compared to the big, strapping Harper men.

Karen smiled, albeit far less warmly than usual. "I'm sure we can oblige you, sir. Two of my sons are currently out hunting, so you can stay in one of their rooms. The cost is two dollars per night, meals included."

He nodded. "Thank you, but I fear you've misunderstood. I have a man with a wagon already on his way to take me back to town."

Karen sucked in a sharp breath. "Come along and help me, children. Sarah needs time to visit with her guest."

"What about our cookies?" Toby slid off the seat. "We always get treats when people come visitin'."

"Not today. Lunch is ready downstairs." Karen waited for her grandchildren, then left the room, stealing a final glance at Sarah.

Emma rose. "I'll leave you two alone to talk and go help Karen."

Sarah's heart thrummed. She'd never been afraid to be alone with Walt before, but his presence now, and in this place, made her tense. Why had he come all this way? "It's...um...good to see you again."

"You've changed." He studied her. "You've got some color in your face."

She touched her cheek, feeling self-conscious. From his tone, she knew he hadn't intended his comment as a compliment. "Why are you here?"

He paced toward the fireplace and back again. "After I had some time to think things through, I felt dreadful about the rushed response I sent back to you. I'm sorry, Sarah. I made a mistake, one I plan to rectify. I've come to take you back to Chicago."

She didn't know what to say. The thought of never seeing Ethan again was like a knife to her heart. More painful, even, than leaving Chicago. But he had never expressed his feelings for her—at least, not verbally. And his treatment of her had been erratic. He had kissed her, yes, but brashly; and, by the way he'd ridden off, she suspected he deeply regretted it. She walked to the window and stared out.

If only she knew how Ethan felt. His kiss gave her hope, but, other than that, she'd always felt his disapproval. If only he loved her, she'd never leave. This place felt like home now. But life here without his love would be miserable. And she'd already hurt Aaron. Maybe it would be best for everyone if she left. *Is this Your provision, Lord? Would You have me leave this place and marry Walt, after all?*

"Sarah, tell me what you're thinking." Walt stepped up behind her and placed his hands on her shoulders.

She tried hard not to stiffen. His touch was as flat as the prairie, and not a whisper stirred inside her. *Oh, Ethan, why couldn't you have loved me?*

Walt turned her around. "There's not much time to deliberate, Sarah. My driver said he'd be here shortly after lunchtime, and we need to head back right away to reach town before sunset." He lifted a hand and combed it through his slicked-back hair. "You're making me nervous, Sarah. I went to a lot of trouble—and expense—to come all this way for you."

She ducked her head, hoping he wouldn't notice the tears she fought so hard to blink away. "I'm sorry, Walt. So much has happened. Aunt Emma really likes it here. I can't make a decision to return to Chicago without talking it over with her."

"I hope you know that she is welcome to come and live with us."

So, there it was. No marriage proposal; just an assumption that his "rescue" would oblige her to marry him. At least he was gracious enough not to toss her aunt out on the street. "Why don't you go down and eat lunch while I talk to Aunt Emma?"

He nodded and started for the door, then turned. "I'll be good to you, Sarah, you know that. You'll never lack for anything, and neither will your aunt. Please say you'll return with me."

She glanced up, sorry to see the worry in his eyes. "I know you'd be good to me, Walt. You always have been." No matter what choice she made, she would hurt someone. She knew Karen hoped she would stay and marry one of her sons. But Sarah was afraid to face Ethan again. If she left with Walt, the Harper family could get back to normal. If only the thought of leaving didn't hurt so much.

She showed him to the inside stairway, then found Emma in the kitchen, washing the soup pot. "Where are the children?"

"Karen took them downstairs with her." Emma turned the pot upside down on the counter to dry and then wiped her hands on a towel. "Sit down and tell me why Walt is here."

Sarah pulled out a chair and dropped into it, her legs feeling limp as noodles. "He's come to take us back."

Emma nodded. "He didn't tell me, but I assumed as much, considering how far he traveled. And how do you feel about it?"

"I don't know." She shook her head. "I just don't know."

"Then, I suggest we pray about it."

Sarah nodded. That was the only way she would find an answer. Stay and hope the man she loved would come to love her, too, or leave and become the wife of a man she didn't love, and never would, though he would treat her kindly. To someone else, it might sound like a win either way. But not to her.

Chapter Twenty-five

"Ma, we're home." Ethan laid the fat turkey he and Aaron had hunted most of the day on the table.

"Come on in here," Pa called from the parlor.

Ethan hurried there, hoping to find Sarah reading to the children. He ached to tell her how he felt—that he loved her. Disappointment lodged in his belly when he found only his parents and the children.

Corrie jumped off the settee, and Toby followed. She ran up and hugged his knees. "Where's Pa?" she asked.

"Out in the barn, tending the horses."

She spun away, though Toby still clung to his leg. "Can we go out and see Pa?" Corrie asked her grandpa.

Ethan bent down and pressed Toby's head against his thigh, enjoying the feel of the boy's arms hugging him. How long would it be before he and Sarah had a child?

"Go on. Just be careful that you don't spook the horses with your squeals."

"I don't squeal, Grandpa. Pigs do that." She pulled her brother off of Ethan's leg. "C'mon, Toby. Let's go tell Pa about Sarah."

Ethan waited until they'd left the room, and then his gaze snapped back to his parents. "What about Sarah?"

Pa lowered his head, his mouth working but nothing coming out.

When Ma stood, Ethan realized her face was red and splotchy, and tears pooled in her eyes. His heart lurched. Had Sarah gotten herself into trouble again? Was she hurt?

"She's gone...." Ma ducked her head and started sobbing.

Ethan pressed a hand to his forehead, trying to absorb her statement. Disbelief made him numb. "What do you mean, she's gone? Where did she go?"

Pa rose and put his arm around Ma's shoulders. She sniffled, and he tugged her against his chest, rubbing his hand across her back. "I told you boys to stake a claim, if you intended to. Now some other fellow has come and carted Sarah and Emma away. Your ma is heartbroken."

Ma sucked in a sob, as if to emphasize his point.

Ethan's eyes went wide as he realized the truth. The woman he loved was gone. "When? Where?"

"A driver from Windmill arrived after lunch to take them back to town." Pa shook his head. "They've probably already arrived."

Ethan rubbed his forehead. It would be dark in a few hours, and riding at night was risky, but at least the moon was close to full. He looked at his parents, knowing his pain was evident. "I love her. I didn't realize it until Aaron asked her to marry him. That's why I had to go find him and make sure things were all right between us. He's still a bit raw over her refusal, but he knows now that marrying Sarah would have been wrong, being as they don't love each other. He gave me his blessing. I've got to go get her."

A flame ignited in Ma's eyes. "Yes, you do. Bring them both back to us." She nudged his pa. "Go out and saddle him a fresh horse while I pack him some food." She gave Ethan a gentle shove. "You go up and change. You smell like trail dust."

He didn't waste time reminding her that he was headed out for another long ride. *Please, God, don't let me be too late.*

⌣

It was mid-morning when Ethan rode into Windmill. He'd hoped to arrive before dawn, but a thick cloud cover had stolen his light, leaving him no choice but to stop. In spite of his anxiety, he'd fallen asleep and hadn't awakened until well past sunup.

He headed straight to the only boardinghouse in town. As he dismounted, he realized his folks had never mentioned the name of the man who'd come for Sarah. More than likely it was Bob Stone, and if that was the case, he could only hope they hadn't yet left for Kansas City.

Hat in hand, he knocked on the door. His body trembled. *Please, God, let her be here.*

An older woman with a kind smile opened the door, unleashing the tantalizing aroma of baking pies. "May I help you?"

"I'm looking for a man that may have arrived here yesterday evening with two women, one of them older, the other rather young."

She pursed her lips and shook her head. "I'm sorry, but you've missed them. He left at first light to go back north. Headed out in a wagon because he didn't want to wait two more days for the train to return this way." Her gray eyes took on a hopeful gleam. "Are you by chance needing a room for the night?"

"No, ma'am, but thank you." He turned and surveyed the town, his heart sinking clear down to his boots. What now? He needed to eat, and he needed a fresh horse. And he needed to hurry. Every minute that passed, Sarah was getting further and further away.

He unhitched the black and led him toward the livery. If he rented just one fresh horse, he'd have no way of transporting Sarah and her aunt back. But if he took a buggy, he wasn't likely to catch them before tomorrow, and he didn't want to have to wait that long to see Sarah. He paid the liveryman to tend and keep his horse and then rented just one—the man's fastest. He'd worry about how the women would travel back later.

Next, he went to the diner and picked a seat by the window. As he waited for his food, he tapped his fork against the salt bowl, willing the cook to hurry. He ached to hop on the horse and go, but his pa had drilled it into him that a man took care of himself because, if he didn't, he couldn't take care of others.

Ethan squeezed his eyes shut and prayed the wagon Sarah was in would break down. On his ride to town, he'd realized his parents hadn't said who it was that had come for Sarah. He'd assumed it was Bob Stone, but what if it was someone else? If Sarah left Kansas City and went back to Chicago, how would he ever find her? His eyes stung. He'd been stupid to wait so long to declare his love. Hadn't he known, deep down, that he'd loved her? Why had he fought it so hard?

The waiter set a plate of roast beef and vegetables in front of him, as well as a basket of biscuits. He took a bite of food, and it lodged in his throat. He was in no mood to eat when the woman he loved was getting farther and farther away. After forcing down half of his meal, he swigged the last of his coffee and stood, tossing some coins onto the table.

Outside, he grabbed the horse's reins and walked him to a watering trough. As he drank, Ethan glanced around the small town. It was growing, slowly. Some of the travelers who headed west ended up here after realizing the hardships of the trail.

Anxious to be gone, he tossed the reins over the horse's head and mounted. He longed to break the horse into a gallop, to close the distance between him and Sarah, but there were too many people out and about. Too many children running around in the street. So, he maintained a walk.

As he reached the end of Main Street, he stopped the horse and looked around. Was someone calling his name?

A group of old men stood outside the general store, watching him.

Ethan twisted his finger in his ear, sure he must be hearing things. Sarah's voice was taunting him, calling to him. Two of the men stared past him, back toward town, and he looked over his shoulder.

Tom Butler, the town barber, shook his head. "If'n I had a pretty gal like that callin' my name, I wouldn't be wastin' no time answerin' her."

Ethan reined his horse around, and his heart nearly leapt from his chest. "Sarah!" He dropped to the ground and ran to meet her in the middle of the street. His eyes devoured her. "I thought you'd left."

"I came very close to doing that."

Did he dare believe she was really standing there, gazing up at him with the light of love in her beautiful eyes?

"Why didn't you go?" He held his breath, afraid to hope.

She glanced down. A man driving past in a wagon stared down at them, and Ethan realized they were drawing a crowd. He took her hand. "C'mon. Let's find some place more private to talk." He tugged her down the nearest alley, over a street, and down another alley, until they'd reached the edge of town. The prairie spilled out before them, grass swishing on the light breeze.

"So, why didn't you leave town?"

Sarah shrugged. "By the time I arrived in Windmill, I knew I couldn't go with Walt. I never mentioned him to you, but he courted me back in Chicago and proposed a number of times. I was never able to say yes, because I didn't love him; and I finally realized I never could, and I told him as much. He was so angry that I had to get away from him for a while, so I left Auntie in our room at the boardinghouse and took a walk. I ended up at the post office and found a letter from Bob." She gazed up at him. "Now that Uncle Harvey is gone, he and Lydia have decided not to leave Kansas City. They've invited us to live with them."

Ethan swallowed hard. "So, you're going back to Kansas City?"

She gazed up at him, her blue eyes filled with emotion. "That depends."

"On what?"

"I can't go until I know how things stand between us." She nibbled her lip, looking vulnerable and very kissable. "Do you care at all for me, Ethan?"

He could no longer contain his smile. "Do I care about you?" He picked her up and swung her in a circle, enjoying her bewildered expression. When he set her down, he put his hands on her shoulders. "I love you, Sarah Marshall. Don't you dare leave town and break my heart."

Her pretty lips quivered, and her chin trembled. Her eyes glazed with tears. "Truly? You love me?"

"More than all the crickets in Kansas."

She giggled and swiped her cheek. "There are thousands of those."

"You'd better believe it, darlin'." He took her hands in his, all humor aside, and gazed down into her cornflower-blue eyes. "Will you marry me, Sarah?"

She sucked in a sob, and then a smile exploded on her face. "Oh, yes, Ethan. There's nothing I'd like more. I love you so much."

He pulled her close and bent down, kissing her mouth, her eyes, her cheeks, and then her mouth again, relief and love pouring forth from deep within him. Before he was ready to quit kissing her, he forced himself to stop and simply held her head against his chest, tears running down his cheeks. He gazed up at the sky. *Thank You, Lord, for keeping her here. And thank You for freeing me to love this stubborn city gal before I lost her forever.*

The wind whispered across the prairie, making the tall grasses sway as if dancing with delight, and the aroma of the wildflowers blended with the scent of the beautiful woman in his arms.

His life was about to change.

Of that he was certain.

A Preview of *Call of the Prairie*
Pioneer Promises ~ Book Two

April 1873 · St. Louis, Missouri

Sophie Davenport held back the curtain and peered out the front window, her heart jolting as a handsome man exited the carriage. He paid the driver, then turned and studied her house. He was taller and nicer looking than she'd expected. She dropped the curtain and stepped back, hoping he hadn't seen her spying. She pressed her hands together and tapped her index fingers against her lips, unable to hold back her grin. Blake had finally arrived!

A knock of confidence, not apprehension, sounded at the main entrance. Sophie hurried to her bedroom door, which opened onto the main entryway, then held her breath and listened. Blake stood on her porch, introducing himself to the butler. Sophie could barely hold back her giddiness. She bounced on her toes as Blake told the butler he had an appointment with her. His voice, deeper than she'd imagined, floated through the open transom window above her like a beautiful cello solo at the symphony.

She patted her hair, hoping the humidity of the warm day hadn't sent it spiraling in rebellious curls. The swish of silk accompanied her as she hurried across the room to the full-length oval mirror that stood in one corner. Pressing a hand over her chest to calm her pounding heart, she surveyed her deep purple gown. Was the fabric too dark? She'd chosen the violet silk taffeta because her brightly colored day dresses made her appear younger, but today, she wanted to look the twenty-two-year-old woman she was. Turning sideways, she checked her bustle and bow, making sure they were straight. Everything was as orderly as it could be. Would Blake like what he saw? Would he think her too short? Her light brown hair too nondescript?

Flicking a piece of lint off her bodice, she turned and faced the door. She would know soon enough. After more than a year of correspondence, Blake knew everything about her, and he had adamantly insisted that none of it mattered. He'd fallen in love with her through her enchanting missives, and he wanted her for his wife.

A vicious knock rattled the glass in the transom, and Sophie jumped. The apprehension racing through her was less about meeting Blake and more about the fact that she hadn't told her parents about him. They would have cut off her correspondence faster than their gardener could lop off the head of a snake. But it was too late now. She attempted to swallow the lump lodged in her throat, but it refused to move.

Her mother walked in, her whole face pinched like a prune, and quickly closed the door. She stood there facing it for a long moment, her head down, then heaved a loud, exaggerated sigh.

Not a good sign.

Finally, her mother turned. "You have a guest, Sophia—a male guest." One eyebrow lifted. "Would you care to explain to me how you are acquainted with this man, especially since neither your father nor I have ever met him?"

Sophie pressed a hand to her throat. She knew this wouldn't be easy. "His name is Blake Sheppard. He and I have been corresponding for over a year."

Her mother's brown eyes widened. "A year? But how? I've never seen a letter from him in the mail."

Ducking her head, Sophie stilled her hands and held them in front of her. "Ruthie sent and received them for me. Blake is her cousin—and a gentleman."

"A gentleman doesn't go behind the backs of a young woman's parents to contact her." Maintaining her stiff stance, her mother puckered her lips. "So, you've been deceiving your father and me?"

Wincing, Sophie turned toward the front window. "Would you have allowed me to correspond with Blake if I'd told you about him?"

"Proper ladies don't exchange letters with men they've never been introduced to, and certainly not without parental approval."

Drawing a steadying breath, Sophie turned to face her mother. She'd known this would be a battle. "Mother, please. Blake is a good man. Ask me anything about him."

"There's no need. We will go out to the parlor, share a cup of tea, and then you'll make excuses that will send him on his way. Is that clear?"

Sophie gasped. "But he's traveled so far, and I've waited so long to meet him." She despised the pleading in her voice. Why couldn't her parents let her grow up like her sister? A wheeze squeaked out of her throat. She had to stay calm. The last thing she wanted was to have an attack in front of Blake.

Her mother moved closer, her expression softening. She took Sophie's hand. "You know how things are, dear. You had no business getting that young man's hopes up."

"That young man is my fiancé, Mother."

"Fiancé—why, that's absurd! You know you can't lead a normal life."

Closing her eyes, Sophie fought back tears. Why did her parents seek to limit her? Given the chance, she was certain she could be a proper wife and mother, but her parents just wanted to coddle her and keep her close. "You have to face the fact that I'm grown up. I want to live a normal life." She hurried past her mother and reached for the door handle.

"But you are not normal, dear. Your father and I only want to protect you. We couldn't bear to lose you, and you know we've come close to doing that very thing on several occasions."

Sophie shuddered at the declaration. Her mother's words rang in her ears: *You are not normal.* Yes, she had a breathing problem; but, as she'd gotten older, the spells had happened less often. Maybe in time, they'd go away altogether. Her parents were afraid to let her live as her sister did. If she didn't get away from them, she'd become a spinster— if she wasn't one already. She stiffened her back and pasted on a smile, trying to ignore the pain of her mother's chastisement. Blake was waiting.

She opened the door and stepped into the entryway, her gaze searching for the man she'd dreamed about so many times. Blake stood in front of the parlor sofa, speaking with her father. He hadn't noticed her yet.

"I'm sorry you've wasted your time traveling all this way, Mr. Sheppard," her father said. "But, as I've already stated, my daughter is not in the habit of receiving male visitors."

Blake's eyebrows drew together, his shoulders slumping, as he looked down at the carpet. Sophie blew out several breaths and tried to calm herself, then hurried through the entryway into the parlor, avoiding her father's glare. Her gaze latched onto Blake's, and she saw the confusion in his hazel eyes. He offered a tentative smile. "Miss Davenport, a pleasure to finally meet you."

She smiled, her cheeks warming, as she curtsied. "I've looked forward to this moment for a very long time." She waved a hand toward her father, and noticed that her mother had followed her into the room. "I apologize, but I failed to tell my parents about your arrival." *Because I knew just how they would respond.* "I fear they are both a bit surprised." An understatement of mammoth proportions, if ever there was one.

Sophie gathered her courage and turned to her father. "I see you've met Blake, Father." Her throat tightened at his stern stare. Another wheeze squeaked out. "B-Blake is my fiancé."

Her father's eyes widened, and his mouth dropped open. A pomegranate color climbed up his neck, turning his ears red. He turned his fiery gaze on Blake. "You presume a lot, young man. Did Sophie not inform you that she is not fully well? She is not in a position to accept an offer of marriage."

Blake cleared his throat and straightened, as if he wasn't ready to give up the battle. "Yes, sir, she told me, but I thought—" His gaze captured Sophie's, and then he glanced at the floor again. He shuffled his feet, as if he were trying to figure out a new dance step. "I thought Sophie—uh, Miss Davenport—was free to make her own decisions, sir. I'm sorry that she failed to inform you of my interest in her."

"Inform me?" Her father puffed up like a tom turkey whose hens were in danger. "A daughter doesn't 'inform' a father that she is planning to marry a stranger. A decent fellow seeks permission *before* approaching a man's daughter."

Blake swallowed, his Adam's apple bobbing. "I'm sorry, sir."

As if an angry fist clutched Sophie's throat, she felt it closing. She expelled a wheeze, and Blake shot a glance in her direction. Her father's tirade blended with the words her mother had uttered, causing an ache within her so painful, she didn't know if she could bear it. She was losing Blake, and they'd only just met. Was she doomed to live with her overprotective parents the rest of her life?

No!

She wouldn't.

She'd fight for Blake. He was worth it.

She opened her mouth to defend her fiancé, but the sound that came out more resembled the bleat of an ailing goat than her own voice. Humiliation blistered her cheeks.

Blake took a step backward, away from her, his handsome face drawn in a scowl.

"You see, Mr. Sheppard, the slightest excitement can set off one of my daughter's attacks." Father turned to Sophie's mother. "Ring for some coffee, if you will. It seems to help our Sophie's spells."

Spells. Attacks. What would Blake think?

Sophie held out her hand to him. Instead of taking it, he cast another worried glanced at her father. She sucked in another wheezy breath, struggling to stay clam in the midst of such turmoil. The room tilte d. Sophie closed her eyes until the spinning stopped. All was silent for several long moments, except for her screeching breaths.

When her eyelids fluttered open, Blake met her gaze with an apology in his eyes. She knew in that moment she'd lost him.

He sighed. "Perhaps I have been too hasty. I sincerely apologize, Miss Davenport, but I must withdraw my offer of marriage. I hope you and your parents can forgive me for troubling you so."

Tears stung Sophie's eyes. She held out her hand again, hoping—praying—he'd take hold of it. "No, please—"

He skirted around her as if she were a leper, nodded to her mother, then snatched his hat off the hall tree and rushed out the door.

Sophie collapsed in the nearest chair and watched her dreams march down the sidewalk and out of sight. Tears blurred her vision as all hope of a future with Blake died. How could her parents be so cruel as to not even allow Blake to express his interest in her? How could they embarrass her so?

Her father walked to her and leaned over. "Try to calm down, Sophia."

She jumped up so fast, her head almost rammed his chin. He stumbled backward. The room swerved as she struggled for a decent breath. "How c-could you, Father?"

A wave of guilt washed over his face. "It's for your own good, you know."

She clutched the end table for support for a moment, then stumbled past him.

He took her arm. "Here, let me help you, precious."

"No! Please." She yanked away. "I can...take care of...myself. I'm a grown woman, and you both need to f-face that fact." She inhaled a decent breath and then charged on, by pure willpower. "I'm twenty-two and not your little girl anymore. Stop sheltering me...let me live my life. It's mine to live, not yours to stifle."

The flash of pain in her father's eyes only made her feel worse. Her shoes tapped across the entryway as she hurried back to her room—the former library, where her parents had relegated her, as if she were a pariah. She shut the door and collapsed on her bed, wanting to cry but knowing that doing so would only make breathing harder. She slammed her fist against her pillow. "Why, God? Why can't my parents let me grow up?"

She'd had such hopes. Thought that when her parents met Blake, they'd see what a quality man he was. But they hadn't even given him a chance. Could she have been mistaken about him? She smacked the bed, a futile outlet for her frustrations and disappointments. Blake hadn't bothered to fight for her one bit; he'd fled out the door the first chance he'd gotten. She'd tried to prepare him—to warn him about her episodes—but she must have failed.

She barked a cough that sounded like a seal she'd once seen at the menagerie in New York City's Central Park. Sophie pushed up into a sitting position, in order to breathe better. Blinking, she attempted to force away her tears, but new ones came like the spring rains that flooded the banks of the Mississippi River. Why had God cursed her with this hateful condition?

The door opened, and her mother entered, carrying a tray. Coffee. She despised the foul-tasting stuff, but it was thought to be helpful to people with asthma, as were garlic, whiskey, and a number of other nasty-tasting concoctions.

"How are you, dear?"

Sophie slid back down on the bed and turned to face the wall. She didn't want to talk—couldn't talk.

"Don't be that way. You need to drink this coffee."

She shook her head.

"Turn over, Sophia." Her mother's tone left no room for refusal.

She obeyed but didn't look at her mother. Instead, she started counting the thin, blue lines in the wallpaper—all nine hundred sixteen of them—as she'd done a thousand other times. Focusing on the task would keep her from weeping and from lashing out in anger.

Her mother blew out a loud breath, then held out the coffee cup. "Drink this."

Sophie shook her head. "Doesn't help." She sucked in a breath, thankful that this episode was a mild one and already beginning to pass, in spite of the day's traumatic events.

Her mother set the cup back on the tray with a loud clatter and stared across the room. "Whatever made you do such a thing? Don't you know that young man must have spent hard-earned money to come here? Taken time away from his job, assuming he has one? You gave him false hopes, Sophia, and now he's wasted a year of his life pursuing a woman he can never have."

Sophie clenched her eyes shut, losing count of the lines. Did her mother not care that her heart was breaking?

Guilt nibbled its way into her mind like a mouse in a sack of grain. She hadn't thought how things would affect Blake if they turned sour. She'd been so certain everything would work out in their favor.

So certain that she could persuade her parents to let them marry, that she hadn't considered the negative side. But her mother was right about one thing. Blake had taken leave from his job as bookkeeper for a shoe factory in Chicago so that he could travel to St. Louis to meet her. He had wasted his time and money to come here.

And it was all her fault.

She sucked in a sob.

Her mother patted her shoulder. "There, there. Things will work out."

Yes, her father would go back to running his company. Her mother would attend her social clubs and church functions. Her sister would continue as a happily married wife and soon-to-be mother, while Sophie would continue her boring existence as a lonely spinster living in her parents' home.

The bed lifted on one side as her mother stood and quietly left the room. After the door closed, Sophie sat up and stared out the window, at the very place she'd first seen Blake. She hated feeling sorry for herself, and she normally didn't, but today, her emotions were raw.

She rose from the bed and crossed the room to her desk, where her Bible lay. She picked it up and hugged it to her chest as she gazed out at the garden. Bright yellow butterflies flitted from flower to flower. A big bumblebee disappeared in a clump of pink azaleas. The beauty of God's creation never failed to cheer her, even on the saddest of days.

Sophie blew out a loud sigh. "Forgive me, Lord, if I've been selfish." She hugged the Bible tighter. "But please, Father, make a way for me to break free from my parents. To prove to them—and to myself—that I can stand on my own. That I can take care of myself. And please, Lord, if it be Your will, send me a man someday who will love me for the woman I am and overlook my...flaws."

Tears pooled in her eyes, and her throat tightened. "But if it is Your will for me to remain in my parents' home and to never marry, help me to accept that and to be content."

If that was the Lord's will, He certainly had a monumental task ahead.

About the Author

Vickie McDonough grew up reading horse stories and dreaming of marrying a rancher. Instead, she married a computer geek who is scared of horses. But those old dreams find new life as she pens stories of ranchers, lawmen, and others living in the Old West. Vickie is an award-winning author of twenty-seven books and novellas. Her novel *Long Trail Home* won the 2012 Booksellers' Best Award for Inspirational Fiction. Her books have also won the Inspirational Reader's Choice Contest, Texas Gold, and the ACFW Noble Theme contest, and Vickie has been a multiyear finalist in the American Christian Fiction Writers' BOTY/Carol Awards.

Whispers on the Prairie is book one in Pioneer Promises, Vickie's first series with Whitaker House.

Vickie and her husband live in Oklahoma. Married for thirty-eight years, they have four grown sons, one daughter-in-law, and a precocious seven-year-old granddaughter. When she isn't writing, Vickie enjoys reading, gardening, antique shopping, collecting quilted wall hangings, watching movies, and traveling. She recently took a stained glass class and is working on several projects.

To learn more about Vickie's books, readers may visit her Web site at www.vickiemcdonough.com or find her on Facebook, Twitter, and Pinterest. Vickie also co-moderates and contributes regularly to the Christian Fiction Historical Society blog: http://christianfictionhistoricalsociety.blogspot.com.